Blackstone Public Library
86 Main Street
W9-AWO-802

The Secret Life of BRYAN

Also by Lori Foster in Large Print:

A Hot Summer (Published in Spanish as Un calido verano)
A Marvelous Lover (Published in Spanish as Una amante maravillosa)

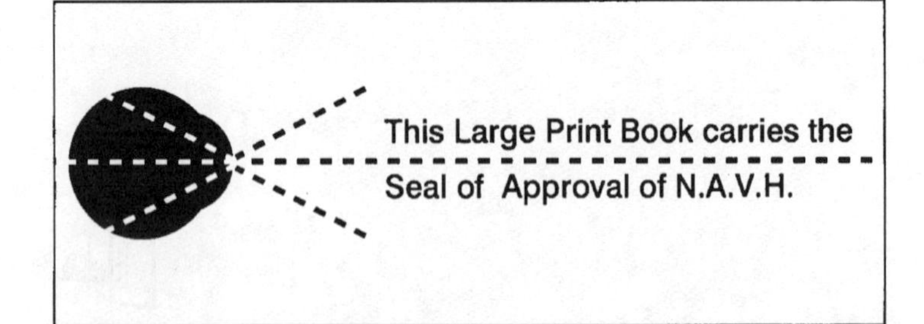

The Secret Life of BRYAN

LORI FOSTER

Thorndike Press • Waterville, Maine

Published in 2004 by arrangement with
Brava Books, an imprint of Kensington Publishing Corp.

Thorndike Press® Large Print Americana.

The tree indicium is a trademark of Thorndike Press.

The text of this Large Print edition is unabridged.
Other aspects of the book may vary from the original edition.

Set in 16 pt. Plantin by Ramona Watson.

Printed in the United States on permanent paper.

Library of Congress Cataloging-in-Publication Data

Foster, Lori, 1958–
The secret life of Bryan / Lori Foster.
p. cm.
ISBN 0-7862-6750-X (lg. print : hc : alk. paper)
1. Impostors and imposture — Fiction. 2. Prostitutes — Services for — Fiction. 3. Clergy — Crimes against — Fiction. 4. Bounty hunters — Fiction. 5. Socialites — Fiction. 6. Large type books. I. Title.
PS3556.O767S43 2004
813′.6—dc22 2004052279

To Barb, Patti, and Morgan.
Good people, good friends,
and obviously, good sports.
Happy hooking!

As the Founder/CEO of NAVH, the only national health agency solely devoted to those who, although not totally blind, have an eye disease which could lead to serious visual impairment, I am pleased to recognize Thorndike Press* as one of the leading publishers in the large print field.

Founded in 1954 in San Francisco to prepare large print textbooks for partially seeing children, NAVH became the pioneer and standard setting agency in the preparation of large type.

Today, those publishers who meet our standards carry the prestigious "Seal of Approval" indicating high quality large print. We are delighted that Thorndike Press is one of the publishers whose titles meet these standards. We are also pleased to recognize the significant contribution Thorndike Press is making in this important and growing field.

Lorraine H. Marchi, L.H.D.
Founder/CEO
NAVH

* Thorndike Press encompasses the following imprints: Thorndike, Wheeler, Walker and Large Print Press.

Chapter One

"Nasty, nasty weather."

Shay Sommers sent her best friend, Dawn, an impatient look. She'd been commenting on the weather for the past ten minutes. Probably her idea of a subtle hint to go. The weather was furious, but then, so was Shay. And she wasn't ready to leave. Not by a long shot.

Dawn pushed back her chipped coffee cup and got right to the point. "Come on, Shay. It's getting dark outside. And I'm cold. There's no point in hanging out here any longer. Leigh's on her way to the clinic, and you know Dr. Martin will take good care of her."

"Of course she will."

"Shay," she said, dragging her name out. "The guy is long gone."

"Probably." Shay drummed her fingers on the scarred countertop. "You should go. Make sure Leigh is taken care of. Tell Eve to send the bill to me. I'll check in with you later."

Dawn's deep black eyes narrowed. "And what will you do in the meantime? Hang around here all night, terrorizing the neighborhood with your frowns? Plotting revenge?"

No answer was answer enough.

Dawn groaned. "Damn it, Shay. She'll be all right now, thanks to you. At least she'll be better than she would have been if you hadn't decided to take up this project."

Shay made a sound of disgust. "Project." Her fingers continued to drum and her frown grew fierce. "It always seems like such a ridiculous word when it's applied to real people."

Dawn squeezed Shay's hand, and her voice gentled. "I know you want to help, Shay. But you can only do so much."

"It's not enough."

"And you're not everyone's mother!"

"I've been thinking . . ."

"Lord help us." Dawn sighed and dropped her head into her hands. "Let me guess. You want to do more than set up a shelter. You want to get personally involved."

Scowling, Shay said, "You know, you have an irritating habit of making my every plan sound stupid."

"Gee, I wonder why that's so easy to

do?" Dawn said. Shay's mouth opened and Dawn snapped, "Okay, okay, forget I said that." She held up her hands in mock regret, which did little to relieve Shay's forbidding expression. "But let's face it, Shay, you don't belong here. You're already spread too thin."

Shay shrugged that off. Somehow, she'd work it out. She had to.

Dawn leaned forward. "Find a manager, let him or her handle the details."

"No way." Shay knew only too well how difficult it was to find a good manager, someone sympathetic and understanding, someone honorable. "This is too touchy. I knew it existed, but . . . Leigh is so young. Even with the heavy eye makeup and that skimpy outfit she wore, I could tell she was little more than a kid." She drew a deep, painful breath, and whispered, "But she'd been prostituting herself."

Again, Dawn took her hand. "Just as I used to do. Until you saved me."

Shay rolled her eyes. Dawn still suffered misplaced loyalty. Shay hadn't saved her. Dawn had saved herself, and she'd turned into a best friend along the way. "Go on, Dawn. I'll catch a cab home. Later. I want to hang out here awhile yet." She wanted to see if there were any more young ladies like Leigh. If so, maybe she could reach them *before* they got hurt.

Dawn glanced around the dining room, then over to the bar. “I’m telling you, it’s not a good idea.”

“It’s an excellent idea.”

“Yeah. If you’re in the market to buy or sell sex.”

The place wasn’t rowdy, Shay noted, merely dark and severe. It suited her mood perfectly. There were a few men, a few women, and the rusty twang of a jukebox. But Shay detected no sense of a threat.

They’d used the phone here to make arrangements for Leigh, then sent her to the clinic. Eve Martin was a formidable doctor who could bully anyone into good health — and often did. She was also a valued friend who repeatedly helped Shay in her efforts.

The excitement was over now, but Shay remained too angry to move. She wanted to understand, to find ways to make things better. She wanted to see if any other young ladies ventured out on this miserably wet September night.

So she stayed, sipping coffee, trying to sort out what had to be done.

Besides, she didn’t want to be alone in her big lonely house with only her anger to keep her company. Even the company of strangers right now was preferable to that. "It'll be safe enough." Then she smiled. "I lead a charmed existence and you know it."

"You're going to be stubborn about this, aren't you?"

"If you mean, am I going to insist on having my own way, don't I always?"

"Yes you do, and it's damned annoying."

Shay grinned. They made an odd team, with Dawn small, her skin as black as her eyes, and Shay tall with a pale, almost Nordic appearance. They bickered constantly, and no small wonder.

Where Shay often acted on impulse, driven by her emotions, Dawn was logic and reason personified. Shay trusted Dawn, and that was saying something, because other than family, Shay didn't trust easily.

They balanced each other, and Dawn did a credible job of keeping Shay in line.

Most of the time.

Giving up, Dawn said, "Do your best to stay out of trouble, all right?" Her stern expression would have been daunting to someone who didn't know her so well. Shay only grinned again.

"I mean it, Shay. Stay inside, but don't

linger in this place too long. If you run into any problems, call me. Or better yet, call the cops."

"My own mother doesn't carry on this much. Will you just go? And stop worrying. I'll check with you later to see how the girl is doing."

Dawn took one last disapproving look around, then shook her head and marched away. Shay watched her go, all the while thinking that if all the women she tried to help were half as wonderful as Dawn, she'd know her husband's money had been put to good use.

Thoughts of her husband, now dead for a little over three years, only tightened the knot in her stomach. She missed him, as a friend, as a companion. But not as a husband. Not as she should have missed him.

That led her thoughts to a dead end, one she visited far too often, so Shay turned her thinking to the problems ahead, to deciding how to handle the situation with the prostitutes. She'd need supplies and a safe place to house the women. A mental checklist formed in her mind.

After an hour had passed and her anger had cooled — but not her determination — she dug through her purse for a few bills, paid her tab and left a generous tip.

Her cell phone had long since gone dead, so with change in her hand, she started to the back of the room for the pay phone.

A woman was already there, her body slouched comfortably into the corner on the small bench. She seemed to have settled in for a lengthy chat. Conspicuously impatient, Shay waited several minutes, but the woman did a convincing job of ignoring her, and finally, Shay gave up. Now that she had a definite purpose in mind, she was anxious to get busy.

She left the bar and grill, thinking to search out another pay phone nearby. The rain continued to fall, the wind blowing it against the building fronts and leaving the narrow streets almost deserted. Earlier, when she'd arrived to get Leigh, she'd seen other women she suspected to be working the streets, too. She'd wanted to talk to them, but apparently, the weather had chased them all away.

Huddling under the faded, tattered overhang of the bar, Shay folded her arms around herself and debated what to do next.

That's when she saw him.

And once seeing him, no way could she look away.

Oblivious to the raging storm, he stood

in front of a small, gaudy barroom on the opposite side of the street. Blinking lights surrounded him, forming a soft glow, giving him the look of a dark, too-serious angel.

Despite the rain, his shoulders weren't hunched, but were straight and wide, his posture confident, even arrogant. Long legs were fitted into snug, well-worn jeans, braced apart as if preparing for battle, though Shay doubted anyone would dare to oppose him.

She knew she wouldn't.

He stood facing her, staring at her in intense concentration. Although she couldn't see his eyes, she knew he looked directly at her, that somehow he *could* see her eyes. It was the oddest feeling, like comfortable familiarity, but with the excitement of the unknown.

Rain blew in her face and she thought to close her mouth before she drowned. She felt flushed from head to toe.

In an effort to see him more clearly, she wiped the rain from her cheeks and eyes — and belatedly remembered her makeup. She probably looked a fright now, but she wouldn't turn tail and run because of it. She wasn't sure she could leave.

There was no sense of danger, no alarm,

only a thrill of awareness that ran bone deep, leaving her breathless and edgy as she instinctively responded to it. Her emotions had been rioting since the call had come in from Leigh. She'd suffered anxiety and urgency, then anger and remorse, all-powerful emotions, only now they were being transformed into something much more exhilarating.

Without changing expression, the man took a calm, measured step toward her, then another, straight into the storm. His movements were unhurried but resolute, and Shay had the feeling he didn't want to spook her with his approach. Her stomach curled in response, her skin heated. She wasn't afraid, but then, she rarely felt fear. Not anymore.

Once, long ago, when she'd been a small child, she'd lived in fear. But she'd gotten over that with a vengeance, and now she kept it at bay with bossiness and a will of iron.

At least, that's what her parents claimed.

Shivering, Shay attempted to smooth her windblown hair, then walked out to meet him halfway. The second she left the protection of the rough-brick building, the rain soaked through to her bones.

At her approach, his step faltered, and

when the neon lights flashed again, she finally saw his eyes. They were such a dark brown as to look almost black. They were narrowed and direct, scrutinizing her from head to toe in a most disturbing way. Their gazes met, and momentary confusion gripped her.

Shay stopped, staring back, breathless and uncertain. Again, his gaze dropped, skimming down the length of her body as she stood in a pool of reddish light, getting more sodden with every gust of wind.

When he looked up again, he seemed almost . . . angry. But why? Hadn't he wanted her to greet him?

Intent on asking him, she scowled and again started forward. She didn't get a chance to move far before a deafening crack rattled the air and a blinding burst of electrical light seared the dark night, lingering, sizzling in ominous threat until one entire side of the street — *her side* — fell into utter blackness. Shay knew the lightning must have struck a transformer. The darkness was absolute, the lights from across the street not quite penetrating so far, making it impossible to see, making her more aware of the noises around her, more aware of the man approaching the shadows with her.

The sounds of people leaving the many bars, the hush of excitement as darkness gave leave to wicked possibilities, was nearly drowned out by the raw severity of the storm. Shay turned to look behind her. She couldn't see them, but the hushed rumblings of curiosity told her that men now hovered in the doorways.

Uh-oh.

Safe within a building was not the same as being outside in a violent storm during a blackout. Her skin prickled with dread. Because she hadn't lost all common sense, she knew the situation could turn lethal. Crossing the street into the light became a priority, but as she jerked about to do just that, she managed only one step before she slammed into a solid wall of warm, unforgiving muscle.

Large, hard hands closed around her upper arms and held her steady when she would have staggered back. Her own hands lifted to brace against a wide chest. Muscles leaped beneath her fingertips, further immobilizing her.

A voice, so close she felt the warmth of breath and smelled the clean scent of damp male skin, whispered into her ear. "It's not safe here. Come with me. Now."

Wow. Not a question, but a command,

and a very tempting one — if she was an idiot. Even before she lifted her gaze, her heart tripping with a mixture of anticipation and excitement, she knew it was him.

Across the street, one of the bars turned on floodlights, probably in the hope of scaring away looters. The illumination fanned out over the wet pavement and filtered onto the opposite sidewalk, providing a soft glow. Through the stinging rain, Shay stared at the man, able to make out his features for the first time. And Lord, was he incredible.

This close, she could see the golden specks in his dark eyes, and his thick, almost feminine lashes. Combined, they should have softened his features, but didn't. He was too intense to be softened in any way.

Dark brows lowered in an expression of grim resolve. His cheekbones were high, his jaw lean with an edge of hardness. Tall, broad shouldered, clean and very commanding, he made a direct counterpoint to most of the men she'd seen in the area, men who skulked about, their postures either humbled or belligerent.

This man was enough to make a woman swoon — if she was the type inclined to such things. But Shay had no intention of closing her eyes for a single instant. He might very well disappear if she did.

His hands still held her arms, his grip firm but not restrictive. And he stood mere inches away, blocking part of the rain with his body. It was that proximity that stifled her usually outspoken manner.

Then another man appeared at her side and said in whining tones, "Aw, Preacher, you sure you want this one? She looks damn fine standing there, soaked to the skin, tall and snobbish."

Shay stared at the little man in appalled fascination. He was wiry, about five-foot-five inches tall, and looked like a geek, complete with black framed glasses, an old-fashioned haircut parted on the side, and a white short-sleeved dress shirt with the top button undone. As he stared at her, looking her over in a sleazy, stomach-turning way, Shay saw the rainwater bead on his lenses.

He swiped it away and all but drooled at her. "Real wet," he breathed.

There were too many possible connotations to what he said, so Shay concentrated on the one she did understand, trying to brazen out the situation, trying to maintain some aspect of control. Glaring, she said, "I may be tall, and I'm as soaked as everyone else, but I am never snobbish."

Both men stared at her.

Shay prided herself on being open and friendly and approachable. That openness was the trick of her trade, what made her so successful in her efforts. Then something else the little man said hit her, and she stared back at the dark-eyed stranger.

Stunned, she managed to squeak out, *"Preacher?"*

He didn't answer her, but instead ordered, "Get lost, Chili. Take your money home to your wife for a change." He hadn't looked away from Shay when he spoke. Evidently, he didn't need to.

Whining, Chili accepted his dismissal and faded back into the shadows.

"Well." Shay cleared her throat. "That was impressive. I gather you're used to giving orders?"

Instead of answering, he scrutinized her. "I haven't seen you here before." His tone was low. Familiar. "So maybe you don't know how dangerous this particular corner is to work."

Shay cocked a brow. She knew. Hadn't she just saved Leigh from working this corner? But . . . surely he didn't mean what she thought he meant, at least in reference to her.

"On a night like this," he continued, "men are more interested in raising hell than paying you for service. Come on. I'll get you out of the damned rain."

Her jaw loosened and her brows came down. He *did*. He thought she was a prostitute. Shay shook her head, but there was no denying his words. This positively gorgeous man with a voice that rubbed rough and raw up her spine and eyes that seemed to see to her soul thought she was a lady of the night. A hooker. A streetwalker.

No matter what term she used, it sounded the same.

But she didn't think he meant to be insulting. In fact, she wasn't altogether sure what he meant. "Are you offering to buy my services for the night?" If he said yes, she'd probably deck him, gorgeous eyes or not. But if he said no, then where did that leave her?

With a growl and a low, muttered curse, he shrugged out of his jacket. "Put this on."

My, my, he was full of orders. "Why? Then you'll just get wet."

His gaze flicked over her body once more, quickly. He looked out over the surrounding area while leaning close, his nose nearly touching her hair. "You look more naked than not." His voice was strained, annoyed. Deep and raw. "Believe me, the men here won't wait for you to name a price before they take what they want. You're wasting your time, and you could get hurt. Take the damn jacket and come with me."

Shay blinked rapidly, thankful now for the darkness and the fact that she had her back to everyone — except the preacher. The floodlights would be against her front, leaving her visible to his view. The snowy whiteness of her dress served as a beacon in the darkness. She folded her arms over her chest and started to look down, but he caught her chin on the edge of his fist.

"Put . . . the jacket . . . on." His expression was fierce, his tone abrupt. When she nodded, he held it out and she slipped her arms into the sleeves, rearranging the strap of her purse over her shoulder. Made of nylon and cotton, the jacket smelled of him, and her heartbeat fluttered, just as it had fluttered when she'd first noticed him watching her.

She held the front closed over her breasts with fingers gone numb from the cold rain and humiliation. She lifted her gaze to his face, but he was busy watching the men around them. He certainly wasn't acting like a customer. Not that she knew how a customer would act. But somehow, she thought he'd be more . . . interested.

"Let's go."

"Where?"

"There's a safe house close by. You can get dry and wait out the storm. No one will bother you there."

A safe house. So he wanted to help her? He'd just solved one of her problems, and her mind buzzed with possibilities. Maybe she could work with him; they could combine their efforts.

She certainly wouldn't object to spending more time with him.

Explanations would have to wait. As he looked up and down the street, watching for danger, impatience throbbed off him in waves. Shay became aware of running feet, then someone broke a window behind her and loud, rather creative cursing was followed by shouts and laughter.

The preacher grabbed her, pulling her close to his chest and turning to move her farther away from the crowd, shielding her with his big body. Her face tucked into his neck and she breathed in his scent. Once again her stomach curled, then tightened. It was a delicious feeling, one she could get used to pretty quickly.

He said against her cheek, "We *have* to go."

Shay nodded, her options limited as more breaking glass erupted around them. "Lead the way."

He grabbed her hand. "Try to keep up," he ordered, and hurried her along down the middle of the street. The rain stung her skin and the wind tried to tear her hair from her head before he darted back into the shadows again, away from the lights and the possibility of being noticed.

Glad of the fact she'd worn low-heeled shoes, Shay trotted along behind him, her steps slightly hampered by the narrow width of her skirt. She'd been at a fund-raising banquet and would have changed before coming here today if there'd been time. But she'd needed to reach Leigh, to get to her before she changed her mind.

She'd met Leigh at one of her women's shelters a few months before. She'd known then that the girl had many problems, but she hadn't known she was a hooker.

Shay had left the banquet in a rush, taking only enough time to grab Dawn on the way. When someone finally reached out, someone desperate, you didn't ask her to wait while you changed into something more comfortable.

Lightning shattered the black sky in front of them, followed closely by the crashing of thunder. The preacher pulled Shay into the recessed door front of a small, seedy motel. "Wait here." Still keeping her hand secured in his, he peered around the corner. "Anyone looking for you?"

"Excuse me?"

He glanced at her, gaze sharp, almost piercing. He repeated, "Do you have a . . ." He shook his head. "A keeper? A *pimp*." He shifted against the building, growling the word in a way that Shay knew it bothered him even to say it.

It disturbed Shay a great deal more, especially after seeing what a pimp had done to Leigh. She leveled an indignant look on his profile. "No."

"I can deal with it," he told her, and his tone reeked of confidence. "I just don't want any surprises."

No one had ever accused Shay of needing a "keeper." Lecturing the preacher here and now on the evils of assuming too much tempted her, but she settled for saying, "I'm capable of taking care of myself."

He turned to better face her, settling all that awesome attention on her until she felt like squirming. “Don’t get all huffy.”

She was indignant, not *huffy*, and there was a huge difference. Not that he seemed inclined to hear about it.

“I’m not judging you.”

“No?”

He shook his head. “I leave the judging and condemning to the society bitches who keep trying to have this area written off.”

Shay took a step back. “Society — ?”

“*Bitches*. You haven’t heard of them? WAM. Women aiming for morality, or some such ridiculous crap. As if they even know what morality means.”

Shay knew them well. They were a group of righteous biddies who had been rather persistent in petitioning her offices, wanting her to back their cause. They considered her one of them: rich and elite and upper class, ready to rid the world of the more unseemly elements, especially the human elements.

But they hadn’t taken into consideration the fact that Shay had come by her money through marriage to a wonderful man, not by familial inheritance. She hadn’t been raised with it, so she had no inbred snobbery. Her own parents were happily middle class, and very supportive of any measure that might help the less fortunate.

She herself had been one of their efforts at helping where and how they could, which added to her determination to spread the goodwill.

When she was six years old, they'd taken her in and smothered her with affection and acceptance, making her a part of their family, giving her a little sister and safety and stability. Now they lovingly put up with her pushy, domineering, take-charge ways, and her unorthodox methods for giving back.

But even they would have difficulty accepting her pretense of being a prostitute.

She should probably tell him the truth. Instead, she said, "You don't talk like any preacher I've ever known."

That observation brought his frown back and flattened his mouth. His eyes looked like flint, his jaw like granite.

Unfazed by the show of hostility, Shay asked, "Is it just a nickname, or are you really a preacher?"

Leaning his head back against the crumbling face of the building, he released her hand to rub the bridge of his nose.

Shay immediately missed his warmth, his comfort.

After what seemed like forever, he growled, "Yeah, I'm a preacher." He fell silent a few moments more, listening as the sounds of a police siren swelled and then faded. "But you don't have to worry about constant sermons and advice at the safe house. You'll get help, not lectures."

"I wasn't worried." Intrigued, yes, but not worried. He had an edge of sharp competence to his manner that seemed more suitable to a gunslinger, not a man of God. Shay knew her own background, the motives that drove her to this neighborhood on such a miserable night, the overwhelming compulsion to help others as she had been helped.

But what motivated him?

She tucked her hands behind her back, resisting the temptation to touch him. "So you've given up on your religion?"

"I didn't say that."

He sounded so put out with her, Shay let that topic drop. "What's your name?"

His gaze zeroed in on her again. "Everyone calls me Preacher."

"So I'm not allowed to know it?"

"You don't need to know. Besides, we have more important things to think about tonight." He started away, but Shay didn't budge.

Glancing over his shoulder, he ordered, "Get a move on."

Shay countered, "Tell me your name."

Impatience rose up, nearly making his dark blond hair stand on end. "This is no time for games."

Oh, boy. And here she'd always thought preachers were supposed to be full of endless, unwavering forbearance. Such a contradiction. But Shay didn't scare easily. "I'll go with you. When I know your name." And then, to soften her insistence: "You can't expect me to just go traipsing off with a stranger."

"And hearing my name is all the reassurance you need?"

His disbelief and suspicion made Shay grin. "Yeah."

Rankled, he rubbed his jaw, dragged a hand over his damp hair. Then he stuck out his hand. "Bryan Kelly." No sooner did he say it than he looked poleaxed, like he wanted to turn around and walk away from her, or curse, or punch the brick wall.

Instead, he just stood there, frozen, his hand extended.

"Bryan." She tasted the name, watched him watching her, and closed her fingers around his. "I like it."

"I meant to say Bruce."

Shay blinked twice. "What?"

With her hand still held in his, he repeated, "I meant to say Bruce. Bryan's . . . my middle name."

"Bruce Bryan Kelly?" And she thought her own name was unique.

His scowl was back, blacker and meaner than ever. "I prefer you call me Preacher."

"Why?"

He appeared to be grinding his teeth. "Because that's what everyone calls me."

"So?"

"I can't show favoritism." He seemed satisfied with that explanation, enough to expound on it. "You can imagine how that'd look, all things considered."

It was difficult not to laugh. "Things being that I'm a prostitute and you're offering to protect me?"

If looks could hurt . . . "Exactly."

"I'll call you Bryan — but only when we're alone."

Seconds passed while he stared at her, probably trying to intimidate her. "Will you, now?"

She met him stare for stare. "Yes."

His eyes narrowed more, his lip curled, and he turned away. "Good thing we won't be alone much, then." He still had her hand caught in his, practically dragging her along, keeping close to the buildings and as far from the blowing rain as they could get.

Pulling the tiger's tail, Shay asked sweetly, "Don't you want to know my name?"

They walked another ten feet before he said in distraction, "What the hell? Go ahead and tell me."

His absent tone was tempered by the protective way he led her down the deserted street. For a preacher, he had incredible instincts, staying alert, constantly scanning the area. Had he maybe served in the service before choosing this vocation? Or was his edgy, suspicious nature just a basic part of the man?

Whatever the reasons for his unique attitudes, Shay liked them. She liked him.

It was the first time since her husband that a man had bothered to show interest in her for any reason other than her money. She was well used to men fawning over her, trying to ingratiate themselves into her life. She had connections and wealth, which meant she had power. The combination served as quite an inducement to most guys.

But Bryan Kelly was unaware of her assets; for heaven's sake, the man thought she was a common hooker in a dirty little neighborhood, desperate enough to be selling her wares on a night like this. It wasn't the most complimentary assumption ever made.

But it was better than being wanted for her money.

And for the moment, she preferred he go on thinking it. Which meant she couldn't give him her full name. "You can call me Shay."

"Shea what?"

No way would she give him her last name. After recent events, she'd suffered some truly awful publicity and he'd probably read most of it. Knowing how he felt about WAM, it wouldn't be a stretch to think he'd leave her standing in the street alone if he realized her identity. "Just Shay."

After a furtive glance, he asked, "Just Shea, like the stadium?" Amusement lightened his eyes. "Or just Shea, like Cher, important enough that you only need one name?"

Was he laughing at her? It didn't matter. Laughter was better than disdain any day. "Just Shay, as in short for Shaina." She spelled out her name for him. No one in the papers had known her full name. No one had called her Shaina since she'd been adopted.

He nodded, then said, "No last name, huh?"

"I like to protect my privacy."

After a look that could cut, he let it go, and for once, Shay was glad. If he didn't ask any other questions, she wouldn't have to outright lie to him.

He led her along until they came to a fully lit section, leaving the blackout behind. The buildings were close together, some rundown, some tidy, all of them showing signs of poverty.

He released her hand and pointed ahead. "See that tall, skinny building at the end of the street? That's the safe house. You're welcome there any time."

"Thank you, Bryan."

His piercing gaze locked on hers, while one side of his mouth curled. It wasn't humor that put that half smile on his hard face. "You're a pushy broad, aren't you?"

Since Shay couldn't deny that, she only shrugged an apology. It was a rhetorical question anyway, given how he turned his attention away.

She liked holding his hand and walking beside him in the rain, feeling his attentiveness to his surroundings and listening to his deep voice and breathing his scent.

She'd like to get to know him better, too, to maybe work with him, maybe be . . . intimate with him.

Okay, so she'd jumped ahead with giant leaps on that one. The timing couldn't be more wrong, and considering that he was a preacher, those thoughts were even more inappropriate. But these things really didn't wait for perfect timing, she supposed.

It had been a long time in coming, and now that desire was finally hitting her again, it did so in full force. She felt it everywhere, such wonderful feelings. And they were intensifying with each second they spent together.

Watching Bryan's long-legged stride excited her. Hearing his deep-toned, rough voice made her insides swirl. Even his ears seemed sexy, and if that wasn't lust, she didn't know what to call it.

With his palm at the small of her back, he ushered her ahead of him. He was easily six feet tall, which left them nearly the same height. Bryan didn't seem intimidated by that. In fact, he didn't appear to notice. His inattention to her as a woman might be a problem, she decided.

He wrestled a set of keys out of a tight,

damp jeans pocket and unlocked the door, then held it open for her. Lights were on inside, and though the room was shabby, it was clean and warm.

Furnished with multiple seating of mismatched couches and chairs and benches, it reminded her of a used furniture store. The scarred linoleum floor had a deep slope and was bare except for an occasional worn area rug. No dust collected in the corners, and no muddy tracks marred the floor. Somehow, the room appeared comfortably lived in, inviting and cozy.

As she slipped out of his now soaked jacket, she watched him. "Do you stay here, too, Bryan?"

"No." He had his back to her, snapping the door shut and turning all the locks to secure the house. With the brighter lighting, she could study him in more detail. His thickly lashed, dark eyes were made for seduction. His dark blond hair, straight and a tad too long, had lighter sun streaks, making an interesting contrast with his eyes.

"Why not?"

"Staying here wouldn't be appropriate, now would it? And you can just imagine how WAM would slant it. By the time they retold the circumstances, we'd all be involved in drunken orgies or worse."

He ran his hands through his wet hair to push it out of his face, and turned toward her. Shay held out his jacket — and he froze.

With his hands still in his hair, his gaze zeroed in on her body. Slowly, very slowly, he lowered his arms. His attention was nearly tactile, heating her, making her heart beat fast.

Belatedly, Shay remembered what he'd told her, that the rain had made her tailored, white silk dress transparent. Oh, no. With dread, she looked down, and almost collapsed with embarrassment.

The light inside the safe house was bright, and not only could he see through her dress, but the rain had soaked through to her white lace panties and bra, too, rendering them transparent as well. She could actually see the pink circles of her nipples, the shadowing of hair between her thighs.

She slapped her hands over herself, but she still felt naked, and she still had his attention. His expression hadn't changed, except that his eyes were black and fathomless.

He wasn't embarrassed. No, he was interested. He was a man, looking at a woman.

Though Shay felt uncertain of herself, she also felt daring. She wanted, for some reason, to hear him admit that he found her attractive. Turning slightly away, she held out the jacket again. "Here you go. Thank you."

Unlike her, he suffered no nervousness or reserve. He accepted the coat. "There're donated clothes folded in the pantry in the kitchen. Down the hall and to your left. Take whatever you need. Use the mudroom to wash up and change into dry clothes."

Shay licked her lips. She was thirty years old, and no one in the last twenty of those years had ever accused her of being timid. She wanted him and the first step in that direction would have to be honesty.

She drew a slow breath, shored up her nerve, and said, "I'm curious about something, Bryan."

He hung the coat on a peg by the door. "And that is?"

"What would you say if I told you I wasn't actually a prostitute after all?"

Chapter Two

His disbelief couldn't have been more plain. "Not a hooker, huh? So why else would you be here, in this neighborhood, dressed like that?" He nodded toward her clothes.

Shay stiffened. Her dress was expensive, stylish, and entirely appropriate — when dry. Now . . . She looked down at herself again and had to admit he had a point.

"Were you slumming? Spying for the rich biddies who want to take away every ounce of assistance these people have so they can pretend they don't exist?" He moved closer to her, deliberately trying to intimidate her with his size and strength. "You want me to believe you're here to visit relatives? To do a little shopping?"

Shay shook her head. "No."

"It doesn't matter to me, all right? No need to be ashamed and no need to lie. Hell, as long as you're not one of those society women or part of that damned WAM group, we'll get along just fine."

Fascinated by these new disclosures,

Shay asked, "You think all society women are like that? Mean-spirited and unconcerned about others?"

"Aren't they? You heard about that rich lady who organizes all the charities, the one the papers call the Crown Princess? She thinks she's so benevolent, yet when a young girl went to one of her shelters for help, she was turned away. It's been the talk of the year, in every damn paper you pick up."

Shay felt a chill of pain slice up her back. She said cautiously, "The papers rarely tell the whole or accurate truth."

Bryan snorted. "The truth is that the girl almost died not forty-eight hours later, alone. If a truck driver hadn't found her, she'd probably be dead right not. But the shelter had refused her help."

Breathing became difficult, from both his censure and her own smothering guilt. "The papers also said that the manager of that shelter was fired, that the lady who'd founded it didn't know anything about the incident . . ."

"Yeah, right." His rude tone ripped apart her excuses. "She set up the foundation, making herself look like a generous god to all her society friends, then didn't bother to make certain things were run the right way. She was probably off shopping somewhere, or having a dinner party while that girl almost died trying to give birth alone."

Shay felt herself shaking in the face of his disgust. *She hadn't known,* she wanted to scream. Excuses choked in her throat: the number of shelters she was responsible for, the number of projects she established, all demanding her time and attention. There were holes in every organization.

But she knew he was right. There was no excuse. And she'd never forgive herself, so how could she expect others to forgive her?

As she turned her face away, Bryan cursed. "Shit, I upset you and I didn't mean to."

Even feeling so horrid, she had to laugh. "You have a terrible potty mouth for a preacher."

He rolled his eyes over that observation.

"And you didn't upset me," she lied. "I'm just surprised at your . . . vehemence. I mean, it's not like you know her personally."

"I know her kind well enough and I know I can trust the desperation that forces a person to make a decision, good or bad, over cold apathy any day."

It hadn't been cold apathy, far from it. She just couldn't convince the papers of that. What the public thought no longer bothered her, not when her own guilt was so heavy.

But . . . what Bryan thought did matter. He was a good man, doing what he could to help others.

Thank God she hadn't told him her last name. She could only imagine what he'd do if he knew the truth. She *was* Shay Sommers, the very woman he despised. Dubbed the Crown Princess, a woman accused of living a charmed life, using her charity functions as nothing more than tax write-offs and society showmanship. If Bryan had known her real identity, he probably would have thrown her into the rioting mob rather than trying to save her from it. And he'd be especially angry when he learned how she'd misled him.

"Christ, how'd we get off on this anyway? Look, how I feel about wealth and all the prejudice that comes with it won't affect you." He gave a halfhearted, feigned smile, trying to reassure her. She'd already guessed that he wasn't a man given to smiles; he looked more at ease snarling than smiling.

"It's all right."

"No it's not. You're shivering. Go get changed and then we'll talk. I'll introduce you to everyone else."

His sudden conversational switch threw her. "Everyone else?"

For the most part, he kept his gaze on her face. But every so often he skimmed her body, lingering in select places. "Barb's the cook and housekeeper. Besides her, three other women are staying here now, but more might come — or they might go." He shrugged. "It changes off and on."

"Three other prostitutes?"

His brows lowered at her blunt question. "They're trying to start new lives for themselves. It can be done, you know."

He didn't have to convince her. She already hoped to start a new project, based on the success of helping these women start over. But she herself planned to stay a prostitute for a while longer. Bryan would forcibly boot her out if he knew she wasn't what he assumed her to be.

And she wanted to stay.

She had enough reasons to justify the deception, at least to herself. She wanted to know how Bryan maintained the shelter, where his donations came from, details on how he worked the safe house. She could use those details in setting up her own shelters.

She also wanted to know all about him,

the past that had molded him, the future he saw for himself, and why he had such a deep hatred for money.

But most of all, she wanted him to know her, to give her a chance to prove she wasn't the malicious, uncaring bitch portrayed in the papers. She wanted him to know she wasn't a Crown Princess at all, regardless of what biased truths were told. She was just a woman who wanted, needed, to help others. But telling him wouldn't do it. She had to show him.

It was odd, but the very thing that had made her so appealing to other men — her wealth — was the one thing that would make this man despise her, and probably before she even had a chance to prove herself to him.

She did care, very much. But she knew the type of rich people he detested. She extorted those people regularly with her many charity functions and benefits. She understood them, how to squeeze sizeable donations out of them, but she didn't really like them any more than Bryan did.

On the other hand, she knew people like herself, people with money who wanted to make a difference, likable people who cared. Her brother-in-law Sebastian was that way, but she didn't tell Bryan that. He had his own prejudices to overcome.

Thoughts of her sister and brother-in-law naturally led a trail to other questions, and before she could consider the impropriety of it, she asked, "Have you ever married? Are you married now?"

Incredulous, he said, "That's —"

"None of my business, I know. But will you tell me anyway?"

He leaned closer, saying succinctly, "No."

"But . . ."

He caught her chin between his thumb and fingertips. "Listen up, sweetheart. Wife or no, you've got no reason to fear me. I only want to help you."

Right. And next he'd sell her a bridge. She'd seen his reaction to her body, to her. Even now, he had a hard time keeping his visual attention elevated above her neckline. He might not want to be interested in any other way, but as a man, some things were unavoidable.

Her silence had him sighing and dropping his hand. "It'd help if you called me Preacher, like everyone else does."

"No," she answered softly. "I don't want to be like everyone else."

He shook his head. "Stubborn."

"And I don't want to think of you as a

preacher." She saw he was ready to walk away, so she rushed through her explanation. "I prefer to think of you as a man, an extremely appealing man. And when you stop making assumptions, maybe you'll start to think of me as a woman."

For someone who made compassion his stock in trade, he sure seemed uncomfortable with it, as if he'd rather be raising hell than serving heaven.

"Trust me, I know you're a woman."

Shay shivered again, this time because of the sensual threat in his tone, the masculine appreciation.

"But —"

She didn't want to hear his "buts." Smiling, she interrupted him to say, "I like you, Bruce Bryan Kelly. Maybe, once we know each other better, you'll start to like me a little, too."

She wanted to stay and talk to him more, but she took pity on the poor man. He'd had a rough day saving a prostitute who wasn't, trying to ignore his own natural inclinations, and now trying to ignore hers as well.

Besides, she needed to call Dawn, to check on Leigh and make sure she got settled in. She left nothing to chance these days, not since that awful debacle with the pregnant girl. She trusted Dawn implicitly, but she still checked and double-checked everything, to make certain nothing like that ever happened again.

She also needed to tell Dawn that she'd be staying in the safe house. The thought had occurred to her that it might be easier to get to know the women, to gain their trust, and for them to give her assistance if they thought she was one of them. And what better way to do that than with the ideal solution the preacher had unwittingly offered her?

With Dawn on the outside carrying out her wishes and Shay on the inside spending time with the women, learning of their needs, she could make real headway. And since no one would know her, the recent taint on her name couldn't affect her efforts.

If Bryan Kelly wanted to shelter a prostitute, she'd be a prostitute.

She thought again of Bryan's reaction when he'd looked at her body and seen her as close to naked as possible. He wasn't indifferent to her. He just needed to remember that, first and foremost, he was a man.

And then maybe he'd be able to help her start being a woman.

When he finally learned that she was rich, that she had more money than any three women could spend in a lifetime, that she was in truth the very same society lady he strongly disdained, it would be too late for him. He'd know that even though she was rich, she did care. And hopefully he'd want her as much, maybe more, than she wanted him.

With a barely suppressed anger common to his temperament, Bryan Kelly entered his brother's small office and quietly closed the door. This room was the only spare room on the ground floor of the house, the only place where he could be himself for a minute.

He leaned back against the door, brooding, annoyed. Surprised. Damn, but hookers were looking mighty good these days.

The plan had seemed so simple, until now. Who could have guessed that playing a preacher would be so tough? Did his twin put up with this crap all the time?

He was a damn saint if he did.

His brother, Bruce, had warned him about a lot of situations.

Sexy bombshells with killer bods wasn't included.

Shay was hot enough to set his blood to boiling, and she was as taboo as a dame could be.

Bruce would have had a conniption if he knew Bryan's thoughts. Preachers weren't supposed to view women — definitely not prostitutes — with lust.

He half laughed. He'd always admired what his brother did, the life he led, but never more so than now.

As a bounty hunter, the only prostitutes Bryan ever met were the ones vying for his money. They'd put on a lot of miles and looked equal parts desperate and hard. Walking away from them had been no problem at all.

Hell, he was picky about the females he invited to his bed. For the most part, he didn't trust people, especially women. They were clever and manipulative and while he felt pity for the women Bruce helped, he sure as hell didn't want to bed them.

But then, none of the others he'd met had looked or acted like Shay.

When he'd started this harebrained plan, he'd known that being surrounded by needy, sex-driven women who were totally off limits would be culture shock. But Shay? No, he couldn't have imagined her if he'd tried.

He'd gone out on patrol, as Bruce often did, because breaking his brother's routine would give them away. People would realize that it was Bruce's twin filling in, not Bruce himself. And that would ruin the plan.

The night was so shitty, Bryan sure as hell hadn't expected to see any working girls. Most anyone with a brain had enough sense to be indoors, out of the vicious storm.

But there she'd been, tall, supersexy, with pale hair hanging in wet tangles to shield part of her lowered face. Her dress, a snug, minuscule white concoction totally unsuitable to the area and any purpose other than advertising her body, left her endlessly long legs on display.

The upper part of her dress had become transparent in the rain, displaying round breasts and nipples stiff from the cold wind. He'd forced his gaze down the length of her body and stalled on her flat dress shoes. They didn't really jive with what most of the prostitutes wore, but then, few prostitutes were as tall as this one.

In the three-inch heels most the hookers favored, she'd be taller than him. Maybe that's why she wore the flats; it probably wouldn't do for her to tower over her johns.

He hadn't wanted to approach her. She'd screamed "Trouble" with a capital T. But damn it, his brother wouldn't have hesitated. Bruce would have seen it as his duty, and he'd have willingly gone to her. So Bryan did what he had to, and made the effort to "save" her.

He snorted. Yeah, right. She was so damn cocky, so self-assured, she'd probably only come along because she thought she might be able to rip him off somehow. He'd keep a close watch on his wallet.

And that nonsense about liking him? Prostitutes liked any guy with money to spend. For fifty bucks, she'd like him as much as he wanted.

But . . . for some reason he didn't really believe that. He'd gotten by on gut instincts too many times to disregard one this strong. Somehow Shay didn't fit the mold, and he didn't mean in the obvious ways. It was more than that.

She seemed to vibrate with energy and something more. She didn't look downtrodden.

She didn't look used.

She was slim but strong, with almost regal features — except for those innocent blue eyes, so huge they could suck a man in. But not Bryan. He'd long since grown immune to feminine wiles.

She hadn't run off as he'd expected, as Bruce warned they often did. He'd been prepared to chase her, but instead of fleeing, she'd stepped right off the curb into the stinging rain to meet him. Crazy broad.

Then, from one heartbeat to the next, her entire side of the street went black as pitch. There'd been no time for gentle urging, as was his brother's custom, no time for explanations. The last power failure in that slummy area had left two people badly beaten and several buildings ransacked. Riots often erupted with little coercing. A blackout could fuel all types of depraved crimes.

Bryan knew the feel, the taste, and scent of danger, and it had surrounded them. Luckily she hadn't argued with him too much. Chili's timely appearance had helped to convince her, no doubt because Chili was a greasy little bastard with a smile like a pig.

The danger had brought out Bryan's instincts, and he'd temporarily abandoned the ruse, acting more like himself than Bruce. Then when she'd asked for his name, he'd screwed up big time. He'd given his own. He didn't make mistakes like that. Ever.

But somehow, with her, he had.

And he'd complicated it further with his half-assed correction. Bruce Bryan? Jesus, even to his own ears it sounded lame.

Not many people knew his brother as anything other than the Preacher, but he didn't like taking chances. He'd have to convince her . . . what was he thinking? To hell with convincing her. She wouldn't be around long enough to cause too much trouble.

Out of all the women his brother tried to "save," he only reached about a fourth. The rest took advantage of his hospitality, his generosity, then returned to work in a few days, a week, a month.

Regardless of how different she seemed, Shay would do the same. He'd just keep his dick in his pants until then.

He recalled his brother's lecture to be like a doctor around the women, immune to them as females. But Bryan only saw women one way and that was the one way Bruce had ruled out.

Still, for a week he'd affected that attitude with ease. Now he felt challenged.

Hell, he couldn't understand the workings of the average female mind, so how was he supposed to understand a trollop?

Knotting both hands in his wet T-shirt,

he jerked it over his head, wadded it into a ball and flung it into the corner. It hit the faded wallpaper with a dull plop, but did little to relieve him.

Outside, thunder boomed, reflecting his mood. At least Bruce had gotten the roof fixed, so there wouldn't be any damp spots in the ceiling upstairs, no need to carry up pots to catch the leaks. It hadn't been easy convincing Bruce to take his money for repairs. But Bryan was a mean son of a bitch, while Bruce was a nice, sensitive guy, so he'd just more or less forced it on him.

Bryan was damn proud of Bruce and what he did, even if he couldn't always agree with it. He supported his brother's efforts and he wouldn't let himself get distracted by a woman with a nice ass and a bold manner, not when Bruce needed him to be on guard, to be the ruthless, calculating hard-ass that their father often called him.

Someone was out to hurt Bruce, someone vicious. Verbal threats had expanded to physical ones. The last attack had put Bruce in the hospital, and that had Bryan pissed. Really pissed.

No one hurt his brother and got away with it.

Soon, another attack would come. But instead of finding Bruce, the bastard would run into Bryan. And that would be the end of that. Bryan just had to wait, then he'd have him.

Which meant he'd have to ignore, or at least tolerate, Shay's invitations. He almost laughed at the irony. Could there be a worse man for this particular job? Since the death of his wife, what he did with women was either apprehend or fuck them. He couldn't do either of those things now. No, he'd have to do the impossible. He'd have to get involved.

Neck deep involved.

The clock on the small table beside Bruce's one guest chair told him time was ticking away. He'd give her twenty minutes to get dried off and changed, then they'd get the rules straight. In the meantime, he could check out a few things.

Because he was soaked, he went to the closet where Bruce kept spare clothes. Pulling out the first shirt he came across, Bryan shoved his arms into the sleeves and quickly did up the buttons, then rolled the sleeves above his elbows.

He dropped into the easy chair, pulled out his cell phone and punched in a series of numbers. He had respect in his field, favors owed him, and connections everywhere. What Shay wanted to keep private, he'd find out on his own.

But the day was rife with frustration. The detective he had called had run a check that came up empty. Far as he could tell, they didn't have a record on any tall blond hookers named Shay. Shelly and Sherry, Scarlet and Selma. But not Shay or Shaina. He checked with other bounty hunters, but no one on the run fit her description.

Maybe she'd worked a different area, even a different state. Whatever — he'd uncover her secrets somehow. Bruce was the trusting sort. Too bad he wasn't Bruce.

For now, he'd follow the mundane routine of registering a new resident to the safe house. He'd play his brother. He'd keep his hands to himself.

And eventually the game would end.

When enough time had passed, Bryan left the privacy of the office. The short hall leading to the kitchen was empty, but he found Shay's sodden purse set on the dryer. It had been emptied so that a comb, lipstick, sunglasses and other female items were scattered about, along with the contents of her wallet spread out to dry.

Bryan didn't hesitate to snoop. Hell,

snooping was what he did.

She had a few bills, a handful of change, a post office receipt, and a grocery list. No credit cards, no drivers license, nothing that could ID her. Not that he was surprised. She really didn't strike him as being stupid. Just brazen. And sexy.

He checked out the receipt, but the rain had faded the ink and he couldn't even make out the total or the location. A dead end.

He laid the receipt back where he'd found it and took two long steps to knock lightly on the wall outside the swinging door to the kitchen.

He called out, "You decent?" then wanted to kick his own ass.

She was a hooker, for God's sake; nothing decent about that.

Shay pushed the door aside and smiled at him. "I was just getting ready to make tea. Would you like some?"

He eyed her fresh appearance. Her damp hair had been combed and slightly curling ends now brushed the tops of her breasts. Her makeup, which had been smeared from the rain, was washed away. She looked young and happy, her blue eyes bright and full of wholesome welcome.

He didn't buy it.

The tattered jeans she'd chosen from the box of donated goods were a little too short and way too tight, fitting her like a second skin. Oddly enough, she'd paired them with an oversized misshapen sweatshirt he assumed to be one of Bruce's cast-offs. So she wasn't advertising her body right now. Maybe it was her off hours.

She shifted under his gaze, and Bryan noticed her bare feet and painted pink toenails. Even dressed in ragged clothes, with all the artificial enticements stripped away, she looked incredibly beautiful.

I'm a preacher, Bryan reminded himself. And not just any preacher, but his brother. What would his brother do in this situation?

For sure, Bruce wouldn't stare at her breasts, which rounded out the sweatshirt real nice. And he wouldn't reach for her hips, thinking how it'd feel to hold her as she sank down onto him, lifted, sank . . . *Damn it.*

Okay, he had it. Bruce would realize that she not only looked sexy enough to eat, but also sweet and innocent and carefree. She may have been just that once long ago, but not anymore. Now she sold herself to any slimy bastard with enough money in his hand, probably out of sheer desperation. Right.

She was desperate and needy.

He pitied her.

He felt sorry for her. . . .

Until he looked beyond her and saw her dress, bra, and wispy little panties draped over the kitchen chairs to dry.

Ah, shit. *Not her panties.*

She'd definitely done that on purpose. Left those lacy little bits of nothing out just to provoke him. And that had to mean she wasn't wearing any underclothes now at all.

All women knew how to draw men in. Hookers would be especially good at it.

But it wouldn't work on Bryan. He was here for his brother, and no woman, regardless of her appeal or lack of underwear, would make him blow that.

Bringing his attention back to her smiling face, he said, "Sure, sweetheart. Tea'd be great. Thanks." *Tea*. Just thinking about it almost made his stomach turn. He'd rather have a beer, but Bruce didn't drink, so there wouldn't be any around even if he dared deviate from his brother's habits.

As he stepped into the small confines of the kitchen, she didn't move. So, she wanted to tease? Fine. Two could play that game.

He skimmed past her, holding her gaze, letting his chest brush her breasts oh so slowly until her breath caught and she moved back.

He contained his smile of triumph. "Where's Barb?" Barb he could handle. Barb was surly most of the time, outrageous the rest. Barb didn't make him hot.

Flushed, Shay leaned against the counter. "She said she had a slight headache. I sent her to put a cool cloth on her forehead. I hope that helps."

Apparently Shay took charge with ease. That didn't surprise him. "Barb suffers from migraines." Bryan lightly tossed the items from Bruce's office onto the Formica table. The spare key made a clinking sound as it landed. The notepad and pen fell beside it. "She has a prescription but hates to use it since it makes her sleepy."

Shay's gaze flickered to the table and back to his face. "She told me. She said she had to stay alert to fix you something to eat and to finish cleaning up afterward. But I told her I'd take care of it."

Giving her a direct, hard stare, Bryan said, "I'm thirty-five and I haven't starved yet. I know how to feed myself." And he wasn't masochistic enough to want to spend his dinner with her.

"But Barb said she cooks all your meals."

"Barb just likes to stay busy. It's in her nature."

"She said you brought her here when she had nowhere else to go."

Bryan couldn't hide his surprise. Bruce had told him all about Barb's situation, but Barb wasn't a person given to sharing confidences. So far, she'd commented on his body, told him it was a shame he didn't share his "sweet self," and she sneered or complained. She set out food, picked up around the place, joked and flattered, or insulted with glee. But she didn't confide.

Bruce said it was all a front, that Barb didn't warm to people easily. Yet Shay had only been in the kitchen a few minutes and already she had Barb talking.

As if Shay knew exactly what he was thinking, she smiled. "Barb's been with you a little over a year now. Unlike the other women here, you pay her wages as a manager."

He propped his hands on his hips, annoyed. "She told you all that?"

"Yes. She feels indebted. Let her do her part to pay you back, Bryan. It would injure her pride to make her think she wasn't needed." As she spoke, the teapot began to whistle and Shay turned her back on him, preparing two cups of tea.

Bryan stared at her ass.

Bruce, or God, or both would probably strike him down for it. But . . . it was a really fine ass. And he wasn't a preacher, automatically immune to such things.

No, he was a bounty hunter, and he'd always been partial to a nice heart-shaped derriere. Hers was of special interest, though, because he could see the small rectangular outline of plastic cards in her back pocket — no doubt the IDs that were missing from her wallet.

Nope, nothing dumb about her.

After carrying the cups to the table, she pulled out a chair and sat. Or more like she sprawled, her body going boneless as she slumped in the seat, stretching out those neverending legs. And still she managed to look elegant and sexy.

Bryan had never seen a woman so comfortable with herself and her surroundings, whatever her surroundings might be. He was already used to the hookers being immodest to the point of being lewd, almost unaware of their bodies, as if they no longer thought of them as their own or as private. Their attitudes carried over to him, and he was able to see them the same way. Not sexy, just very used to showing skin.

But Shay was impossible to ignore. She just didn't behave like he'd expected, like Bruce had predicted.

If he didn't know better, he'd think she had no idea how sexy she looked. But as a hooker, that wasn't possible.

He took his own seat. "This house wouldn't run smoothly without Barb."

"I hope you tell her that. Often."

Her chiding tone grated on his nerves. His brother did what he could. Sometimes, to his own mind, it wasn't enough, but Bryan knew that Bruce was as honorable and considerate as they came.

He didn't like anyone, especially this pushy bimbo, judging his brother. "Shay . . ."

Teasing, whisper-soft, she replied, "Bryan?"

The reprimand died on his tongue. *I'm a preacher. I'm a preacher.* Bruce would reassure her, not set her straight. Bruce would make her feel welcome. "You're not like the other women here."

That made her laugh, but she quickly stifled the sound. "Sorry." She rubbed away her smile. "How am I different, do you think?"

She said it like a challenge, but then

everything about her, from her smile to her openness, challenged him. *You don't seem wounded. You seem much too confident and sure of your actions. You're too damned bossy.* He couldn't say it, of course. Bruce wouldn't say it.

"Well?"

He had to tell her something, so he said, "You're more relaxed than most of the women." Then a thought struck him. "You haven't been working long, have you?"

"Since I was fourteen."

An invisible fist squeezed his larynx. He choked, wheezed in a breath, and choked some more. Fourteen! Holy shit.

Brows raised at his reaction, she said, tongue in cheek, "Oh, you mean prostituting."

Feeling duped, he pondered the pleasure of putting her over his knee. She deserved it. But of course, his brother would have a cow if he did something so outrageous. Through his teeth, Bryan said, "Most of the women prefer to call it *working*."

"Really? I prefer to call it what it is." Her eyes were serious, but her soft mouth still sported that teasing smile.

He wanted to lick it away. When this damn switcheroo was over, he just might. "Have you been prostituting long?"

"Actually, I'm fairly new."

He hadn't realized how tight his stomach felt until she answered. He'd dealt with a lot of ugly shit in his life, most recently in Visitation, North Carolina, where he helped to save Joe Winston's ass. A woman and two kids had blindsided him then, ruining his plan to use Winston as bait to get the fugitive he wanted.

They'd found a soft side he hadn't known he possessed. Now Shay did the same. It shouldn't have mattered, but knowing she hadn't been selling herself long filled him with immense relief.

It also made sense, because a woman like her couldn't be easily ignored. If she'd been around long, Bruce would have already found her and brought her to the shelter.

And that thought really perturbed him.

Bruce wasn't like him. Bruce was a hell of a lot nicer and therefore more susceptible to female wiles. She would have had Bruce wrapped around her little finger in no time.

With his own humorless smile, Bryan said, "I'm glad I happened along when I did, then."

"Happened along? I had the feeling you were patrolling the area."

"I watch out for trouble," he told her. And for once, he gave the undiluted truth. He sought out criminals, brought them to justice — but usually with a nine-millimeter in hand. Not a Bible. "In this neighborhood, I can usually find it."

Hell, he'd found her, hadn't he?

"What kind of trouble?"

A few truths about her newly chosen profession wouldn't hurt. It might even set her back on the straight and narrow, where she'd be safer. "Sometimes the women refuse help because they're supporting a boyfriend's habit, or children, and they figure they can't make enough in a conventional job, not with their backgrounds."

"Meaning?"

He shrugged. "They lack acceptable work experience and education." He hoped she would disclose her own reasoning for being here, but she disappointed him.

"I like how you say that, how nonoffensive it is. You go to great pains with your wording, don't you?"

Bruce did — and Bruce had coached him on what to say. Bryan studied her. She didn't squirm, didn't pose or posture herself — just remained lounged back in that stiff little kitchen chair, at her leisure, perfectly comfortable with the conversation, with the situation, with him and with herself.

"Why would I want to insult or offend anyone?"

"I don't know." And then with a crooked grin: "You have the look of someone who normally wouldn't care."

That's because normally he wouldn't.

"But you're actually pretty good at this." She took another sip of tea. "So go on. Some of the women refuse your help . . . ?"

Her prompt made him want to reach out and shake her. He wasn't used to being led around verbally or otherwise. And he wasn't comfortable giving control, even of a simple conversation, to someone else. Especially not a woman. Especially not a hooker. "They go back on the streets. Sometimes they end up hurt, beaten . . ."

He drew a breath. In this, at least, he and Bruce were alike. Neither of them could stomach brutality against women or children.

Their methods for dealing with it, though, varied by a mile. He told her Bruce's method. "I try to watch out for them, see that they get help if they need it, when they need it. But it isn't always possible. Some of the women's pimps cause trouble. Sometimes I'm not there when I should be."

Avoiding his gaze, her eyes on her teacup, Shay said, "A person can't be everywhere at once." Then her lashes lifted and she caught him with her innocent gaze. "I think you could use some assistance here."

Didn't he know it. Bruce left himself vulnerable far too many times. "That's asking for the impossible. Most of society wants to write off this area and pretend the problems don't exist. If they ignore it, it'll go away. They're not interested in finding solutions."

Shay nodded, very introspective for the moment. Then she leaned forward, propping her elbows on the table. "You said I seem different from the other women here. Well, you're certainly unlike any preacher I've ever met."

Not good. Back up, Bryan. "Because I work in the field, instead of a church?"

"Working in the field," she repeated. "I like that. But no, I meant because you don't preach about the evils of the flesh."

"No." Their father preached, endlessly, on everything under the sun. He was good at it, both effective and entertaining. People who would normally doze in the pews would be alert and engrossed when his dad got started.

His sons didn't seem to have the same charisma when it came to relating, though Bruce was certainly heads and tails ahead of Bryan, who, according to his dad, tried to communicate with grunts.

Bryan grinned, thinking of how his dad and Bruce always harassed him about his lack of social skills. Then he caught Shay watching him and pulled himself back to the present.

What was it Bruce always told him? Oh, yeah. In righteous tones, Bryan repeated, "These women won't accept words, so instead I try to offer options. Maybe a few solutions."

"Like what?"

Because he was familiar with Bruce's operation, he could answer without hesitation. "Safety and physical comfort have to come before they can be spiritually content."

Shay reached out and touched him, her fingertips light against his wrist.

Yeah, she was asking for it. But for the time being, he'd have to refuse her. He slowly pulled away.

"What happened to you, Bryan? Why aren't you in a nice little church somewhere?"

If he hung out in a church, the roof would probably cave in. He snorted. “Why should I be?”

She raised a brow.

“Everyone deserves a safe place to go for spiritual guidance. It’s just that . . .” *Damn it, Bruce, I’m going to kick your ass when I see you.* He sighed, locked his jaw, and murmured, “I want to do more.”

She stared at him, her expression rapt. “Why here? Why this cause?”

Good question. Why couldn’t Bruce have taken in stray dogs, or assisted the elderly? Why did he have to enmesh himself in overly sexual floozies who all wanted to torment him, this one more than the others?

He drummed up the last speech Bruce had given him. “There’s a lot of misery in the world. But this is in my own backyard. I want to change things and I can’t do that from a safe distance in a safe little church, with safe people. To put out a fire, you have to get close to the flames.”

“That doesn’t mean you have to live in them.”

Damn. He’d told Bruce that exact thing many times, and always gotten the same answer. “Maybe not, but it’s difficult to survive in both worlds, the tidy little communities and the crumbling ones. It scares people on both sides. They're afraid you'll carry something back with you, that you'll somehow spread a disease they won't be able to run away from."

Shay nibbled at her bottom lip before nodding. "I suppose you're right. People fear things they don't understand. Maybe if they were aware of how the problems originated, that no one chooses to be born into poverty, then maybe they wouldn't fear it so much."

Her forthright speech threw him. She sounded just like Bruce. "Maybe," he said, conceding the possibility of truth in her words.

"It's difficult to teach ethereal ideas like morality and pride when you have no electricity and no food on the table."

He couldn't remember the last time he'd had a lengthy, meaningful discussion with a woman. And damned if she didn't have an uncanny insight into the obstacles Bruce faced every day.

"An awareness program is real low on the list of priorities, with so many other things to be done."

"So what's high on your list?"

He tried a smile that fell flat. "Right now, you are."

Her eyes were big and soft, eating him up. Her hand slid up his wrist to his biceps. "Good."

Again, Bryan leaned out of her reach. "Damn it, stop that." Pointing a finger at her, he growled, "You need to understand a few things, lady."

She held her hands up in the air. "I'll behave. No reason to panic."

A cynical smile curved his mouth. "Women don't panic me, even pushy women like yourself. But I've got some questions for you, and we need to get started on them."

"Sure. I'll fix us something to eat while you grill me."

He watched her rise from her seat, then became engrossed with the way her behind moved as she roamed the kitchen, opening cabinets and drawers, as if she'd lived in the safe house for an eternity. "I don't intend to grill you. I just need some information."

She bent into the refrigerator. "There's cold chicken and potato salad. That sound okay to you?"

Distracted by her stance, which he considered a real money-shot, he said, "Yeah, sure. Whatever."

"Good. It'll be ready in a jiffy." Then she

peered over her shoulder. "Well? Fire away with the inquisition. I'm ready."

She looked ready. He decided to get the most pertinent questions out of the way. "When was the last time you were examined?"

She straightened out of the fridge, a little appalled, her cheeks heating. "Examined?" she asked on a whisper of sound.

Was there a better way to ask? If so, he didn't know it. He wasn't cut out for this sentimental, heart-to-heart crap. "Yeah. By a doctor."

She blinked, and looked away from him.

Bryan persisted. "You know, to make sure you're . . . healthy." He'd almost said clean, but caught himself in time.

Turning her back, she asked, "Do I look ill to you?" She was so tall, she didn't have to tiptoe or use Barb's stepstool to reach the top shelf of the cabinets.

Bryan sighed. "You know that's not what I mean."

She pulled down two plates, cleared her throat, and said, "It wasn't that long ago. I don't have anything contagious."

Now he felt like an asshole for asking, like he'd insulted her as well as embarrassed her. But hell, Bruce had it on the list.

Clasping the ends of the pen in both

hands, he attempted to clarify *why* he'd asked. "There's a woman — a doctor — who works with us. Dr. Eve Martin, from the clinic. She gives free examinations to the women."

Shay jerked around with renewed interest. "You said Dr. Martin?"

"That's right." He frowned at her. "You know her?" If she did, then that had to mean she was from the area after all. Maybe Shay was an alias. But why?

She ducked her head and turned away again, then plopped two heaping servings of potato salad onto the plates. Instead of answering, she asked another question. "Why would I need to see a doctor?"

She made it harder than it had to be. "You're not dumb. You know there're a lot of health risks these days."

"No problem with me. I'm always, uh, careful."

The pen threatened to snap in his hands. "Still," he insisted, trying not to growl, "if it's been a while since you've been checked, I'd feel better if you let Dr. Martin look you over."

"No."

He straightened in his chair. "What do you mean, no?" Few people dared to refuse him. In the normal course of things, he wouldn't accept a refusal. "Why the hell not?"

"I don't want to, that's why."

His hand curled into a fist and an uncertain dread began. His voice was even lower when he said, "If there's a problem, you can tell me. It's nothing to be ashamed of. And hiding it won't help."

She turned to face him, her eyes wide.

He stared back, unblinking.

"There's not a problem."

Then why didn't she want a free checkup? "I can get you a private appointment with Dr. Martin. No one else would have to know."

Shay looked from his eyes to his mouth, and damn it, he knew exactly what she was thinking. She made him think it, too.

She blinked, focusing on his eyes again. "This is totally unnecessary. I really am a responsible person."

He gave one sharp nod. "Great. Then you'll agree to see the doctor."

That uncanny stare held him again, as if she could do battle with a look. But he wasn't a pushover like his brother; he wouldn't be budged. Finally, she rolled her eyes in annoyance. "Oh, all right. But I don't need an appointment. I'll just go to the clinic on Saturday."

Dr. Martin would let him know if there were any problems, and Saturday was only three days away. "Does that mean you'll be staying with me . . . with us?" *Whoa, what a slip.*

"If it won't inconvenience anyone."

When he'd started this sham, he hadn't expected to really care about any of the day-to-day stuff. He'd figured on filling in, chatting when necessary, until he found the son of a bitch who was harassing his brother.

But he'd already developed an easy familiarity with the other women. They didn't suspect him of being an impersonator, and he didn't hassle them when they broke the minor rules his brother had set.

But this woman . . . it would be a mistake to get too close to her. He couldn't treat her like he did the other ladies. Probably because she was so different, she got to him in a way no woman had since the death of his wife.

Actually, her effect was unique even beyond that. He'd loved Megan, and his grief, guilt and anger hadn't abated enough with time. But never had he lusted after her like this. His need for Megan had been tempered with uncommon gentleness and an affection that had grown over time.

Shay, on the other hand, hit him like a tropical hurricane. Urgent. Instant. Even if her vocation didn't put him off — and it did — he would never betray his brother's trust by touching her.

"There's plenty of room with six small bedrooms upstairs. Unfortunately, only two baths, one upstairs, and one down here."

If anything, she looked intrigued by the idea of close company. "I don't mind sharing." She bit her bottom lip again. "What about you?"

He didn't like it when she looked at him like that. Or rather, he liked it too much. "What about me?"

"How often will I get to see you?"

"I'll be around. I use the room on the other side of the kitchen as an office when I'm here."

"This is going to be fun."

Like a lobotomy. "Ya think so?"

"Sure. I get along with everyone. It'll be like a girls' night out. When do I get to meet the other women?"

How the hell did he tell her that the other women weren't like her? They were sarcastic, lusty, often raunchy and loud — and those were the nice ones. He shook his head. "You and Morganna will get along.

She's the redhead." And he meant red, as in flaming red. "She's . . . flamboyant."

"You saying I'm flamboyant?"

"In a pushy, disrespectful way, yeah."

She laughed.

"You've already met Barb. And Patti's nice enough." Just too damn grabby. She made him feel like raw meat set before a hungry pit bull. "But Amy is . . . different."

"Different how?"

Bryan remembered his reaction when he'd first met Amy. He looked away. "She'll be okay, but she's still a little wounded."

"Wounded how?" Shay's voice had turned as cold as death. "What does that mean?"

Bryan set the pen aside because otherwise he knew he'd break it. "She's young and scared. Her pimp is not a nice guy, and he had control of her for far too long." He shrugged, trying to relieve some of his own tension, then added, "She's afraid. Of just about everyone and everything."

How Bruce managed to keep his cool in this job amazed Bryan. When he'd seen the bruises on Amy, the utter dejection in her green eyes, he'd wanted to find the fucker who'd hurt her and pound him into the dirt.

But Bruce had been clear on what he

could and couldn't do, and mangling anyone was on the "couldn't do" list.

Besides, for some reason he couldn't understand, Amy blamed only herself. She'd thought she was special to the guy, thought he cared about her more than the others. Bryan wasn't sure she'd given up on that fantasy.

If she were his daughter, he'd —

Shay made a small sound of distress. Bryan turned to her, saw she was rigid with anger, and in the next second, she exploded.

It was so unexpected, her previous manner so laid-back, so relaxed, that he jumped in surprise at her ferociousness. She turned to the counter and slammed down a fist. "It's so damned unfair."

Her hand would be bruised, he thought as he rose from his seat.

With two long strides, he reached her. He grabbed her shoulders, trying to turn her. She might be tall, but he probably outweighed her by eighty pounds or more. She was no match for his strength.

Still, she tried to brush him off and Bryan hesitated, not wanting to hurt her but not wanting her to hurt herself, either. "Calm down, Shay."

"No."

She looked feral and dangerous, a

woman to be reckoned with. Bryan raised a brow, admiring her temper despite himself. "It'll be —"

She rounded on him in a fury. "Don't you dare tell me it'll be all right, that things'll work out." She squeezed her eyes shut tight, and in the meanest voice he'd ever heard, rasped, "I hope the guy who hurt her is miserable now, I hope he —"

"Rots in hell? Yeah, me too."

Her eyes snapped open and she gaped at him.

Bryan's hands were still on her shoulders, and somehow he was caressing her with his thumbs, soothing her without even meaning to. "Close enough. They couldn't nail him for what he did to Amy, since she wouldn't testify against him, but he got busted on a drug-related charge. He should be doing some jail time."

"Good."

Bryan grinned. "My thoughts exactly."

She looked startled, then exasperated. "You are the oddest sort of preacher."

Wondering if he'd ever survive this, Bryan said, "Yeah, I know."

As he watched her, she pushed her hair away from her face. Her hands were shaking. "Sorry for losing it. It's been a long day."

"Yeah?"

Her thoughts flitted across her face before she came to some decision. "I had a friend get hurt earlier. I've been edgy ever since."

"A friend you work with?" He hoped like hell she'd open up a little. He detested mysteries. He detested secrets. He wanted everything laid out where he could examine it.

Her lips quivered, and he had to lock his knees to keep from pulling her against him. Holding her seemed like a real good idea, when he knew it'd be dumb as dirt.

She shook her head, but he didn't know if that was an answer or a gesture of futility. "She was afraid to go to the police."

"That's tough." He'd prefer her harassment over this show of emotion any time.

Taking Bryan by surprise, she leaned into him. Her hands fisted in his shirt and she tucked her face into his neck as if she'd done so a hundred times. Softness touched him everywhere, the softness of her body, her scent, her hair, her breath — and her compassion.

He stood there, stiff, appalled, incredibly turned on and feeling like a sick bastard because of it. "Shay." He pressed her shoulders, intent on moving her away.

Her lips touched against his throat; he

felt her mouth tremble, felt her breath become jerky, and then she slumped into him and began to cry in near silence.

"What the hell?" He was lousy with crying women. Hell, he ran away from women when they started blubbering. He couldn't take it. But Shay had a death grip on him and wouldn't turn him loose.

She even curled closer. "I'm . . . I'm sorry."

Bryan's cynicism melted on the spot.

The rest of his body was rock hard and throbbing.

She'd seemed so indomitable that her vulnerability was amplified. He stopped thinking about right and wrong, about his brother and propriety. He gathered her in and held her tight.

He didn't know if it helped her any, but he sure as hell felt better.

His hands rubbed up and down her slender back as he attempted to offer reassurance. He wasn't very good at it, and he felt awkward as hell. The nonsense he whispered to her brought his lips close to her ear. He breathed in her scent; his cock twitched in temptation.

Pressing his mouth to her hair, then her cheek, he tried to offer comfort, while at the same time wishing she was naked, wishing he was naked, too.

It didn't make any sense. He was a damn good bounty hunter because, despite the sob stories he always heard, he could stay untouched. He had a keen sense of right and wrong, of his own terms of justice, and he never confused the issues.

At the moment, he was lost in confusion.

He knew only one way to make women feel better, but he doubted a screaming climax would work in this instance.

Then she turned her face up to him, drawing in a slow, shuddering breath. Her gaze was soft and liquid, her lips open.

And somehow, despite his intelligence and cynicism, despite his loyalty to his brother and everything he knew to be right and wrong, he let her kiss him.

And damn it, he even kissed her back.

Chapter Three

The shock of feeling him pressed against her body, the power in his arms, his warmth and caring, swept away all caution. Shay's hands lifted and her fingers tangled in his silky, still-damp hair, holding him closer, refusing to let him escape when he tried to pull away. This was a revelation, a unique experience she didn't want to give up.

A preacher. A man. A hunk. Her lips opened more, inviting, and his tongue came inside, slow, warm and wet. Nothing had ever felt so right. Nothing had ever made her so warm and alive and —

A raw groan escaped him, and he thrust himself away. He was breathing hard, and his face mirrored his struggle — a struggle he won. Holding her back the length of his arms, he rasped, "Damn it, *no.*"

"Yes." Blindly, she reached for him.

With something close to a shove, he paced away from her, both hands thrust into his hair. He looked narrow-eyed and mean.

Not good.

"Bryan?"

Even though she still ached, Shay could feel the heat of his anger — at her or at himself?

She swallowed, and without even meaning to, whispered, "Please?" Not since her days in the last foster home had she ever begged for anything, but God, it felt like she'd been turned inside out, like she needed a man. This man.

He couldn't say no.

But he did.

"Knock it off, Shay." He had resistance written in every line of his hard, rugged face. "This isn't what you want, and it sure as hell isn't what I want."

"But . . ."

"You don't even know me," he accused. "You're just confused." His intensity was back, his gaze probing and hot, his voice thick.

Her heart beat so hard, it shook her. "I'm not a child, Bryan," she whispered. "I know what I want."

"A blind fool could see you're not a kid." The words were heavy with irritation. "But this is *not* going to happen. You're here under my protection, and you're my responsibility."

Shay drew a slow breath, feeling like a fool who'd dug a hole for herself and now couldn't climb out. He wouldn't touch her because of what he believed her to be, yet she'd repulse him if he knew who she really was. That left her with few alternatives, none of them to her liking.

She straightened her spine and looked at him squarely. "I'm not a prostitute."

His disbelief scorched her. "This isn't about what you do. You don't have to lie to me."

Between rejecting her and insulting her, he batted a big fat zero. "Pay attention, Bryan, okay? I am *not* a prostitute."

His brows pulled down. "Is that right?"

This part wouldn't be easy, and she'd have to do a little verbal dancing, but she had to convince him. "You assumed I was a prostitute," she said with a shrug, "so I let you believe it. But I'm not."

Folding his arms over his chest, he studied her. "Okay. Then what — I mean *who* — are you? A biochemist? A fighter pilot? What?"

She winced. "I can't tell you."

"Right." A cynical smile curled one side of his mouth. It was obvious he still believed her to be a hooker, but for now, he'd play along. "So why'd you lie?"

She lifted her chin with scathing disregard. "I didn't exactly lie. I just let you believe what you wanted to believe."

"Uh-huh." And then he reiterated, "Why?"

The words rushed out, a little too urgent, a lot too desperate. "Because if I told you the truth, you'd hate me. And you were being so nice to me, I didn't want you to send me away. I wanted to get to know you better and —"

He took one hard stride toward her, effectively cutting off her rambling explanation. His expression was forbidding, his eyes almost black. Shay started to back up, but it just wasn't in her nature to retreat. So she braced her legs apart and waited.

Though they were of a similar height, he was all solid muscle, wide shoulders and throbbing power. Their gazes were nearly level, yet he seemed to tower over her. "You actually believe I would have sent you away?"

Shay blinked in surprise. He hadn't lambasted her for lying. He hadn't lost his temper. He was just . . . insulted by her lack of faith in his scruples?

"Answer me, Shay."

She jumped at the lash of his demand. “Yes.” His tone would have angered her — *no one* talked to her like that — but with him so close, it was damn difficult not to touch him again. There was no room in her thoughts for anything else. “You would have sent me packing, but I don’t want to go.”

“And I guess that means you won’t tell me why you were really at that bar, dressed the way you were, hanging around outside in a storm?”

“My business is my own,” she said, and before he could start growling about that, she explained, “Until my dress got soaked, it was in the best of taste. It’s just that the rain made it transparent. Otherwise, it would have been fine.”

She thought that might sidetrack him a little, but he wasn’t moved one bit. If anything, his jaw hardened in that now familiar manner of annoyance.

“Shay?”

He managed to say her name without his lips moving. Probably a bad sign. “I can’t tell you.” And then, going on the defensive, she added, “Why does it matter so much? I’d like to stay. Here, at the safe house.” She bit her bottom lip, then really pushed. “And if you wouldn’t mind too much, I’d prefer the other women believe I’m a hooker.”

With droll sarcasm, he said, "You're not a hooker, but you want everyone to think you are?"

That did sound idiotic, but so what? "Yes. They wouldn't like the truth any more than you would." It looked like his eyes might cross. "I'm only telling you this much so you won't think you're taking advantage of me."

He stared at her so long and hard, Shay felt rattled.

"Could I stay? Please?"

It seemed to take him forever to come to a decision. "Shit." His frown seared her. "Yeah, of course you can stay." She had just started to relax when his jaw jutted forward. "But your reasons for being here won't change anything. While you're here, you're off limits. So you can just keep your hands to yourself."

"Oh, but —"

"Just don't cause any trouble." Struck by his own words, his back straightened. "Speaking of trouble — you're not a reporter or something, are you?"

Taken aback, and highly insulted, Shay gasped, *"No."*

He leaned closer, his gaze flinty and his manner challenging. "If I find out otherwise . . ."

The threat went unsaid, but she knew he'd think of something dire. Shay shoved him back a step, out of her personal space. "I'm not, so quit trying to bully me."

He grunted. "As if anyone could." He said it more to himself than her, then turned back to the table. "Whatever problems you have, they won't matter, not to me and not to anyone else in this house. What you tell the other women is up to you. But I mean it — *no trouble*."

Shay crossed her heart. "Scout's honor." She felt a little ashamed of herself for taking advantage of him. But not enough that she'd relent. She still wanted him. And once he got over his noble streak, he'd admit he wanted her, too. "Thanks." And for good measure, she added, "I'm sorry for misleading you earlier."

He dropped into his chair without replying, probably because he still didn't believe her. After a long stare, he said, "As long as we're apologizing . . . I'm sorry for what happened. It won't happen again."

"The kiss?"

His brows lowered. "You took me by surprise with the tears."

Shay actually felt herself flushing. "I'm doubly sorry for that. I'm not a person who ever cries much. But sometimes I just get so frustrated . . ."

One eyebrow arched up.

"I don't mean sexually! Well, that, too."

He snarled in exasperation.

"But I meant when I try to do things and they don't work out the way I want them to."

"That's what happened tonight?" He tapped the pen against the table. "Things didn't work out, your friend got hurt, and you ended up stranded in a rainstorm during a blackout?"

Shay could just imagine all the ridiculous conclusions he drew. She shrugged, wondering how much she should tell him about Leigh. She'd tried to help the girl but it wasn't until after Leigh had gotten hurt that she'd finally accepted Shay's offer.

"Do you mind if we eat while we talk?" She picked up both plates and joined him at the table. "I'm starving."

The sharp look he sent her way made her roll her eyes. "It's an expression, Bryan. I'm not literally starving. It's just that I didn't have much breakfast, and then lunch was ruined by a crisis, so —"

"Your friend?"

Well, now she definitely had to tell him. She only hoped he'd at least know something about Leigh's background, something Shay could use to help the girl.

She took a bite of her potato salad, giving him leave to start on his own meal while she contemplated how much to share.

"She's been having some problems with . . . a guy." Though Leigh had called him her boyfriend, Shay couldn't say the same. The man was a conscienceless animal who'd used Leigh as a sexual bartering tool, and he deserved to be locked away. "He'd threatened her a few times, shoved her around, bullied her. But it got worse suddenly."

"I get the picture. He was pissed about something and taking it out on her?"

"He said she hadn't brought in enough money lately, money he needed to support them both. He accused her of not doing her share. Today, he threw her out — but not before . . ." The words stuck in her throat, and she shook her head twice before managing to say, "Not before beating her up."

His eyes flinty, Bryan asked, "Who is she?"

Very softly, Shay said, "Her name is Leigh."

Rising from his seat, he leaned forward,

his palms flat on the table. "Where is she?"

Stunned by the menace he exuded, and by the fact that he obviously knew Leigh, Shay rushed to reassure him. "She's safe, and she'll be okay."

"That's not what I asked."

No doubt he was used to commanding fast answers. Too bad she couldn't accommodate him. Shay asked, "You know her?"

"Yeah. And I told her this would happen." He sounded furious with himself. "I tried to get her to stay here, but she wouldn't." He loomed over Shay. "So where is she?"

With a shrug of apology, Shay said, "I can't tell you." Before he could insist further, she explained, "She's afraid, Bryan. That's why she wouldn't go to the police. I had to promise not to tell *anyone*. Maybe she didn't mean you. But maybe she did. All I can tell you is that she is okay now. You have my word."

Bryan's stare held her a moment more, then he sank back into his seat. "If she's really away from him, that's a start."

"A very good start," Shay agreed, and with a sigh: "But it's been an upsetting day. Seeing someone hurt like that makes me feel so damned helpless, as if there's no escaping the bad stuff."

Bryan leaned forward again. "I don't know what's going on with you, Shay, how you're tied in with Leigh or why you were hanging around the bar. But if you stay here, I won't let anyone hurt you."

She'd only meant she felt helpless in her inability to help the others, but he'd taken it as personal fear. And now, with him offering his protection, she saw no way to correct the misconception. "Thank you. That's very . . ." What could she say? Gallant? Heroic? She shook her head. "Thank you."

He picked up his pad of paper, all business again. "Tell me about yourself."

For such a big, hard, macho guy, he was damned endearing in his attempts to help. She peeked at the paper he held, saw it had pretyped questions on it, and shrugged. "Sure. What do you want to know?"

"Start with family."

"Okay." Shay continued to eat, waiting for him to begin, but he hesitated. "What is it?"

Rubbing the back of his neck, appearing uncomfortable with his task, he said, "If I hit on a sore spot, just tell me, okay?"

"I'm not shy."

"I noticed." Their gazes met and held, until he looked back at the paper. "What about your father?"

"My birth father or my adoptive father?"
"You have both?"
"Unfortunately."
She had no idea what he was thinking, but it didn't look good. "Start with your father. Do you think he's interested in where you are?"
The rude sound she made was answer enough. Her father was slime. But her adoptive father, if he had any idea what she'd gotten herself into, would probably give her enough lectures to last a lifetime. Not that it would do him any good. He knew she couldn't be stopped once she'd set her mind on a course. So he usually just ended up offering his full support.
"Shay?"
She gave Bryan a smile of reassurance. Her father, and his lack of interest, had no impact on her life. "He's a world-class pig. I haven't seen him since I was five, and that was when he left me at the bus station."
His expression hardened. "What do you mean, he left you?"
"He said he was going to buy us something to drink, but he never came back. I sat there almost the whole day waiting, until I had to go to the bathroom. Then I didn't know what to do. When I started to

cry, a woman offered her help, and the next thing I knew, I had everyone's attention."

She hadn't meant to say quite that much. She hadn't talked about those long-ago days since she was a child. But with Bryan's undivided attention, the words just seemed to come out. "The police figured my father had abandoned me, and after a few months, they finally located him three states away, living with a woman and her sister." Her smile went crooked. "He denied being my father."

Bryan's expression didn't change, but there was now an alertness in his dark brown eyes that hadn't been there earlier.

"What about your mother?"

She shrugged. "The reason my father had me with him in the first place was that my mother refused to keep me any longer. She was what the authorities termed 'emotionally abusive.' That was after they found me in the bus station and did a thorough checkup into my past."

Bryan had the paper and pen out in front of him, but he hadn't written a word. His jaw looked like granite again. "And after they did the checkup?"

She tried to skim over details while still giving him a truth or two about her past, enough that she wouldn't get tripped up in it later. But she didn't want to hurt him with her truths, not when they no longer hurt her.

"I spent some time passing around foster homes and was in an orphanage for a bit." She left out the people who pretended to care but didn't. She left out a chunk of little girl hurt and fear and desperation.

"Jesus."

He looked so outraged on her behalf, she jumped straight into the happier parts. "When I was almost seven, I got lucky. I got adopted." Just thinking of her first few weeks with her new parents had her smiling again. "Mom and Dad are incredible. They didn't think they could have kids, so they took me into their home and treated me like I was their own. Later, they did have a baby. So I also have a little sister."

He finally made a few notes, his gaze repeatedly coming back to her face as if he couldn't stop looking at her. "Won't these people worry?"

"They know I can take care of myself. I've been doing it for a long time."

"Do they know *how* you take care of yourself?"

She wouldn't outright lie, and if he

chose to make more assumptions, it was no more than he deserved.

"They know." Thinking of all the times her parents had lamented her stubbornness, she grinned. "They gave up on telling me what to do when I was about fifteen."

His brows snapped down. "You've been on your own since then?"

"No. I didn't move out until I was seventeen. But I've been fairly self-sufficient since before I was in high school." Mostly because she'd always needed a challenge, because she'd been innovative in making her own money through one scheme or another, because she'd gone on to college only months after turning seventeen with a full academic scholarship. Even as a young child she'd been driven by demons to *do,* to make a difference, to fulfill promises to herself that no one knew about and no one would understand.

Her parents would have gladly given her the moon if it were possible, but they knew she wouldn't accept it, not if there was a single chance she'd be able to get it on her own.

After a few tense, silent moments, Bryan asked, "What about your sister?"

"Her name's Brandi."

"You two close?"

"We are." But then, thinking of the last vacation Shay had forced on her sister, and the results, she winced. "At least, when I don't interfere too much in her life."

"What the hell does that mean?"

He sounded offended on her behalf. It felt odd because usually she was the one trying to take care of everyone, whether they wanted her to or not. Normally she rebelled against anyone worrying for her, but she liked Bryan's concern.

"It means I can be a real pain in the patoot. Brandi isn't like me. She's sweet and shy and quiet."

"And you're not?"

That made her laugh. "What do you think?"

"I think sweet and shy has its place, but on you it'd be ridiculous."

"Gee, thanks." She couldn't help but chuckle over that backhanded compliment. "Brandi takes after our parents, who are small with dark hair and eyes. She's pretty. Not a big gangly girl like myself."

"Gangly?" His mouth curled in wry amusement. "Fishing for a compliment?"

Shay grinned. "Would you give me one?"

"No. You're cocky enough as it is." He tapped his pen with growing impatience.

"So the two of you are different and that causes problems?"

"Sometimes. Where I'm too outspoken and brazen for my own good, Brandi is always circumspect and proper. At times, I try to force her to be more outgoing. We're opposites, but she's my sister and I love her."

"Your stepsister."

"If you want to get technical. But I don't think of her that way."

The devotion and love of her family had never been in doubt. She was considered their firstborn, and Brandi *was* her little sister, in every way that mattered to the heart.

"My life isn't an unhappy one, Bryan. And the truth is, I'm much luckier than most people could ever hope to be."

He disregarded her reassurance with a shake of his head. "Is there anyone who might be interested in helping you?"

Stubborn man. "I don't *need* any help."

"No?" His gaze challenged her. "Then why are you here?"

Oops. Caught in a web of her own making.

She couldn't tell him that no one in the media trusted Shay Sommers right now. If she got involved as herself, the press would be everywhere, and they'd make mincemeat out of Bryan's efforts.

But in the name of fair play, she had to let him know what he was getting into. She owed him that much. She got to her feet, circling the table so she stood right beside him. He, too, stood up, as if having her over him made him uneasy.

Wise, as well as stubborn.

"All I can tell you is that I have my reasons for wanting to stay here, for needing to stay here, but they have nothing to do with why I want you."

He gave her a sharp look of censure. "You're a regular broken record, aren't you?"

"I'm thirty years old. I can't claim to be innocent or pure. Far from it. I'm ambitious and determined to have my own way. Once I set my mind to do something, no one can stop me. But I'm not a hooker."

"Whatever you are, you're too damn pushy."

Bold she'd always be, and she believed in going after what she wanted. She wanted Bryan. "I know."

She put her hands on his chest, felt his strong heartbeat, the clench of muscles. He gripped her wrists, holding her still, ready to put her away from him.

And a woman burst into the room.

Hugh green eyes took in the kitchen scene in a flash as she skidded to a halt. With an expression of delight, she leered at the preacher. "Hey, sweetcheeks. You weren't about to do something naughty, now were you?"

Shay stared. The woman looked to be in her mid-twenties, had dark red hair sprayed and gelled and teased to stand out like a wavy halo around her oval face. Her lips, painted crimson and with enough shine to blind passersby, were open in a wide smile. She wore a white tank top with no bra, and her stretch shorts were much *too* short, proving she didn't wear underpants. Paired up with chunky wedge sandals, it was quite an eye-catching outfit.

Aggrieved, Bryan said, "Morganna," by way of greeting. "I was about to call you down to ask if you'd show Shay a room to use. She's moving in."

Cocking out one well-rounded hip, Morganna teased, "Yeah, sure, dollface. That's what it looked like you were gonna do."

Bryan winked at her, which seemed to startle the woman, then he disengaged Shay's hands. "I'm heading out. Morganna, help Shay get settled in, okay?"

"You betcha."

Shay almost panicked. "But where are you going?"

Morganna snorted. "He's afraid of gettin' raped if he hangs out with us at night. Not that I blame him." She gave Bryan a lingering once-over, then blew him a kiss. "It's a waste, not to be using that prime bod."

"Behave, Morganna."

"Now, sugarplum, what fun would that be?"

Bryan gave up with a rusty chuckle. "Lock the door after me, and remember —"

"Don't open it to no one unless I know they're supposed to be here."

"Exactly."

Shay watched him stride off, and not once did he look back at her. She didn't realize her expression was so wistful until Morganna rudely elbowed her in the side, nearly knocking her off her feet.

"You're gawking, tootsie, but then, that man is fine to look at, isn't he?"

"He's gorgeous."

"Yeah, but don't waste your time. Even when the offer is free, he never touches any of us, except to joke around every now and then, or to offer a shoulder to cry on. Besides, that man is made of ice. I swear, it doesn't matter what a body does to try to attract him, he just treats us all like pals, or little sisters maybe. Now I ask you, do I look like anyone's little sister? Hell, no."

Shay felt herself warming inside. Bryan had covered his reaction well in front of Morganna, but the kiss he'd given her earlier hadn't been friendly or familial. It had been hot, assuring her of eventual success.

In a fine frame of mind now, Shay turned to address Morganna. This is what she'd been waiting for, a chance to get to know the women. How was it Bryan had put it? Oh yes, she'd now be *working in the field*. The idea was almost as exciting as Bryan himself.

She sent a beaming smile to the younger woman. "Why don't I make some tea and we can get to know each other a little better?"

Eyeing her up and down, Morganna said, "My, you're a fancy one, ain't you?"

Shay blinked, unsure what that meant. "I, ah . . ."

Morganna curled her lip in distaste. "Sweetie, if you want me to choke down tea, we'll have to spice it up a little." She moved the stepstool so she could reach a cabinet over the refrigerator, and drew out a bottle of whiskey, waving it toward Shay with a happy grin. "This is guaranteed to help a body sleep on a miserable night like tonight." She climbed down and went for some teacups. "A little of this mixed in our tea and we'll be able to get to know each other real well in no time at all."

It was an offer Shay couldn't refuse.

Chapter Four

The preacher had finally left, and this time he hadn't even sought her out to say good-bye. But she wasn't hurt. In fact, she was glad. Yes, glad! His constant coddling was annoying, filling her with guilt, making her think . . . No. She knew better, damn it.

Damn him.

But lately, God, he made her nervous. He wasn't as . . . warm as he used to be. Sometimes he even seemed glacial.

When he looked at her, it was like he could see clear to her soul. Like he knew what she was, what she wanted and what she did. She shivered, filled with sick dread.

Her hiding place beneath the stairs was stuffy, filled with cobwebs and dust and the stench of her own fear. But this way she could hear the chatter of the new woman and that bitch Morganna.

Stupid Morganna, always acting so friendly with everyone, always flirting with the preacher. She never learned.

Who was the new lady, anyway? Not a

whore. Though the stairs muffled some sounds, she'd heard every word said. She couldn't believe the preacher still thought the new lady was a hooker.

She was up to no good, that much was plain.

It would be smart to keep an eye on her. Later, she'd join them in the kitchen. Maybe ask a few questions. If she could find out anything, it might earn her some points.

"I'll be right back, okay?"

"Don't disappear on me now, Shay. There's no fun in drinking alone."

Shay laughed. "I wouldn't miss it for the world."

With a hand over her mouth, she ducked farther back into the corner, until the unfinished wall dug into her spine. Her heart was pounding, her legs shaking, her underarms had grown clammy. Why did everything scare her so much? As footsteps neared her, then stopped, she didn't dare breathe. After a moment, she worked up the courage to peek between the steps.

Shay paused by the mudroom where she'd plugged in her cell phone to recharge it. She glanced around, making sure she was alone, then dialed a number.

"Dawn? Hey, it's me." With a laugh, Shay said, "I'm better than okay. I'm staying at a safe house." She paused, smiled, and said, "Seriously!"

She watched the woman pace as she talked, and from her hiding spot, she tracked the movements with envy. Shay was tall, slender, beautiful. She'd be valued. She'd be loved.

Even though she knew she had no choice, she felt wicked for listening in. But information was all she had now, and she had to get it when she could.

"How's Leigh?" Shay listened, closed her eyes a moment, and sighed. "Wow, that's a relief. Tell her I'll come to see her tomorrow. I don't know when, but I'll definitely stop by." Shay ducked her head, paced the length of the hall, and said, in a whisper, "Hey, call my realtor for me. Tell her to start scoping the area for any property suitable for a safe house. Yeah, I know, but I want my own, too. If one is good, two would be better, right?"

She listened a moment, then rolled her eyes. "Don't worry so much, and don't call my cell phone. In fact, I'm going to turn it off. But I'll check in with you each day, okay? Yes, I promise. Hold down the fort for me. Love ya, too. And Dawn? Thank you." She tucked the phone deep into her purse and headed back to the kitchen. "All right, Morganna. Where's that drink?"

Oh God, she'd mentioned Leigh.

Spots danced in front of her eyes — from fear, anticipation . . . elation. If she knew where Leigh had gone off to, she could really make him happy. He hadn't meant to lose his temper. He sure as hell hadn't meant to lose Leigh, even if he had kicked her out.

A long time passed, and still she stayed hidden, breathing in the thick air beneath the stairs, gleeful of what she now knew, scared spitless at the idea of getting caught. But she had no choice.

It wasn't until much later, when the others joined Morganna and Shay in the kitchen, that she finally crept out of her special place. No one saw her.

No one suspected a thing.

After taking his time, walking around the block and down a few dark alleys, deliberately leaving himself open to an attack, Bryan gave up. There'd be no outlet tonight, damn it.

He needed some physical activity, some way to release the pent-up energy induced by Shay and her kamikaze-style flirting. The woman didn't even try to protect herself. She just kept coming after him, leaving herself open to hurt and rejection.

But he was the one who felt battered.

Right now he'd welcome a brawl. The last time he'd thrown any punches had been against Joe Winston, in Visitation, North Carolina, and that hadn't been very rewarding because he hadn't really wanted to hurt Joe. Their situation had been one big misunderstanding, with both of them after the same man.

This time the situation was crystal clear, and he was the only one hoping to get hold of the jerk who'd hurt his brother. But the coward didn't show himself. Yet.

Bryan let himself into Bruce's apartment in the old run-down building only three doors down from the safe house. The walls were thin and the decoration total crap, but there were no bugs and the windows were secure.

The second he stepped inside, he knew he wasn't alone. His hand paused on the light switch and he went still, soaking in the feel of danger, seeking it out, all his senses alert.

Then he relaxed. "Damn it, Bruce. I'm not fifteen anymore. You could get hurt lurking around in the dark."

From his lounged position in the worn-out easy chair, Bruce laughed. "How do you do that?"

"What?" Bryan flipped the wall switch

and the room filled with light. He looked toward his brother, and grimaced. Dressed in baggy brown slacks, a ragged flannel shirt and with his hair long and stringy, Bruce made a foul sight. "Good God, you look like a deranged hermit."

Bruce rubbed his patchy beard. "Yeah, I know. Nifty, huh?"

"Nifty? What the hell is nifty about it?" Bryan stepped inside and secured the door.

"The disguise conceals the real me." Bruce pushed to his feet. He was healed now, but it hadn't been that long ago that he'd been too injured to walk on his own. "So how'd you know it was me?"

Shrugging off his jacket while heading toward the kitchen for a beer, Bryan said, "Because any real threat smells dark and murky and mean. It sticks to your skin, burns your throat."

"Yeah?" Bruce followed behind. "What do I smell like?"

Grinning to himself, more than ready to twit his brother, Bryan said, "Cookies. Santa Claus. Hell, I don't know. But nothing close to evil."

Not at all insulted, Bruce pulled out a chair and straddled it. "In my line of work, that's a good thing." He seemed full of energy, but then Bruce usually was. "So how'd it go?"

"Pure fucking hell, if you want the unvarnished truth." Bryan aimed the neck of a tall beer bottle toward Bruce. "You're sick, you know that? Only a sick man would surround himself with loony broads who eat, sleep and drink sex — when he's not supposed to touch any of them."

Bruce chuckled. "Like you even wanted to."

"There's the hell of it." Bryan pulled out his own chair and dropped into it with a groan. "I wanted to." He ignored Bruce's snap to attention to down half his beer in one long gulp. If he couldn't fight, maybe he could at least get drunk.

"You . . . ?" Bruce couldn't seem to finish that awesome thought.

"I was on my best behavior."

"Which isn't saying much!"

"Quit squawking." Bryan set the beer aside with a sour expression. Hell, he knew he wouldn't get drunk. He never did. Only an idiot reduced his reaction time with alcohol. "All your fallen doves are unsullied by me."

"I never thought otherwise." Bruce rose and went to the refrigerator. He popped the tab on a Coke, set it beside Bryan, and dumped the beer in the sink.

It was a routine they often went through, something Bruce had started when they were little more than kids and he'd taken it upon himself to keep Bryan out of trouble. He'd steer him away from fights, pull him back from smiling girls, prod him into doing homework.

His efforts weren't always successful, but since Bruce seemed to take such utter satisfaction in making decisions for him, Bryan occasionally let him have his way.

Besides, it was nice to know his brother had his best interests at heart — not that Bryan would ever admit that to Bruce. That'd ruin most of his fun.

Bruce slapped mayo on wheat bread, loaded on three pieces of cheese, and handed it to Bryan.

"I already ate." But he took the food all the same.

"Really? With the women?" Bruce rejoined him at the table with his own sandwich in hand. "Barb cook for you?"

"No, Shay did."

He paused with his mouth open for a bite. The sandwich got lowered. "Shay?"

"A new one." Bryan eyed the sandwich, realized he was hungry after all, and dug in. Eating when Shay sat so close that he could smell her hadn't been possible. He'd barely managed three bites, then. "Found her tonight."

"I see."

That had Bryan laughing. "No, I doubt you do. She's . . . not like the other ones."

"No?"

"No."

"Is she pretty?"

"Stunning." The Coke actually tasted much better than the beer had. Bruce was a good influence on him. "Tall, built like a brick shithouse, legs up to her armpits, long blond hair . . ." Just talking about her made him hot. He shrugged. "Stunning."

Bruce nodded. "And so you're attracted to her?"

Not even close. He wanted to fuck her lights out. But then . . . he'd enjoyed holding her, too. And talking to her.

Shit.

"Look," Bryan said, glaring at his smiling brother, "if it was just the looks, I could ignore her."

"Hmmm."

God, he hated it when Bruce said "hmmm" in that sanctimonious way of his. "She's . . ." Bryan hesitated, trying to decipher his own thoughts, but he shook his head, at a loss. "I don't know what she is, all right? Annoying, for sure. Cocky as hell. Pushy."

"Sounds like a real charmer."

Feeling unsettled, Bryan left his seat, paced to the cabinets and rummaged around for some chips. "She's outspoken — but not in a defensive way. More like she's just very self-assured. But she's hiding something, too."

"Most of them are."

"I don't mean that." He found stale nachos and dumped them in a bowl. "She needs to be at the safe house, that much I believe. But the rest . . . I dunno. She's not telling me the whole truth, but I can't pick out the lies." He shook his head again. Damn it, he hated being confused.

Bruce propped his bearded chin on a hand. "Let's get back to that part about you wanting her."

He didn't want to talk about that. "Totally fucked up, huh?"

With a scowl, Bruce said, "Your language is fucked up. I swear, you make my ears burn. If Dad heard you —"

Bryan shrugged. "I curb it around him."

"But you figure I can take it?"

"You haven't fainted yet." Bryan started to grin, but it ended in a groan. "I should admit that I'm having a problem watching my mouth around Shay, too. She keeps telling me that I'm not like any preacher she's ever known."

That worried Bruce a bit. "You think she's guessed?"

"No way." At least, he hoped not. "There's just something about her that pushes my buttons. All my buttons. She makes me forget what I'm doing, lose my temper . . . and hell, you might as well know I let her kiss me."

Bruce choked. He appeared more fascinated by the moment. "You let her . . . ?"

"Like I said, she's pushy." Disgruntled again, Bryan explained, "I told her no. Hell, I *kept* telling her no. But then she got upset about something and turned on the tears and the next thing I knew, I was too damn close to her, and she —"

"Kissed you."

"Yeah." And what a kiss. He'd sank into it, let his mind go blank while every nerve in his body had jumped to attention. A mind-blowing kiss — *from a hooker.*

Bryan took another vicious bite of his sandwich.

"So what?"

Doing a double take, Bryan growled, "What do you mean, so what? I'm supposed to be *you.*"

Bruce looked thunderstruck, and he even paled a little. "Did anyone see you kissing her?"

"No." With Bruce's good humor shot, Bryan went back to eating. "And it was the other way around. She kissed me."

"Semantics." Bruce relaxed again. "I repeat, so what? You obviously like her."

"Like her?" Bryan snorted. "I'd like to get her naked, yeah. But she's most likely a *hooker,* Bruce. She's supposed to be under your protection. Doing the horizontal rumble with her sure as hell wouldn't do the safe house's reputation any good."

"Assuming anyone found out, which maybe they wouldn't."

"You're trying to talk me into this?" Bryan sat back and stared at his brother. In his experience, now was the time for Bruce to break out the long talks. Not encourage him. "Why?"

Bruce shrugged. "Never met a woman who rattled you before."

"I never had to play a preacher before."

"Maybe that's it." Bruce dragged his finger through the frost on his Coke can. "But maybe she's just special."

"God save me." Crossing his arms on the table, Bryan glared. "You think a hooker is special?"

Bruce grew serious real quick, matching Bryan's dark frown. "Don't judge, Bryan. Don't do that. They're human beings like the rest of us, with flaws and worries and —"

"Yeah, yeah. You gave me this lecture once already. That wasn't what I meant." But it sort of was. He wasn't a chauvinist and he didn't mind a woman who enjoyed her sexuality, but a guy had to draw the line somewhere.

"If I met a woman," Bruce intoned, looking down his nose at Bryan, "who *pushed my buttons,* I wouldn't care about her past."

"No?" But it wasn't surprising, because Bruce was different. Bryan had never met another human being with a bigger, more forgiving heart than his brother. Strange how identical twins could be so different.

"And it's not like your life has been all lily white anyway."

"True." Bryan's past overflowed with dark memories that fell just short of legal, and a few that didn't even come close. In the line of duty, he'd done things he regretted. In his personal life, he'd made mistakes that had turned deadly.

But in the end, he knew he'd do them again.

"So?"

What did Bruce expect him to say? That he wanted Shay enough to change his life and settle down? Idiotic. "So I'm not interested in getting involved with any woman right now."

"Sounds to me like you're already involved." Bruce smiled with satisfaction.

"You better hope you're wrong," Bryan told him, "because after I catch the son of a bitch who jumped you, I'm walking away. And *you're* going to be left to deal with her."

Thunderstruck, Bruce said, "And she'll think that I'm you. . . ."

"Exactly."

"All right, all right." Bruce held up his hands. "Then stay away from her."

And therein lied the biggest problem: He didn't want to. "Easier said than done. She's pushy."

"So you keep saying," Bruce grouched. "You telling me you can't handle one little woman?"

Despite the seriousness of their conversation, Bryan grinned. "She isn't all that little. In fact, she's as tall as me."

"Really?" Bruce rubbed the disreputable whiskers that couldn't seriously be called a beard. "Maybe I could clean up, drop in and see for myself."

Bryan's chair scraped back and he towered over Bruce. "Do *not* even think it." Only to himself would Bryan admit that it wasn't just fear of his brother getting hurt that motivated him. He didn't want Shay rubbing up against Bruce, maybe coercing him into a kiss, maybe even . . .

Unconcerned with his brother's bluster, Bruce raised a brow. "You've got me curious."

"Curious enough to get yourself killed?" And he played his ace in the hole, the one thing he knew got to Bruce quicker than most. "To maybe endanger those women, too?"

"No." Bruce turned quiet, thoughtful. "But I'm going to be keeping an eye on things. No one recognizes me because they think you're me. Keeps them from looking too close. I'm safe. But I want you to stay safe, too."

"Don't worry about me." Bryan churned with anticipation. "When I finally meet up with your villain, I'll be able to lose some of this tension."

"If you ever meet up with him. He could be long gone by now. It could have been a random attack, an attempt to steal from me, when I had nothing of value."

"You don't believe that any more than I

do." He stared at Bruce while thinking things through. Now that Shay had entered the picture, he felt more desperate than ever to see an end to things. The less time he spent around that one, the better for his sanity.

Bryan rubbed a hand over his eyes. "Ah, hell. Maybe I should call that damn spook, Jamie Creed, see if he has any leads."

Bruce leaned forward with new interest. "The guy from Visitation? The one you told me lived on the mountain and showed up just to give cryptic clues to problems?"

"Yeah. That's him." When he'd been in Visitation chasing down that bastard Bruno Caldwell, Bryan had found his hands full dealing with Joe Winston; Joe's woman, Luna; and crazy Jamie Creed. In some ways, he missed them all. He definitely missed Visitation.

"I thought you didn't believe in Jamie's supernatural skills."

"I don't. The guy was creepy, but lucky at guessing stuff." Bryan snorted. "The women sure fell for him, though."

"Maybe you could consult him."

Bryan stared at Bruce as if he'd grown two heads. "I was being sarcastic. No way in hell am I asking that lunatic anything. The last time I spoke with Joe, he carped on and on about Jamie. Not that Jamie comes off his mountain any more often than he ever has, but he's there, like a damn scar that won't heal, bugging the hell out of everyone."

"Bugging the men, you mean."

"Yeah." Bryan took a long gulp of his Coke. "Don't worry about your pesky enemy. I'll take care of him. And then some."

That alarmed Bruce, enough that he pointed his finger at Bryan. "You'll follow the law."

"Right." After he gave some payback for the injuries done to his brother. That should be easy enough to accomplish. Few people gave themselves up without a fight. Bryan stretched, trying to relieve the tension in his tight muscles. "I'm beat. I think I'll turn in."

"Meaning I have to get lost?"

"Or camp out on the couch. I don't care." In fact, he'd prefer Bruce stayed where he could keep an eye on him.

"No, I'll go home. Or rather, to my temporary home. I'm enjoying all this cloak and dagger stuff, actually. Slipping in and out of shadows. Being in disguise. I can see why you're drawn to it."

Bryan stared heavenward. "God help us."

"He always does." Bruce slapped him on the shoulder, pulled on his tattered jacket, turned up the collar, and slipped out the front door.

Bryan counted to twenty, then followed him out. Bruce didn't know that he was being followed because Bryan was too good for that. But someone had hurt Bruce once already. No way was Bryan going to let it happen a second time.

When Bruce reached the seedy motel that served as his temporary residence, Bryan waited in the shadows. He kept his attention on the upstairs window until a light came on, and even waited a minute more, just to make sure everything seemed routine before disappearing into the darkness again.

As a bounty hunter, he'd tracked everything from robbers to rapists and murderers. Until recently, he'd been content with the nomadic lifestyle, always on the go, heading wherever the criminals took him. But when his last job, his most important job, had taken him to Visitation, he'd found a home.

Something about the area made his heart feel easier than it had in years. The sun shone down from the sky as if calling to him. Despite the drama that had occurred there, despite crazy Jamie Creed looming on his mountain, it was peaceful beyond belief.

Someday he'd settle there, maybe even get out of the bounty hunter business altogether — if he could find something he was good at. He'd already bought the perfect property — an acre of prime land, nicely secluded and dotted with a variety of trees, close to a clear, churning stream. The water was cold, the fish were fat, and the wildlife liked to hang around.

He'd parked a rusty trailer there, for when he visited. Joe kept an eye on it when he wasn't around, but the trailer was temporary. In Bryan's mind, he'd already designed the perfect home. He knew how big it'd be, how close he'd have it to the stream. But until that day, the trailer worked when he wanted to get away.

He hadn't lied when he told Bruce he was beat, but now the humid night air had revived him, so he didn't go straight back to the apartment. He wandered the dark streets awhile, wishing the coward who had jumped his brother would show himself. When he encountered nothing more than rowdy teens and bar noise, he found himself drawn back to the safe house.

To Shay.

The rain had finally stopped, but the blacktop streets were shiny and wet, reflecting ribbons of light from street lamps and passing cars. The steady drone of dripping gutters and leaves seemed somehow soothing. Mosquitoes buzzed, fireflies blinked.

He stood a good distance from the house, next to a large oak tree, undetectable beneath the moonless sky. Through the kitchen window, he watched Shay flit about, going from woman to woman. So she'd met them all now, and she seemed to be organizing some kind of gathering.

It looked like . . . maybe a tea party?

He'd never seen a woman move like her, fluid and unrehearsed, teeming with energy but still so damn feminine it made his teeth ache. Morganna stood and, hefting a bottle of whiskey, poured another round of drinks into chipped teacups. The ladies toasted each other.

Ah ha. No ordinary tea party.

Bryan found himself smiling. Crazy broads. Were they all getting smashed? Was Shay? He knew it wasn't wise, but he inched closer still, until he could hear the soft buzz of feminine conversation. It had the lilt of women's voices, but with bawdy comments and a hefty dose of swear words to keep it amusing.

Because he was in the dark and they were in the light, he could view them as easily as a screen in a movie theater.

Amy sat off by herself, sipping her drink and shyly watching the proceedings. Patti and Morganna were egging Shay on. Barb held a mirror. And Shay . . . he shook his head, then chuckled. Shay was putting makeup on Barb.

Bryan stared harder and realized she'd already done up the other ladies.

Gone were the garish colors, overdone in the extreme. Comically arched eyebrows now held a natural curve. Ruby-red lips were now mauve or pink. All the women looked . . . pretty. Subtle. Not so much like streetwalkers.

Propping his hands on his hips, Bryan considered what she did and maybe why she did it. He'd seldom seen all the women congregated together. Morganna liked everyone, but because she could talk your ear off, the others sometimes dodged her. Amy was reserved and withdrawn, slipping off by herself whenever possible. Barb constantly bossed the others around. And Patti couldn't keep her hands to herself.

Yet here they were, all laughing together. Having fun. Sharing company and drink.

Doing their makeup.

It was such a "woman" thing to do, when he hadn't seen them act that much like ordinary women. Mostly they acted . . . outlandish. Bryan watched for a few minutes more, then decided to go before he got caught playing Peeping Tom on his own safe house.

Or before he did something stupid, liking joining them for a drink.

When he entered the apartment for the second time that night, he was still smiling. The place was silent and empty. He secured the locks, stripped off his clothes and took a quick shower, letting the cool water relax him. He thought about Visitation again — and found himself wondering if Shay would like the area.

Damn it. He would *not* think about her.

But the minute he stretched out naked on the rumpled sheets, she crowded into his brain. If, as she claimed, she wasn't a hooker, then what did she do for a living? Why did she need to be at the safe house?

And why did she keep claiming to want him?

It was a long time before he finally fell asleep, but even then his subconscious dwelled on her. Somehow sexual dreams, so vivid he could taste them, *taste her,* got slowly tangled into a nightmare.

One minute he was making love with her, both of them breathing hard, gasping, straining together. Then the same intangible force that threatened his brother tore Shay away from him. Bryan couldn't see the man, couldn't find him, but he knew he had Shay, that he was hurting her.

Bryan fought to get to her, determined to protect her. Only he turned into Bruce, and he was praying . . .

With a low, hoarse shout, Bryan jerked upright in the bed. Sweat dampened his throat, his chest and shoulders. His hands were fisted in the sheets, his muscles pulled tight. He struggled against the urge to kill — yet he was alone in the small room.

He had no one to fight but himself.

With a growl, he fell flat again, still breathing too hard, feeling a little sick. His stomach was in knots; his brain throbbed. After a moment, he dug the heels of his hands into his eye sockets. Jesus. A nightmare, a stupid dream. But it had felt so real.

A glance at the clock showed it was six-thirty. No way in hell was he going back to sleep. When his breathing finally calmed, he sat up on the side of the bed.

It was stupid, he knew it was stupid, but still he picked up the phone and dialed Bruce.

Sounding drowsy and confused, his brother answered on the first ring. "H'lo?"

Bryan hesitated.

New awareness filled Bruce's voice when he said again, "Hello?"

"Sorry."

"Bryan?"

God, he felt like an idiot. "Yeah. Go back to sleep."

"What is it?"

"Nothing." He walked to the window and pushed aside the blinds. The sun was a bright crimson ball that blinded, making its way to the sky. "An idiotic dream. I just . . ."

"Wanted to make sure I was okay?"

So fucking lame. "Yeah, something like that."

"Thanks."

Though he couldn't see his brother, he knew he had a gentle, understanding smile on his face. "Anytime. Later."

Bryan hung up before he or Bruce got too sappy. They'd always been close, and there had been times when Bryan had just known his brother needed him. And vice versa. It wasn't mystical. Wasn't a special bond of being twins.

It was a bond of being brothers.

Bryan headed for the bathroom, determined to put the stupid dream from his mind.

Of course, he couldn't. He knew Bruce was okay now, but Shay had been in the dream, too, and he was a man who lived by his gut instincts. Right now, those instincts were nagging him. And the longer he thought about it, the more they nagged. His shower was accomplished in record time. He shaved so fast, he almost cut his own throat.

Finally he gave up, threw on clean clothes, and went out the door in a rush. It was ridiculous, but he couldn't seem to help himself. He actually jogged to the safe house. His fingers fumbled with the many locks.

He refrained from calling out once he got inside. All he needed this morning was a passel of angry, hungover women giving him hell. He hesitated at the bottom of the steps, but had enough sense not to go up.

No way did he want to invade the somewhat sacred ground of hooker bedrooms.

Coffee. That'd be a start.

He entered the kitchen, faltered in stunned disbelief, and stared. The grin came first, but it was soon followed by a chuckle, and finished with a hard laugh.

Shay twitched as something intruded on her peaceful dreams. She started to move, but her neck felt like it had broken sometime during the night. Then her head started aching and her stomach pitched. She moaned.

"That's what you get for sleeping in a chair."

Her heart almost stopped.

She ceased all movement.

She didn't even breathe.

Peeking one eye open, she found Bryan standing over her, his hands on his hips, his dark eyes shining, his sexy kiss-me mouth curled in a grin.

She blinked but he didn't go away. "Hi."

His grin widened. "Do you need some help?"

She started to move, and winced. Sounding like a sick frog, she rasped, "I think my neck is broken."

His hot palm curled under her skull and his other hand caught her upper arm, helping her to straighten. He let go of her far too quickly to suit her.

"No wonder. When I first walked in, I thought someone had killed you. Did you sleep with your head back like that all night?"

Given the way her body felt, she must have. She was in a straight-backed kitchen chair, her legs stretched out in front of her with her feet propped on the kitchen table, her arms hanging almost to the floor.

And her head . . . her poor head. She groaned in discomfort. She'd let her head drop back on her shoulders, with the top of the chair digging into her nape, and she'd fallen asleep. All night. "I'm dying."

"Just sit still a minute and I'll start coffee."

Cautiously, slowly, she slumped forward, holding her head in her hands because she doubted her neck could support it properly.

Not only her head ached, but her back and shoulders, too. She was a lousy drinker. One glass of wine and she fell asleep. But last night, she and the ladies — each of them a delight — had finished off a bottle of booze. Cheap booze. Really *potent* booze.

True, she had drunk less than the others, only sipping hers while pretending to keep up, but apparently she'd drunk enough to think the chair would make an adequate bed. "Make the coffee strong, will you?"

"You got it."

He was back in only a few minutes. Shay could hear the hiss and sputter of the coffee machine and already the delicious scent filled the air. Heaven.

"Sit still."

Shay cocked a sluggish brow. Did she look particularly capable of movement? Even breathing hurt.

With a strange gentleness, Bryan's big, rough hands moved her hair aside, laying it over her shoulders, smoothing it out of the way. Her heart did a little flipflop and awareness chased away the remaining cobwebs. She was now awake — very awake.

His callused fingertips touched her sensitive nape, slid around to the tops of her shoulders. His thumbs pressed in, moved, circled . . .

"Ohhhh," she moaned as the tension and pain melted away. "That's orgasmic."

Bryan paused, made a sound that was part amusement, part chastisement, then continued. "You're all knotted up."

She hung her head, letting him do as he pleased. It was wonderful.

"Why were you sleeping in the chair, Shay?"

"Late night. The ladies and I were . . ." She bit her tongue. Booze was forbidden, or so they'd told her. "We stayed up late. Talking."

"Uh-huh. Anything else?"

Did he already know about the alcohol? Oh hell, the cups! They were in the sink. She swiveled to look, but no, they'd been washed and set upside down in the drainer.

Could he smell the drink on her? How humiliating. First he'd thought her a hooker, and now he'd think her a wino.

"Shay?" He brought his hands up to frame her head, rubbing her temples, filling her with bliss.

"Hmmm?" If she couldn't go back to sleep, she'd settle on having him touch her like this.

"What else did you do last night?"

"Makeup."

"Makeup, huh?"

She started to nod, but couldn't, not with the way he rubbed her head and neck. "Yeah. The ladies let me make them up. It was fun."

His long fingers tunneled through her hair, massaging her scalp, turning her boneless. Turning her on.

"Why'd you want to do that?"

It was all she could do to keep from moaning. "To show them how."

"How to what?"

Would he guess her intent if she told him? Her goals were altruistic, but if he figured out that much, he might start wondering who she really was and then he'd put two and two together, and he'd kick her to the curb.

She wasn't ready to go. Choosing her words carefully, she explained, "I wanted to show them how to be a bit more subtle, and to look more attractive in the bargain."

"And they let you?"

Shay heard his astonishment, and satisfaction settled over her. It hadn't been easy at first, but she'd cajoled them and after Morganna agreed, the others had fallen in line. "Yep." She looked at him upside down. "I told them the highest paid prostitutes don't look like prostitutes."

His fingers stilled a moment before resuming their gentle massage. "Like you?"

That made her chuckle. "Why, thank you. I'm glad you've finally decided I don't look like a hooker."

"It wasn't exactly a compliment."

"I know." She couldn't help but laugh. He was trying to snoop, to get her to admit to things. But even hungover and drugged by his magic fingers, she had better sense than to spill her guts.

He shook his head, and she saw him

smile before he tilted her face back down. "So after you worked them over, they wanted a turn on you?"

"No, they just watched."

Devilish satisfaction filled his tone when he said, "I don't think so, Shay."

Her brows puckered. "What do you mean?" She'd done their makeup, showing them how to apply it right, and they'd tried their best to get her drunk. Morganna had told some really raunchy jokes, with Patti egging her on. And Barb had grumbled at all of them. Amy had been the most reserved, but she'd seemed to enjoy her appearance after Shay finished.

Shay had to admit, they all looked very pretty when the heaviest makeup had been removed.

Bryan caught her elbow and lifted her from the seat, leading her toward the stainless steel toaster. "Why don't you take a look while I pour your coffee?"

A little apprehensive, Shay hesitated, then bent and peeked at her reflection in the stainless steel.

Oh. My. God. Smudged, kohl-lined eyes blinked at her. A bright red mouth opened in surprise. She choked — and her back snapped straight again. She covered her face with her hands. She wasn't a vain woman, but wow. Halloween had come early.

Grinning like a sinner, Bryan pulled her hands down and handed her a cup of sweetened coffee. "Drink. It'll help to clear your head."

She gulped down half a cup, aware of Bryan chuckling at her.

"They did you up real nice," he teased. "I almost didn't recognize you. You could stand on any street corner around and make a fortune."

She groaned. "Shut up, please." She handed the cup to Bryan, drew a deep breath for courage, and bent to look again. She had enough eyeliner for Bozo the clown. Her cheeks looked like someone had slapped her. Hard.

And her mouth. With the crimson lipstick, which had smeared during her sleep, her lips looked too full, her mouth too wide.

"Here you go."

The coffee wasn't helping, Shay decided, after swilling another cup. She peeked at Bryan, knew he was waiting for her reaction to her appearance, and decided a thorough scrubbing was the order of the day.

"Delicious coffee. Now, if you'll excuse

me." She leaned into the sink bowl, turned on the water and started splashing. Behind her, Bryan laughed out loud.

"Get me something," she demanded, "a washcloth or a paper towel or whatever."

"Given that paint job, you could probably use a mop." He wasn't gone long. "Here you go."

Half of Shay's hair was wet with the furious way she splashed. Blindly, she reached out, bumping Bryan's abdomen and chest before finding and snatching the hand towel from him. She stuck it under the water and scrubbed hard.

"Easy," Bryan told her. "You're going to take off a layer of skin."

"You're a wicked, wicked man for not saying something sooner."

He carefully gathered her hair together and held it back from her face. Shay could feel his warmth, smell his scent. "You couldn't move, Shay, so what could you have done about it?"

"I could've just died and got it over with."

"Now what a shame that would've been."

Her splashing stopped. It seemed she wasn't even breathing.

Damn it, he hadn't meant to say that, to

egg her on or encourage her in her infatuation. But watching her furious efforts to remove the war paint amused him.

Seeing her rounded backside jutting out turned him on.

And the damn dream had his emotions all churning, way too close to the surface.

Finding her safe, drunk, and the brunt of a joke had given him so much relief, he wanted to fold her in close to his chest and promise to protect her so he never had to worry again.

Idiotic.

She didn't need his damn protection. Like cats, women had a knack for landing on their feet, no matter what. He should have learned that lesson by now. Not since his wife had he indulged his inflated noble streak by trying to protect a woman. And look where that had gotten him. Megan, who had been young and naive, had screwed him over in the worst possible way. If she could manage that type of deception, what was someone like Shay capable of?

So maybe she wasn't a whore, but she still had deep secrets, and secrets were always a dangerous thing.

Very slowly, her face dripping, Shay straightened and turned to him. Her lips were open, her breathing harsh. Bryan knew he should resist temptation, but he couldn't get his feet to move. In fact, the only things moving were his pounding heart, his laboring lungs, and his cock — which strained with interest.

They stared at each other.

The night's debauchery had left her eyes bloodshot and some of the smeared makeup remained. The hair around her face was sodden. She *looked* hungover — and still he wanted her so much that he shook with it.

"I have to leave for a little while today."

That brought him out of his sensual revelry and nudged his worry right back to the surface. "Leave where?"

Shay lifted one shoulder, and avoided his gaze by looking at his throat. "I just have a few things to do. I won't be gone long."

He crossed his arms over his chest. "What things, Shay?"

She shook her head. She couldn't tell him that she wanted to check on Leigh, talk to her realtor, arrange to have new clothes dropped off, that she . . . had so many things she was dying to accomplish, things that would help him, the shelter, and the women. "It's private."

He caught her chin and tipped her face

up to his. He looked darkly determined, riled. Shay licked her lips in nervousness — and his gaze dropped to her mouth.

Taking the hand towel from her, he used a wet corner to wipe around her lips. "You missed some," he whispered.

"Oh." Shay's heart kicked hard, but not in fear. She just felt so alive, so excited.

"When are you leaving?"

She tried to think, but somehow, it was his thumb touching her lips, and not the towel. "I . . . I thought I'd go now, so I could be back before the others start waking."

"Don't want them asking questions either, huh?"

"I'd rather they didn't."

Bryan released her, letting his hands drop to his sides. "You're coming back?"

He really didn't trust her at all. "Yes." Her smile felt shaky. "I promise."

"All right." He took a step away from her. "I have some stuff to do, too."

Shay twisted the towel in her hands. "Like what?"

Her audacity had him lifting a brow. "I have to tell, but you don't?"

The heat of a blush warmed her cheeks. "Unless it's private."

"It's not." Shay watched him go to the

refrigerator and open the door. "Today is grocery day. I need to restock" — He slanted her a look — "minus the whiskey."

Oops. Shay covered her mouth. So he *did* know. "Sorry about that."

"You're not the one who brought it here. Just try not to get so sloshed next time that you pass out in the chair. God only knows what they'll do to you if it happens again." He moved around the various jars of condiments, making note of what had to be bought and what didn't. "I've got to check out a few prospective employers, too."

"For who?"

"The ladies. If I can find them a better place to work, I'll have better odds of keeping them off the street."

"Great idea." Her thoughts churned. She knew some people she could contact, some arms to twist. Thinking out loud, she said, "You need a place willing to train. Where there's room for advancement. Someplace local, so they won't have to travel too far. . . ." She realized Bryan stood there, the refrigerator door still open while he stared at her. Another oops.

Without a word, he closed the fridge and went to the cabinet. "You know anyplace like that, Shay?" He shook a box of cereal, counted cans of vegetables.

"I might." She did, but didn't want to give him names. She'd rather contact the people herself, maybe have them get in touch with Bryan, keeping her involvement quiet.

Glancing at her watch, she said, "Well, I should be going."

"How do you plan to get wherever you're headed?"

"Bus."

"Why don't I drive you?" Crossing his arms over his chest, he leaned back on the counter. Today he wore a black T-shirt that hugged his muscular chest and showed off really impressive biceps.

How in the world did a preacher get built like a bouncer? Shay sighed. His jeans fit him like a dream, worn thin in all the right places.

When she looked back to his face, his eyes were narrowed in that special way of his that showed both impatience and awesome attention to detail. She had no doubt he knew her thoughts, but he wouldn't acknowledge them.

"I have a station wagon. We use it to get the women to the clinic and back. Nothing fancy, but it's reliable."

Riding with him would give them more private time to talk, but then he'd know where she went, and she couldn't have that. Feeling real regret, she denied the offer. "Sorry, no. The bus is better for me. You can get your errands done, I'll take care of mine, and . . . maybe we can visit again later?" She hoped so. She really wanted to spend more time with him.

Her evasions displeased him, she could tell. He pushed away from the counter. "Maybe." Then he went right past her. A few seconds later, she heard the front door close.

Shay missed him already.

She shook herself out of her melancholy. If she hoped to accomplish everything in the short time she'd have here, she couldn't waste a single second on moping.

Using the downstairs bathroom, she found a bar of soap and removed the remainder of makeup, then combed her hair and put it into a ponytail. A supply of new toothbrushes were in the linen closet, along with a variety of other things women might need. She pulled out lotion. It wasn't the expensive brand she normally used, but for today, it'd have to do.

Picturing Bryan in a store, sorting through all the varieties, stocking up on feminine products, brought a smile to her face. What a guy.

She turned on her cell phone. While she was out, she'd call Dawn. Her friend did like to fret.

Not bothering to change clothes — since she had nothing to change into — Shay threw her purse strap over her arm and headed out, facing the day with a whistle and a lot of anticipation.

Chapter Five

Wearing a low-billed cap and mirrored sunglasses, Bryan watched Shay leave the safe house. She looked young and energetic and full of purpose. His instincts insisted that he follow her, not only because he didn't trust her, but because he still couldn't shake off the damn dream. He wanted to see what she was up to, and he needed to make sure she stayed safe.

Idiot.

Even as he cursed himself, he kept her in his sights. She headed for the bus stop, drawing a lot of attention along the way. Shay wasn't a woman anyone could ignore — male or female.

Chili was still at the bar, hanging outside, looking for ways to waste his money. His shirt was more out than tucked in, and he barely managed to stay upright on his feet. He eyed Shay as she passed him, his expression covetous behind his glasses. Bryan made a mental note to have a talk with the little cretin, especially since he seemed to be skulking about a lot more often.

Men in recessed doorways, in various stages of drunkenness, tracked Shay with their blurry gazes. The pawnshop owner, a fifty-year-old woman, stopped sweeping her walk to stare. The newspaper vendor did the same.

Oblivious to them all, Shay slipped on sunglasses and continued on her way, her expression lost in thought.

She wasn't wearing a see-through dress today, but still she captivated one and all. It wasn't the clothes; it was the woman.

Bryan groaned. Hell, he was doomed.

He waited until Shay got on the noisy bus, then he followed along in the station wagon. At each stop, he waited to see if she'd depart, but it wasn't until they reached the nicer area on the outskirts of downtown that he spotted her bright hair and long-legged stride among the crowd leaving the bus. She separated herself, striding up the main street to a family-style Italian restaurant. Bryan pulled to the curb and kept the car running while he watched her go inside.

It was almost half an hour before she came back out, accompanied by an older, rotund man in an apron who kept his arm around her with obvious affection. Shay smiled down at the shorter man. She kissed him on the cheek, accepted his hug, and walked away.

The sun was already high in the sky and despite a gentle breeze, the day had warmed considerably.

It had nothing on Bryan's temper.

Rather than return to the bus stop at that point, Shay traipsed across the street to a tidy clothing store, then into a coffee shop, and after that, a private gallery.

After each visit, she left grinning.

And so the morning went. Bryan followed her from one destination to the next. She spent anywhere from twenty to forty minutes in each establishment.

After visiting no less than ten places up and down the main street, she hailed a cab.

What the hell was she up to?

In the back of Bryan's mind grew the ugly thought that she might be servicing regulars, gathering up some ready cash. His hands fisted on the steering wheel and his guts cramped.

He hated the idea so much that he talked himself out of it. After all, she wore no makeup this morning, had her hair in a plain ponytail, and wore the used clothing he'd given to her yesterday. Logically, she couldn't be working.

But then, even dressed down, Shay looked more edible than any woman he'd ever seen.

His anger simmered. All her dealings were with men, of all ages, build and familiarity. Hell, she seemed to know everyone in this neck of the woods. Why she had to visit them all now, if not for business, he couldn't guess.

But he'd figure her out sooner or later.

The cab left the business area for the suburbs, and Bryan, a pro at tracking, held back so Shay wouldn't notice him.

Finally the cab pulled up in a residential area. Small brick homes lined the street, each nearly identical to the one beside it. Only the trim colors on shutters and gutters offered any variety. Enormous trees were everywhere, dating the area. Family-style cars, mostly older, were parked all along the street.

Bryan stopped several yards away, inching the wagon in behind a minivan that helped conceal him. A group of kids ran down the street kicking a ball, chased by a dog. It was the type of neighborhood he'd grown up in: far from wealthy, but wholesome and clean.

His dad had done a hell of a job with them. Raising two kids alone couldn't have been easy, but not once had Bryan ever heard his dad complain.

After paying the cabbie, Shay strolled up a cracked walkway lined by colorful flowers, to a concrete porch shaded by a massive elm. It was a small yard, lush with vegetation, flanked by another house on the right only two yards away. On the left was an empty building, and a narrow alley that led to another street and more houses.

A young, quite petite woman met Shay at the door. Of course, standing next to Shay would make most women seem short. Bryan guessed the woman to be in her late twenties. She had very dark skin, stylishly short hair, and a wide smile of welcome. They were obviously friends.

She held the door open for Shay to enter, and Bryan caught a glimpse of Leigh, the girl he and Shay had discussed the night before. She hovered in the doorway, anxious to see Shay.

Shay drew her into a warm, friendly hug.

Bryan stared so hard that he almost missed the shadow at the side of the porch, by the alley. Unlike the shade of the tree that moved and shifted with the breeze, this shadow remained still, too still. Bryan pulled off his hat and glasses, then leaned over his steering wheel, keeping his attention divided between the front door and the side yard. He waited, his senses on alert.

The shadow shifted and a shrouded head appeared.

Well, well, well, Bryan thought, already sliding from his car in silent fury. The hot September sun beat down on him, yet the intruder had dressed in dark clothes, complete with a loose-fitting sweatshirt and hood. The clothes were so concealing that Bryan couldn't catch a single distinguishing feature.

He crept forward, his movements silent, undetectable, as he skirted from the car to a tree, waited, and then moved along the length of the van, staying out of sight of anyone from the house. Tuning out the sounds of kids, barking dogs and running cars, he concentrated on his timing, preparing to lunge so he could take the guy by surprise. He waited, gathering his control — and suddenly Shay was there.

She stepped around the end of the van, hands on her hips, sunlight glinting off her fair hair.

Bryan was so startled to see her, he didn't at first move. She managed to look down her nose at him. "I knew it! You followed me. How dare you!"

Goddamn it. Knowing she'd already scared off the intruder, Bryan thrust Shay behind him. "Get in the wagon and lock the doors!"

In the distance, he could see the guy shooting down the alley. He was small and wiry, his feet flying over the ground. Bryan ran hard. He heard Shay call to him, but he ignored her, keeping his attention on the quickly disappearing body. If he got distracted now, he'd lose him.

As Bryan ran past the house he yelled to Shay's friend on the porch, "Get inside!"

The man skidded around the end of the alley and was out of sight. But Bryan didn't stop. In his mind, he remembered the shape his brother had been in after being attacked, the bruises and cuts . . . This had to be related somehow.

He'd be damned before he let a woman get hurt like that. He shot around the corner — and stalled. There was confusion everywhere. Youths were shooting basketball, a woman was unloading groceries from her car, two older folks were talking. But he didn't see the man. He turned a fast circle, bouncing on the balls of his feet, ready to break into another run . . . but he had no idea which way to go.

Damn it.

One boy, around ten or eleven years old, stared at Bryan.

"Where'd he go?" Bryan demanded.

The kid pointed up the street, but didn't say a word. The road was long, with side roads cutting across every ten houses and numerous large trees, fences and detached garages.

Running a hand through his sweaty hair, Bryan asked, "Did he turn anywhere? Did you see where he went?"

The woman stepped away from her car, her expression growing suspicious. "What's going on? You a cop?"

"No, ma'am. I saw that guy sneaking around your neighbor's property, and then he took off running." Bryan shrugged. "So I chased him."

"Well, he's gone now. I doubt you'll find him." She caught the bag under one arm, and with the other, corralled the kids like a small herd of cattle. "Inside. Let's go. All of you."

She didn't look at Bryan again. He ground his teeth, so frustrated he wanted to shout.

Someone touched his arm. Even before he turned, Bryan knew it was Shay. His temper snapped and he rounded on her. *"I told you to get in the car."*

Her eyes widened in stunned disbelief. "I don't take orders from you."

Her defiance was like gasoline on a blazing fire. Bryan snagged her arm and started walking her back the way he'd come, through the alley and toward the house where Leigh and the other woman waited.

Shay tried to pull away, and when he didn't immediately release her, she gave up. "You're making a spectacle of yourself."

"Do I give a damn? Someone was stalking you."

"Yeah. *You.*" She stumbled to keep up with him.

He snorted. Because he needed a minute to calm the adrenaline rush, he didn't answer. He was afraid he'd say things he'd regret.

Shay didn't own an ounce of caution. "I knew you were following me, Bryan."

"Not a chance." He was better than that. Hell, he followed people for a living. *No one* ever caught on to him.

Shay nodded. "From the time I left the house, though I didn't see you at first. I just felt you watching me. When did you get the wagon?"

Bryan stopped and stared at her. They

were under an enormous oak with chatty squirrels overhead. He knew Leigh was on the porch, peering around to watch them. Bees were buzzing, the grass was hot from the sun.

Clenching his teeth, he struggled to keep his voice low. "I was in the wagon the whole time."

She frowned. "No, at first you were following me in a cab. Then on foot. Then in the car —"

"No, Shay." He rubbed the back of his neck, so annoyed with himself he could have chewed nails. "You probably caught on to that other bastard following you. And if I'd been on my toes, I'd have caught on to him, too."

"The guy you were just chasing?" She sounded very perplexed. "And why *were* you chasing him?"

Bryan thrust his face close to hers. "He was hanging around the side of the house, snooping, trying to listen in. It's hot as Hades out here, but he wore a hooded jacket. Maybe to conceal himself. But maybe to conceal a gun."

Her mouth fell open. "You mean . . ." Worry replaced her indignation. "Oh God, then he knows where Leigh is? Maybe that's why . . ."

Idiot, Bryan called himself, because more than anything, he wanted to reassure her, to promise to keep her safe. To hell with it.

He took her elbow again. "I won't let anyone hurt either of you. You have my word on that." He got her walking again, headed for the house. He'd made enough mistakes for one day, no reason to keep her standing out in the open, too. "Damn it, I should have seen him."

"Why would you?" She hustled along beside him, full of questions and curiosity. "It's not exactly a preacher's job to be aware of stalkers."

They started up the steps of the porch. "You noticed him," he pointed out.

"Yeah, but I . . ." Her words fell off into silence and she bit her bottom lip.

"Got enemies you don't want to tell me about?"

She didn't reply.

"That's what I thought." More secrets. He led her into the house while Leigh stared at him wide-eyed and the other woman just got out of his way. "I would have noticed him if I hadn't been busy watching you flit from place to place. I'm damn curious about what you were doing, but we'll talk about that in a minute."

"No we won't."

Ignoring that, Bryan turned and faced the other two women, both of them mute. "Leigh." His voice softened. She was young, too young for what she did. "You okay, hon?"

She blinked big blue eyes at him. Belatedly, Bryan remembered that Bruce never called the women by endearments. But damn it, she was only a kid, not even twenty yet. She should be grounded in her room. She should have two parents coddling and protecting her.

He couldn't help but treat her the same way he would a child.

"I'm okay now, thanks to Shay."

Bryan eyed Shay, saw her face was red, and narrowed his eyes. "Yeah, she's a regular Wonder Woman, isn't she?"

He'd meant it to be sarcastic, but Leigh nodded. "She is."

The other woman stepped forward with a determined smile. "Hello. I'm Dawn. And I presume you're the preacher?"

Bryan took her proffered hand. "Guilty."

"It's very nice to meet you. Leigh has told me a lot about you."

He winked at Leigh, confounding her again. He'd never get the hang of being a preacher.

With the introductions out of the way,

the women started shuffling their feet.

Shay cleared her throat. "Dawn, would you mind taking Leigh in the other room so Bryan and I can talk?"

Leigh said, "Bryan? That's your name?"

He rolled his eyes. "Only pushy broads insist on calling me that. You can still call me Preacher."

"Oh." Leigh looked more uneasy by the moment. "Okay. Sure." She twisted her hands together in worry.

"You sure you're okay?" Bryan asked her.

She nodded, but then blurted, "I'd heard you were hurt. That's why I didn't come to you. I didn't want to cause you more trouble."

Everyone seemed to know about Bruce being attacked. Luckily, they didn't realize his speedy recovery was due to Bryan impersonating him. "I'm fine now — and, Leigh? You can always come to me."

"But the rumors on the street were that you got hurt real bad, that you were even in the hospital. . . ."

Shay stiffened. "What's this?"

"As you can see, I'm fine," Bryan said in what he hoped was a soothing tone. "I had a concussion, that's all." *Bruce had also suffered a cracked rib, and fractured ankle . . .*

Leigh's bottom lip began to tremble. "It

was my fault, wasn't it? I asked Freddie if he did it, if he was the one who hurt you, and he said no, but he got so mad at me for going to you that last time, and then when I asked him about it . . ."

If she so much as shed one tear, Bryan was going to kill someone. Preferably the miserable Freddie.

Then Shay was there, holding Leigh close, rocking her from side to side. "It was not your fault, Leigh." She looked at Bryan over Leigh's head. "The preacher is a big guy. Just look at him. He can take care of himself."

"Damn right I can." It amazed him that Shay treated Leigh like a daughter. And it made her all the more intriguing — and special.

"But —"

"No buts." Shay smoothed Leigh's hair. "You're doing the right thing, Leigh. It might not feel like it now, but it will once you get your life settled. And Dawn's going to help you with that."

"No, she's not."

The second Bryan spoke, three sets of female eyes settled on him. He knew Shay was about to start arguing with him. He sighed, and circumvented her.

"Dawn, thanks for watching over Leigh,

but she'll have to leave here now. Today."

All three women began squawking at once. Bryan turned away, looking for a phone.

Women. They were never easy. And thanks to his brother, he was stuck right in the middle of the brassiest bunch of women imaginable.

Shay rushed after Bryan. What a day it had been! Waking with her face painted had set the tone for doomed intentions, or so it seemed. Being followed hadn't alarmed her because she'd thought it was Bryan and only Bryan. She was always aware of being followed because the damn reporters were so persistent. No reporters this time, and not Bryan either, but a real threat — and now this. "Bryan, what do you think you're doing?"

"Looking for a phone." He glanced around Dawn's home. "I'm going to call Dr. Martin and see if she can put Leigh up for a little while, until I can make more permanent arrangements."

Shay almost stumbled over her own feet.

"Why can't she stay here?" Dawn demanded. "I like her company."

"I'm sure you do." Locating the phone on the kitchen wall, Bryan went in and picked up the receiver. "But someone knows she's here now."

Leigh twisted her hands together. "It was probably just Freddie."

"Maybe. But if it was him, and he had only good intentions, why sneak around? And since he ran off, I can't ask him."

"I could maybe call him," Leigh offered, but as one, Bryan, Dawn and Shay said, "No."

Bryan huffed out an impatient breath. "Look, hon, I have no idea if the guy I chased was after Shay, or if he was following her in hopes of finding you. Hell, I have no idea *what's* going on. And until I can figure it out, we're going to be extra careful. With everyone."

Shay smiled at Dawn, thrilled with Bryan's concern. "You see? He's very kind-hearted and sweet and protective."

Dawn smiled back. Leigh licked her lips nervously.

"Sweet, Shay?" His words dripped with disgust. Not taking the compliment all that well, Bryan viciously punched in a series of numbers and waited. "Dr. Martin, please." He covered the receiver and glared at Shay. "Don't you dare make me out to be a damn saint. I'm only —" He lifted his hand. "Hey, Doc."

Shay watched him smile and wondered if Eve Martin was as smitten as every other woman. Probably. Just because the doctor was stern and professional didn't make her a cold fish, and who could resist Bryan, especially when his smile went all the way to those dark and sexy bedroom eyes — as it did now?

He explained the situation to Dr. Martin, glossing over things. He listened in turn, and his shoulders relaxed. "Great. We appreciate your help. And remember, don't say a word to anyone."

He hung up and turned to face Leigh. "There. You're all set."

Blond hair hung down, hiding Leigh's face. "I hate being such a bother."

Shay rushed to reassure her. "But you aren't! We're all happy to help."

Leigh blushed. "It's so much trouble."

Dawn smiled at her. "I felt the same way once." She put her arm around Leigh. "But there's no shame in accepting a helping hand, especially from people who care about you. Now let's go upstairs. We'll get your things together, and Shay can have a private talk with the preacher."

Shay watched them go with overwhelming relief. She'd been on pins and needles, waiting for Leigh to say something that'd give her away. If Bryan found out who she was now, it'd ruin everything.

"Now I get it."

Uh-oh. Had she counted her blessings too soon? Avoiding that probing gaze that always saw too much, Shay turned to the cabinet and got down two glasses. Cautiously, she asked, "Now you get what?"

"Why you're here." He pulled out a kitchen chair and sat down, and though she didn't look to verify it, Shay knew he was watching her. "Dawn helped you out, didn't she? She's the one who got you off the streets?"

Sheer surprise brought her head up. He thought Dawn was the one . . . *Wonderful.* Bryan had just supplied her with the perfect story. He had things a bit backward, but she didn't mind. Dawn had helped with a lot of women since they'd become friends.

Refusing to tell him an outright lie, she grinned and patted his shoulder. "How clever you are."

"It was pretty damn obvious." He tipped his head. "So what were you doing in town today?"

Oh no, you don't, Shay thought, refusing to give away too much. "Lemonade?"

He made a face. "Got a cola instead?"

She bent into the refrigerator. "Root beer okay?"

"Yeah. And no glass. I like it from the can."

Shay made a face, washed the top of the can, and handed it to him. "I'm glad Dr. Martin agreed to help out, but how long can she keep Leigh?"

"It shouldn't be for long — just until I can get things figured out." He tipped up the can and swallowed about half. Shay watched the way his strong throat worked, and felt herself warming. "Damn, that's good."

Amusement filled her. He was such a very strange preacher. Not by word or deed did he behave like a man given to strict religion. "Glad you liked it."

"Now . . ."

"Where will Leigh go after she leaves Dr. Martin's?" Shay hoped to keep him distracted so he couldn't continue questioning her.

"She's so young." He traced the top of the can with a fingertip, lost in thought. His gaze lifted and locked on hers. "It'd be nice if I could convince her to try going home again. If not, maybe we can get her relocated to another area, with a job and a small apartment. I have some friends I'm going to call to see if we can get this thing figured out. But in the meantime, Shay, I don't want you going off by yourself, okay?"

She seated herself beside him, making a point to let her knee bump his. "You can't keep all the women under surveillance, Bryan."

"I didn't say all of them." He shifted so they weren't touching. "I said *you*."

Shay left her chair to move closer again. She put a hand on his shoulder. "You telling me I'm special?"

"You were followed — yeah, that makes you special."

"That's not what I meant."

He set the can aside and pushed to his feet. With his hands on her waist, he backed her up a step. "I know what you meant."

His voice was deeper, thrilling her, adding to her own awareness. "What Leigh said . . . I didn't realize anyone had hurt you." She touched his chest, felt the solid thumping of his heart. "Are you still in danger?"

Long fingers wrapped around her wrist. "I sure as hell don't need you worrying about me."

"I will anyway."

She put her other hand on him, spread

her fingers wide and enjoyed the feel of solid, warm muscles under soft cotton. His nostrils flared with his deepened breaths — but he didn't push her away.

"Bryan?" She went on tiptoe, slid her hands up to his shoulders then around to his neck. His skin was so warm, his hair silky soft. Power and determination mingled with his delicious scent, pulsing off him in tangible waves.

His eyes closed. His jaw tightened. "This is wrong," he ground out.

"Then let's be wrong." Shay touched her mouth to his, tentative and soft, and just that slight contact had her knees weak and her stomach tumbling. She kissed him again, more firmly this time, parting her lips, tasting his bottom lip, touching with her tongue . . .

The next thing she knew, he had her pinned against the hard counter, his hands holding her face still while he devoured her — and it was heaven.

She groaned aloud, amazed and instantly aroused. He felt so solid and comforting and safe. His chest crushed her breasts until she could feel the firm thudding of his heartbeat. His hips tilted in, making her aware of the solid rise of his erection.

For one of the few times in her life, she felt small next to a man. But she also felt wanted, and she liked it.

He released her mouth with a rough sound.

Crowding close so she couldn't move, he smoothed her cheeks with his thumbs and stared into her eyes, studying her expression — and he came right back, kissing her again, softer and deeper this time, sinking his tongue in, exploring, moving his mouth over hers.

Shay would have been happy kissing him just like this for the rest of her life.

He lifted his mouth, but stayed so close that she could feel the heat of his breath, smell the scent of his skin. "You're making me crazy, Shay," he whispered against her lips.

"I'm sorry." She tried to draw him closer, but he didn't allow it.

"Tell me what you were doing today." He punctuated that demand with a soft kiss that lingered and enticed. "Why did you go into all those businesses?"

"No, I —"

His mouth smothered her protests, warm and damp and delicious. He eased back, though his mouth still brushed hers. "Tell me."

She groaned. "Unfair, Bryan."

"Tell me." With his eyes holding hers prisoner, his hand moved to her shoulder, then boldly down over her breast.

Her back arched and she caught her breath.

Oh God, he wasn't even moving, just holding his palm over her, and everything inside her tingled and tumbled and her lungs constricted. . . .

Staring at her, seeing her reaction to that simple touch, Bryan began caressing her. His eyes were barely open, dazzling bright, full of purpose. "Tell me."

Like a bucket of ice water, Shay realized what he was doing. "Bastard." She started to shove him away but he locked her close with one hard muscled arm, as tight and inflexible as an iron band, and he kissed her again.

She tried turning her head, but the way he had her backed to the counter afforded her no room to maneuver. And his hand never left her breast. No, it stayed right there, firm, teasing, his thumb now rubbing up and over her nipple until she wanted to cry out with the excitement and frustration of it.

She made an incoherent sound of fury that didn't affect him one bit. His leg wedged between hers, pressing hard against her, and Shay went weak all over.

She'd dated plenty in her lifetime, even been married once. But never had she felt like this, so alive and full of sensation and need.

There was no option but to give in.

"I was . . . I was looking for a job."

He went still, then he tilted back, putting a small space between their upper bodies. But the new position pushed his lower body even closer, emphasizing the press of his erection. "A job?"

Shay nodded. Her lips were tingling, swollen. She could still taste him. She wanted to taste him again. All over. She had his full attention now, but still his hand worked her breast, so careful, keeping her dizzy with pleasure. Breathing was difficult, thinking more so.

She didn't explain that the jobs would be for the women at his safe house.

When she said nothing else, his thigh pressed in, making her go on tiptoes. She gasped.

With silky menace, he asked, "What kind of job, honey?"

Oh, given that tone, she knew what kind he thought. The man really did have a rather uncomplimentary opinion of her ability.

"A starting position," she whispered, struggling to keep her eyes open in the face of such overwhelming need. "Waitress, cook, cleanup, secretarial . . . anything legitimate that would pay well, offer opportunity for advancement, and some benefits."

"Since when does waiting tables offer benefits?"

"Some do." The people she'd gone to were willing to help her — because she could help them. In exchange for giving one of the women a good job, Shay would use them for her charity events. Catering, displays, advertisements . . . she put on functions of all kinds. In fact, her sister had met her husband at a male auction that had raised a lot of money for abused women.

Companies loved to be included in her events, because it showcased them and gave them more business in return.

Bryan put some respectable space between them, stepping back and letting her feet touch the floor, at the same time releasing her breast. But he didn't leave her. He pressed her head to his shoulder and hugged her, surrounding her with his warmth. "I'm sorry."

Shay instinctively knew that he didn't

apologize often, and she took pleasure in the special moment. Being hugged by him was special, too, and comforting. "For using me?"

"For doubting you." He tilted her back, and one corner of his mouth lifted in a crooked smile. His fingers trembled the tiniest bit as he touched her cheek with incredible tenderness. "I wasn't using you, Shay. I was fighting myself. If we weren't here, now, I probably wouldn't have stopped, because stopping now is about the hardest damn thing I've ever done."

Her heart swelled in yearning at that awesome admission, but the others were coming back and Bryan moved away from her, reseating himself at the table. He finished off his root beer just as Leigh and Dawn walked into the kitchen.

"You two ready?" he asked, and if Shay hadn't known better, she'd think he'd been sitting there the whole time, rather than ravishing her.

But Dawn was no slouch. She'd been in the flesh business too long to miss the signs. She took in Shay's rumpled hair, swollen lips and dazed expression, then cast a suspicious glance at Bryan. Shay shook her head, warning her friend not to say anything.

Leigh, for some reason, kept grinning. She even looked at Shay once and giggled. It was nice, making her sound like a regular nineteen-year-old, instead of a cynical, wary woman of the night.

Within seconds, Bryan had them ready to go. He thanked Dawn, put a solicitous hand at Leigh's back, and started out the door.

Shay said, "Go on. I'll be right there." She needed a minute to talk to Dawn in private.

Reluctantly, his expression dark with suspicion, Bryan escorted Leigh outside. The moment they were out of sight, Shay rushed into a speech. "I have to hurry before Leigh says something she shouldn't."

Dawn shook her head. "No, I told her that the preacher thought you were a hooker, too. I have to tell you, Shay, it's the first time I've heard Leigh laugh like that."

Awareness dawned. "So that's why she kept giggling?"

Her friend nodded. "You gotta admit, the idea of you being a call girl is hilarious."

Shay started to frown, but how in the world could she take offense at that? She waved away Dawn's teasing comments. "First, call Eve and tell her I'll be with

Bryan but that she doesn't know me."

"Oh yeah, and that'll make a lot of sense."

Shay laughed. "I'm sure you can explain it to her. She'll play along." At least, Shay hoped she would. In the past, Eve had helped a lot with Shay's efforts. "And can you get some clothes together for me?" During the bus ride, Shay had compiled a list of what was needed. Pulling it from her back pocket, she handed it to Dawn.

"Sure. I'll run by your house today."

"No, I mean for the other women. Well, clothes for me would be good, too, but nothing fancy. Just more jeans and some casual shirts. Some sandals, too, maybe. Underclothes and something to sleep in. But here's what I really want." She went over the list with Dawn, hoping she had guessed correctly at the sizes. "What did the realtor have to say?"

"There are three buildings you can look at. One's just down the street from the preacher."

"Really?"

Dawn laughed. "Yeah, I thought you'd like that." Dawn handed her the addresses so she could check them out herself. "There's no rush. The buildings have been up for sale for a while."

"Thanks." Shay tucked the piece of paper away, and gave her friend a hug. Through the front door, they could see Bryan standing by the old station wagon, his impatience almost palpable. Shay already had fantasies of working side by side with him, each running a shelter of sorts, confiding in each other — and spending each night together.

Dawn cleared her throat. "Leigh tells me that the preacher never gets involved with any of the women."

Without taking her eyes off Bryan, Shay said, "Some of the women told me the same."

"Seems he was pretty *involved* with you."

"I'm working on it." Shay headed for the door. "Wish me luck, okay?"

"I always do. Just be careful, all right? He's a good man and he's not going to like it that you're playing this game. I don't want to see you get hurt."

"I'll tell him everything soon, I promise." But not before she felt sure that he liked her, that he'd trust her, and that he'd want to keep on seeing her.

After that scorching kiss and the tender way he'd held her afterward, Shay knew she'd already made considerable headway.

If she could just get him alone, she

might be able to build on their growing closeness.

And then maybe, when he finally heard the truth, it wouldn't drive him away.

Chapter Six

Bryan went around to the rear entrance door of the clinic that led to Eve Martin's office. Thanks to the clinic's location in the less auspicious part of town, they were always busy. There seemed to be no end to the illness and injury among the underprivileged. He'd always known that, of course, because his brother discussed his work often enough. But seeing it firsthand was something altogether different.

He knew this was Eve's lunch hour — the only break she got — and he regretted his timing, even while considering it beneficial. No one would see them entering, and that would mean less risk to Eve.

Unlike before, he'd kept his eyes open and so he knew they hadn't been followed.

Being smart made Eve the cautious sort, and she peeked out through the miniblinds before opening all the locks.

"Preacher," she said in greeting.

"Hello, Dr. Martin. Thanks for seeing us."

She waved them inside, and once the door was again secured, she turned to Leigh.

Leigh, bless her heart, looked pale and uncertain and embarrassed. He didn't know Eve Martin as well as Bruce did, but his brother assured him that, although she seemed strident and all business, she had a big heart.

Bryan witnessed it now as she took in Leigh's expression and reserved posture.

"You must be Leigh," she said with a smile. "It's very nice to meet you."

Leigh stared.

"Have a seat, please. All of you."

Shay, acting very maternal, hovered over Leigh.

And Bryan, damn it, found himself hovering over Shay. Eve raised a brow at him and he moved back, taking a chair opposite Leigh.

Leaning against the edge of her desk, Eve smoothed her slim dark skirt before folding her hands over her lap. "I have a garage apartment that you can use, Leigh. It's small but private."

Without raising her head, Leigh whispered, "Thank you."

Poor girl. Bryan wished for some way to reassure her. He saw Shay put her hand on

Leigh's shoulder, offering silent comfort and reassurance.

Eve continued. "The preacher told me you're looking for a job and I could really use some help here in the office. I can't pay much, but it's not hard work and I'd be deeply appreciative. In fact, the timing couldn't be better for me. I was going to have to start interviewing people soon, but if you're willing, I'll be saved all kinds of time and frustration."

Bryan relaxed. Bless Eve, she made it sound like Leigh would be doing her a favor. And that tactic must have worked, because with a trade-off in the offering, Leigh perked up. "Oh, I'd be happy to help out. You don't have to pay me."

To her credit, Eve didn't let the girl grovel. "You won't be out around the patients since your location is to be kept quiet. But here in my office, there are always papers to be filed, mail to be sorted, supplies to be restocked. That sort of thing. Your contribution will be most valuable to me."

Leigh looked overwhelmed with the offer. "I've . . . I've never worked in an office before." Her shoulders slumped a little and she swallowed. "I've never done a real job anywhere. Freddie said I wouldn't know how."

"Freddie's wrong. Everyone starts new, and I'll show you everything you need to know." Eve pushed off her desk. "So that's settled. Preacher, was there anything else?"

Bryan was amazed at how quickly and easily things had been resolved. In his experience, people weren't so helpful or giving. In his experience, everyone had an ulterior motive, which made them suspect and worthy of caution.

More than ever before, he felt the difference in his world compared to his brother's. Bruce had his share of creeps to deal with, but he also knew some incredible people with generous hearts.

Now Bryan knew them, too, and he felt humbled. He took Eve's hand in gratitude. "You've covered everything. Thank you."

"My pleasure."

Shay stepped forward. "I'd like to give you my cell phone number, just in case anything comes up."

Raising a brow, Eve inquired, "And you are?"

Damn, he'd forgotten his manners — about ten years ago, actually. But playing Bruce, he needed to recall them real quick. "Sorry. Dr. Martin, this is Shay. She's staying at the safe house, too."

Eve's expression was comical. "She's . . .?"

"Staying at the safe house," Shay repeated. "It's a wonderful place." She grabbed up a pen off Eve's desk and jotted her number down on a notepad. When she handed it to Eve, their gazes held. "Leigh and I are friends."

No way could Bryan miss the significance in their exchange. It held a wealth of innuendo. So Shay knew Eve already? He remembered her reaction when he'd asked her to go and get checked out. Had she been to the clinic before, maybe to be treated? Or had she met Eve while helping someone else?

How well did they know each other? And what made Shay think he was dumb enough to be fooled? He was both insulted and throbbing with curiosity.

Shay gave Leigh a hearty hug, whispered in her ear, then stepped away.

"We won't keep you any longer," Bryan said, and he took Shay's arm. "You already have my number. Call with any concerns at all. I'll check in with you tomorrow."

Eve opened the door to let them out. "We'll be fine. Take care."

Shay was far too quiet as they walked to the car. It bothered Bryan. He was used to her being chatty and brazen and confident, not introspective. He opened her car door and watched her slide in. Leaning down, he said, "All right. What is it?"

"What? Oh, nothing." She smiled. "I'm just worried about Leigh. I hate shuffling her around like this."

Bryan shook his head in wonder and went around to the driver's side. "She'll be safer here, in case that was her ex hanging around outside your friend's house."

"I know."

As Bryan drove into traffic, he asked, "What's going on, Shay?"

She twisted to face him as much as her seat belt would allow. Eyes direct, she said, "I like you and what you're doing. I want to help. The world needs more men like you and I find it very appealing that you, a very manly man, could be so helpful to women used to selling their bodies. Most men wouldn't be able to behave. Or they'd be filled with disgust. But you . . . you're compassionate and understanding and kind."

"I'm not a damn saint." Bruce might be, but being twins didn't make Bruce's qualities his own.

"No. You're sexy and macho and strong — and that only makes what you do that much better. It shows the women that good men do exist."

"Do you know much about good men?"

She grinned. "Yeah, I do. My sister is married to an astounding man. Like you, he's really big and capable and very handsome."

Bryan frowned. He didn't like hearing her compliment another guy, even a guy married to her sister.

"He's also very aware of the injustice in the world. I love him. He's terrific."

Hands tightening on the wheel, Bryan asked, "How does he feel about you?"

"I asked him that once. He said I was pushy and shrewd and too outspoken." She laughed. "But he hugged me when he said it. We were actually friends long before he married my sister."

Most of what she said didn't sit well with him. The insults, even tempered by hugs, bugged him. And the hug itself made him see red. Shay was a beautiful woman, sexy as hell, and he found it hard to swallow that any guy would hold her and not want her. Men were men, and Shay was too appealing.

He knew zip about her past other than the sketchy details she'd shared about her childhood. He knew other men had wanted her, that she hadn't lived in a cocoon, but that didn't mean he had to like it.

What really got to him, though, was one particular word.

"Shrewd?" Megan had been shrewd, more so than anyone might have guessed. He'd figured Shay for being an open book, but what her brother-in-law said contradicted that.

She was looking out the window, the sun on her face and shining in her fair hair. "I admit it, I like to get my own way." She turned her head and those incredible blue eyes caught his. "I'm too stubborn *not* to get something, when I really want it."

And she'd already told him that she wanted him.

It was time for a serious chat with his conscience. He only hoped his conscience was smarter than various other parts of his body.

Eve closed and locked the door, while still absorbing the absurd notion of Shay in a safe house. The woman owned and ran three shelters for abused women. She was wealthy beyond belief. Her philanthropic tentacles were spread far and wide. The last thing she needed was a free place to stay.

What was she up to now? Whatever it might be, it was surely to benefit someone else. Shay was a remarkable woman, and Eve counted her as a friend.

She turned to smile at Leigh. The girl stood back, her eyes wide, her manner uncertain. "Have you had lunch?"

"Yes, ma'am. At Dawn's."

Getting to know each other over lunch would have been nice, but she'd make do anyway. "All right. Then we can go over your duties while I eat. If you have any questions, just let me know. And Leigh, thank you. I can't tell you how helpful this is going to be to me."

Eve watched Leigh smile with a combination of hope and gratitude, and realized she was quite pretty when one ignored the shadows in her eyes — and the shame that she couldn't quite hide.

But now, thanks to Shay, she'd have a chance to be a happy young woman. That seemed to be Shay's biggest goal in life — helping others, especially women, who otherwise might have to struggle their entire lives. Eve knew that was in part due to Shay's own tragic past as a child, but also because she had an enormous heart and a capacity to understand and empathize, which few others could ever claim.

So, what was Shay doing with the preacher?

And as to that — what was the preacher doing with Shay? In all the years she'd known him, Eve had never seen Bruce Kelly look at a woman quite the way he'd looked at Shay.

Eve smiled. She'd have to give Dawn a call back when she had more time to talk. This seemed like a very interesting situation, and she couldn't wait to hear the nitty-gritty.

Bryan finished dragging the razor over his chin, then rinsed his face. He could use a haircut — hell, he looked almost as shaggy as Bruce — but he doubted he'd take the time for it right now. He had more important things on his mind. At least, the majority of the time he did.

With iron control, he managed to block most thoughts of Shay. It wasn't easy. In the last five days, he'd only seen her in passing. He'd avoided being alone with her, hadn't let her get within touching distance, and had steered any conversations — all of them brief — away from intimate talk. Yet . . . soft images, bits of conversations and fleeting smiles kept creeping back to him, and he'd find himself smiling for no reason at all.

She was an enigma. A beautiful, kind-hearted enigma.

He could ignore her beauty, but the rest . . .

Clean-shaven, he stalked into the kitchen for more coffee. Maybe a rush of caffeine would exorcise her from his soul.

He'd just finished refilling the cup when, through the archway, he saw the doorknob turning on the front door. Very still, he listened for just a moment, and recognized the sound of his brother's attempts at stealth.

With a sigh, he got down another cup.

The door crept open and Bruce slipped in. His brother seemed to enjoy his furtive role in their switch.

When Bruce turned he saw that Bryan was aware of his entry and watching him. He also noted that Bryan wasn't dressed, was in fact buck ass naked in the kitchen. Bruce's jaw fell open.

Smirking, Bryan ignored his surprise and strode forward to hand him the second cup of steaming coffee. "You look like you could use this."

Bruce accepted it automatically, still somewhat stunned. "Is there a reason you're not dressed?"

"Hadn't gotten to it yet."

"But . . . you're in the kitchen." He sounded scandalized, and that amused Bryan.

Just to irritate Bruce, Bryan shrugged in nonchalance, blew on the top of his coffee, and sipped. "If I'd known you were coming, I could have pulled on jeans." Carefully carrying the steaming mug, he headed into the bedroom to do just that.

Bruce followed. With awe in his tone, he said, "It just never occurred to me to leave the bedroom naked." And then, more thoughtfully, "No wonder you're so popular with the ladies. You're rock solid with muscle."

A laugh caught Bryan by surprise. He set the coffee aside to open a drawer and pull out boxers. "I have to stay in shape."

"*I'm* in shape. *You're* a brute."

"Now don't make me blush."

It was such a ridiculous comment that Bruce snorted. Bryan hadn't suffered a blush since he was a green kid, ogling his first naked female. He'd been sixteen at the time, and the female in question had been nineteen. Of course she'd thought he was nineteen, too.

That wasn't the first example of how he differed from his brother and father, but it was certainly one of the more memorable ones.

Making himself at home, Bruce stretched out on the unmade bed, crossed his ankles and folded his arms behind his head. "I miss this bed," he said with a groan of pleasure. "The one I'm using at the motel is lumpy and has some suspicious smells."

"So go stay with Dad." Shuffling through a drawer, Bryan located a snowy white T-shirt and tugged it on over his head. "No one said you need to hang around here, watching my every move."

"Right. No reason at all."

His tone held a wealth of insinuation, and Bryan couldn't resist teasing him. Holding his jeans loosely in his hand, he faced his brother with a raised brow. "You don't trust me?"

"Of course I do. You're my brother."

Bruce's naivete never ceased to astound him. "And that means I have unplumbed scruples?" He laughed. "You're smarter than that."

"I see." Unconcerned, Bruce sighed and closed his eyes. "So you've done something heinous and that's why you're avoiding the safe house?"

Bryan froze. If wanting Shay was heinous — and considering he was supposed to be a preacher, it very well might be — then he couldn't be more guilty. "Who says I'm avoiding it?" Bryan eyed his brother's stretched-out form while threading a thick black leather belt through his belt loops.

Bruce was solid, but a bit leaner than Bryan. With his blond hair so long and unkempt, and his whiskers more disreputable by the day, they shared little resemblance to the unsuspecting citizens in the area. No one who saw Bruce now would realize he was the preacher. Their ruse was safe.

"You've avoided it enough that you haven't noticed some of the changes."

"Such as?"

Bruce cracked one eye open. "How the women are dressing. Their makeup. Mealtime."

With his big feet now shoved into low boots, Bryan was fully dressed. He crossed his arms over his chest and frowned at Bruce. He already knew about the makeup, and he supposed new clothes seemed like a natural procession to the changes Shay had instigated. But . . . "Mealtime?"

"It's now a formal affair. Proper place settings, linens, etiquette, the whole nine yards. You'd think the safe house was a finishing school for privileged young ladies, rather than a haven for prostitutes."

"No shit?" Shay was more ambitious than he'd figured. But why? By the minute, she became more interesting and more mysterious.

Bruce glared at his language, then sat up. "Ever since you dropped Leigh off at the clinic five days ago, you've barely visited."

"I've been busy scoping out the streets."

"And finding nothing?"

Bryan shrugged. "No more young ladies, and no sign of your attacker. Mostly I just run into Chili everywhere I go. Does that fool ever sleep?"

"He's not around as much during the day, because believe it or not, he holds down a job. But he and his kind keep the area thriving with their drinking, whoring and gambling." Bruce's disgust showed through. "With fewer women working the corners, he probably spends more time drinking."

"Since he's around so much, I figure he ought to be good for some info now and then. I might have a little chat with him, see if he knows anything useful."

"I don't want to talk about Chili." Bruce shoved up to one elbow. "Tell me what's going on. Why haven't you been back to the house?"

"I've been there."

"Yeah, in and out like the hounds of hell were on your heels. Is Barb driving you nuts with her bossiness?"

Bryan shook his head. "Barb's easy enough to understand."

"You think so?"

"Sure. She's bossy to cover up her insecurity. Even though you've given her a job and responsibility, she's distrustful of it. She's not sure it'll last, and that scares her."

His brother looked surprised that he'd realized so much, as if he had no sensitivities at all. And for the most part, Bryan admitted, he didn't. But Barb was so obvious he couldn't have missed it.

"All right, you and Barb related on a higher plane. I'm glad to hear it."

His brother was always so dramatic. Bryan dropped down to sit on the edge of the mattress.

"So," Bruce continued, "is it Morganna's crude jokes that are getting to you? I admit, she's embarrassed me plenty of times and she always has a new one to tell, worse than the one before it."

"I think her jokes are funny."

Bruce rolled his eyes. "You would." Then, with false concern, "So, is Patti too grabby? She's like an octopus sometimes. It's hard to believe she only has two hands. But I think it's just that she —"

"She wants attention, yeah, I know. So I give it to her." Bryan winked. "While dodging her hands."

A slow smile turned up the corners of Bruce's mouth. "Wow, you've got a handle on all of them, don't you?"

Bryan shrugged. Not all. He didn't understand Shay, but he wanted to.

"Maybe," Bruce teased, looking decidedly evil for a preacher, "it's just that Shay is too irresistible?"

Judging by his brother's expression, there'd be no point in denying it. "Bingo."

Bruce laughed. "That's what I thought."

"It's hardly funny." Frustrating, certainly. Maddening even. But not funny.

"Not to you, maybe." Bruce stared off in the distance as if lost in thought. "She really is a beauty."

Bryan shoved himself up from the bed. "Hell, if that's all it was, it'd be no big deal. But it's more than that."

Bruce put on his best preacher face. "Want to talk about it?"

"No." Bryan snatched up his cup and stalked into the kitchen. The bed squeaked, and a second later, Bruce was right on his heels. Without even meaning to, Bryan heard himself say, "She's different from any woman I've ever met."

"How so?"

"I don't know." He rubbed the back of his neck in annoyance. "More open, honest." And feeling sheepish, "Beautiful on the inside, not just the outside."

"Ah." Bruce took a chair. "You're falling in love with her."

"No! Jesus, Bruce. I barely know her." He threw himself into the seat opposite his brother. "Don't talk stupid."

"Love is not stupid, but it is unexpected. Hits you broadside sometimes. You're walking along, minding your own business, and boom, you're on your butt, reeling."

"Oh for the love of . . ."

Bruce laughed again, then leaned forward and rubbed his hands together. "So obviously you've done something you think you shouldn't have, right?" No answer was answer enough. "Have you slept with her?"

Bryan stared at him, feeling mean and put upon. "No. I have *not* slept with her."

"I'm glad. You shouldn't until you come to grips with how you really feel." His head tilted. "So what have you done with her? Something you're regretting?"

Bryan felt like a kid again, called on the carpet with his dad frowning down on him with so much disappointment. Only his father and brother could make him feel that way. He looked away. "Nothing for you to concern yourself with."

"But you feel tempted?" Bruce nodded. "I can tell you that she seems to be making great strides with the ladies. Even from a distance, I see how they react to her. No one leaves the house without Shay standing on the front stoop with a wave. She welcomes them when they return. She hugs them." A new depth of gratitude shadowed his brother's features. "She accepts them. To my knowledge, more so than anyone else ever has, even their families. Of course, I wouldn't have to tell you this if you'd spend more than fifteen minutes there."

"I go over every morning."

"Right." Bruce quirked his mouth. "When the women are still asleep. You creep in, take a tally of groceries, see that everything is secure, then sneak back out."

"I do not sneak."

"Do too."

Exasperated, Bryan snapped, "I check in every damn night."

"Zip in, zip out, no time for personal contact." His smile was back. "No time for touching."

Bryan narrowed his eyes. "Maybe I need to remind you of our little deception. I'm playing you. And *you* wouldn't be touching any of them."

"I would if I were in love."

Bryan's head felt ready to explode. "I am *not* in love, damn it."

"Thou protesteth too much."

"Shut up, Bruce."

"Okay, okay." Sensing he'd pushed enough, Bruce held up both hands. "But don't blame a brother for being happy at the signs of resurgent emotion. After Megan, I thought you'd never really care about a woman again."

Every speck of tolerance drained away, leaving Bryan rigid on the outside, raw on the inside. "Don't bring her up, Bruce."

His brother had no sense of self-preservation, not around Bryan. "Why not? You were married to the woman. You loved her. Despite the awful things that happened, she's an important part of —"

Unwilling to discuss it, Bryan scraped back his chair and stormed out of the kitchen. But that didn't deter Bruce. He just followed, as determined and adamant as only a brother could be.

"What happened to her wasn't your fault."

Bryan rounded on him in a fury. *"The hell it wasn't."*

Unmoved by the show of rage, Bruce flattened his mouth. "Save it, Bryan. That red-eyed evil look doesn't work on me. I'm your brother." He landed one heavy hand on Bryan's shoulder. "I love you and I know you love me."

Hearing those solemn, sincere words took the wind right out of Bryan. "What is it with you and love this morning?"

Bruce's arms spread wide. "It's a beautiful day," he intoned in his best preacher voice. "We've been blessed with lots of sunshine and an incredible blue sky. It's a good day for talking about love."

With theatrical exaggeration, Bryan held his head. "You sound more like Dad every damn day."

"Thank you."

"It was not a compliment."

Bruce grinned. "If you don't want to hear me, then go to the house. See how the women are doing. Encourage them. Encourage Shay. Talk to her. If it makes you feel better, I give you permission to kiss her. God would like for you to kiss her, I promise. I think you both could use a little more affection."

The way Bruce said that set off warning

signals popping and zinging through Bryan's already overwrought nervous system. His eyes narrowed. "What exactly do you know of Shay?"

"More than you, maybe. But then, I'm not blinded by emotion."

Bryan took two steps forward until he stared his brother in the eyes. "What the hell does that mean, Bruce?"

"It means that you're not paying attention, and that's unlike you, especially in a circumstance where you should be noticing every little thing. That's why you insisted I play this ridiculous game, remember? Because you're more observant."

"And meaner."

"There's that," Bruce agreed.

"And tougher."

"Tough as nails," he conceded.

His brother was definitely up to something, maybe hiding a few things as well. "Has there been another threat, Bruce? Do you know something about the bastard that jumped you?"

Bruce shook his head. "Only that he's laying low, because I haven't seen him. But if he doesn't do something soon, I'm ready to call it quits. I'm tired of skulking around and playing the coward."

"You are not a coward. You're just not a tough guy."

Teasing, Bruce flexed his arm, making his biceps bulge. "Oh ye of little faith."

Bryan had to laugh. His brother was about the corniest person he knew, and he had the biggest heart. Today there was no stopping him. "Okay, so you could maybe hold your own if you had to. In a one-on-one, face-to-face fight, you'd do okay. But you're not used to criminals the way I am. They don't fight fair."

"I know. I got the lump on the back of my head to prove it." As if the ache remained, Bruce rubbed his head. "Hard to fight someone who sneaks up behind you."

"True enough. Just give me a little more time. I'll ferret him out."

"By dodging the safe house?" Bruce caught Bryan and dragged him to the couch to sit. "Be reasonable, Bryan. You need to be seen there, not just seen on the street. Everyone who knows me, knows my routine. That was the whole point, remember?"

"All right, quit nagging. It just so happens I was heading for the safe house this morning anyway."

That surprised Bruce. He reared back, then asked, "You'll stay awhile?"

"Yeah, sure," Bryan said, as if it were no big deal, while inside he cringed. If he hung around, he'd see Shay, have to talk to her, smell her, listen to her soft voice. . . .

Remembering that kiss and the feel of her breast and the way she moaned had his hands shaking.

Bruce took the chair across from him. "And you'll go back tonight? Maybe hang around and have dinner with them?"

He was not a masochist. "You're pushing."

"Actually, I'm manipulating. But hanging around is what I'd do, so that's what you have to do, too."

Bruce looked far too satisfied by that conclusion.

"I'll stay," Bryan said through his teeth. "But you'll have to be responsible for the consequences."

"As a man of God, I spend my life dealing with consequences. Yours won't add to my burden."

On that bit of nonsense, Bryan shoved up from the couch and escaped the apartment, but behind him, he could hear Bruce laughing. His brother had developed a warped sense of humor.

Bryan only prayed Bruce wasn't starting

to get more like him. That would really make dealing with him impossible.

Shay jumped up from the table when she heard the front door opening. All the ladies were present and accounted for, so it had to be Bryan. He was the only one, other than the women staying at the house, who had keys.

Her heart immediately sped up and her stomach tightened. She'd missed him so much. The quick, casual encounters she'd had with him recently had been far from satisfying. Had she scared him off? Probably. She just hadn't suspected that he'd avoid the safe house.

"Go on," Morganna told her with a grin. "We can manage without you."

Shay caught herself. She'd been on the verge of racing for the door like a lovesick teenager. Dashing after Bryan was totally inappropriate on many levels. She was trying, subtly, to teach the women some manners and decorum. What kind of an example would she set by leaving the table unexcused and chasing after a man who, by his absences, had made his disinterest clear?

But then he stepped into the kitchen doorway, filling up the space with his tall, muscular body and his sheer male presence. He had his hands propped on his lean, denim-clad hips, his feet braced apart in a confrontational stance. The pose pulled his T-shirt tight, showing off impressive biceps and a hard, wide chest.

He emanated power and dominance. He was so masculine, so strong and self-assured.

His dark eyes seemed fathomless, his sun-streaked hair hanging smooth to his shoulders.

Everything around her came to a throbbing halt, leaving the air charged and her body humming with awareness. His eyes moved all over her, then settled on her mouth. Shay burned from the heat of his interest. She remembered his kiss, the way he'd touched her, as if it had happened moments ago instead of days ago.

He wanted her. He just felt compelled to fight it.

Barb slapped a hand to the table. "Now that we've got this fancy table set, are we gonna eat or ogle each other? I'm starving."

Morganna laughed. "You are so bad, Barb." Then, to Bryan, "Come on in, Preacher. We're getting ready to dine in hoity-toity style. Patti, keep your hands to yourself. The preacher won't eat with us if you start pawing at him."

Patti scowled, but drew back the hand she'd extended toward Bryan's rear.

Bryan pulled his gaze off Shay and looked around. As Shay watched him, his eyes widened in disbelief. "Barb?"

She fluffed her newly styled hair. "It's me. Shay just gave me a new do. You like?"

Bryan cleared his throat. "Yeah. It — I mean you — look . . . nice."

"Don't choke saying it."

"Sorry."

She stood and thrust out her chest. "What do you think of these clothes?" Her sour expression made it clear what she thought. "Shay says it looks nice, but I feel like a nun. You can't even see that I have boobs, can you?"

Bryan's mouth opened twice, but nothing came out. His eyes seemed to be glued to her face, unwilling to venture down near her "boobs" to give an opinion. Shay grinned.

Barb had an overblown figure that no amount of classy clothing would hide, but with the right outfit — a loose, button-up blouse and straight blue skirt that just skimmed her knees — she looked sexy instead of sexual. Her long brown hair had new highlights and had been blow-dried into a silky curtain to fall down her back.

"Well?" Barb demanded.

He looked to the heavens, as if begging divine intervention. None came. "All right, you want the truth?"

Barb shriveled a little, and in a small voice, said, "Yeah?"

"You look a hell of a lot better. Men like to guess what's underneath, not have it shoved in their faces." He warmed to his topic, making all the women sit up and take notice. "No one is going to miss your figure, Barb. But any guy who's interested in a better peek is going to have to get your attention, and then your cooperation, by being nice to you."

"Why?"

"So that you'll want to show him what you have to offer. It puts you in control instead of the other way around."

Barb chewed on that and finally nodded. "Yeah. I think I'd like taking a little control for a change."

Patti scoffed. "I get paid extra for that." Then she blanched. "I mean, I used to. Back when I still did that." Her apologetic smile had them all smiling in return.

Bryan turned his attention to Morganna.

Shay watched him take in the changes she'd so meticulously wrought. Morganna's red hair, now toned down to a richer, deeper shade, hung in a tidy braid down her back. Rather than hoop earrings the size of a plate, she wore small golden studs. Without the garish makeup her eyes were a clear, bright green. She was tall, lush on the top, and the romantic peasant blouse and matching white slacks emphasized her height, giving her new dignity.

"You look great, too, Morganna."

"I know, sugar. I can't help it." She winked. "It's not the digs, but the body underneath."

"Exactly," Bryan said, agreeing with her.

She gave an evil grin. "I probably shouldn't tell, but it's only the top layer that's spiffed up anyway, because I ain't giving up my sexy undies for no one. I just wouldn't be me without a little leopard print or peekaboo lace or leather."

Bryan raised a brow. "Leather?"

"Yeah, you think that's sexy, doncha?"

Patti swatted at her. "He's a preacher, idiot."

"He's still a man." She drawled that out, trying to make Bryan blush, Shay knew.

Instead, he said, "Actually, I'm more partial to cotton. Soft cotton. But every guy is different."

The women went mute for a single second before Morganna roared with laughter. "A simple man, huh? Well, as you said, to each her own."

"You should wear whatever you want underneath, Morganna," he said in encouragement. "Whatever makes you feel good."

Patti giggled in coy, rehearsed delight. "Nothing at all makes me feel good, so I'm bare as a baby underneath."

Bryan looked dumbfounded.

"Shay said it was okay, long as I remembered not to bend over —"

"So Bryan," Shay rushed out, interrupting Patti's awesome admission. Discussing underwear, or lack thereof, was not something Shay had ever expected to do with Bryan. She rushed into speech, hoping to get the conversation back on track. "They've each had a makeover. I told them they looked wonderful, but they needed to hear it from someone else, too."

"You were right. Very nice." Bryan's attention skimmed over Patti, and he smiled. She wore a black silk blouse and beige slacks that complemented her light brown hair and eyes. She looked ready to grab at him, so Bryan sidestepped toward Amy. She sat quietly, taut with nervousness.

Bryan nodded at her. "Amy? I like your new clothes, too."

Shay had taken extra care with Amy. The girl was still jumpy, and thin in a gaunt, sickly way. Dark colors or pale pastels would have only made her more so. Instead, Shay had chosen a simple tan dress with three-quarter-length sleeves. The flowing skirt fell to mid-calf, showcasing cute flat sandals. Simple gold jewelry completed the look.

Amy ducked her face more without replying.

Shay understood Amy's reserve and saved her from further unwanted attention. "Would you like to have breakfast with us, Preacher?" She hoped he appreciated her effort. She'd promised only to call him Bryan in private, and she'd keep her promise.

"Well . . ." He wanted to escape, she could tell, but Shay wasn't about to let him.

"It'll be delicious, I promise," Shay said.

Barb shoved back her chair. "Sit down, both of you. I'll get it. After all, I cooked it. And damn right it's good. With Shay nagging over me, how could it be anything else?"

Morganna laughed. "Barb doesn't like all the fuss, but I'm starting to enjoy it." With her baby finger bent just so, she waved a linen napkin at Bryan. "Makes me feel special."

"You are special," Shay assured her while returning to her chair.

Patti grinned, and said to Bryan, sotto voce, "Shay says that a lot."

"Only because it's true." Shay grinned at each of them. "And I don't want any of you going to your interviews today with an empty stomach."

"I don't wanna go at all," Amy muttered without looking up.

Shay ignored that. Everyone was enthusiastic about the job possibilities — except Amy. Shay hoped that more encouragement and support would get her through her difficult adjustment.

Bryan waited until Barb had returned to her seat, then he joined them at the table. "What's this about interviews? How many of you are going?"

As usual, Morganna spoke up before anyone else could. "Just me, Amy and Patti. Since Barb already works for you, she don't need a job."

Shay leaned close and whispered in Morganna's ear, and a second later Morganna said, "*Doesn't* need a job." As everyone began passing serving bowls of scrambled eggs, potato casserole, and platters of ham and toast, Morganna added, "I'm going to this fancy restaurant to apply. If I get the job, I'll have this dorky uniform to wear, and I'll be cleaning tables and stuff at first. But if I can pick up all that nonsense about different sized forks and where all the silverware goes, I can be a waitress. Know what they make?"

Bryan shrugged. He looked like a wary mouse dropped into the middle of a field of hungry cats.

"Not as much as I make a night, that's for sure." Morganna gave an exaggerated wink. "I'm good, so I make plenty. Just goes to show you that flesh is better than forks any day. But sugar puss, I know putting out forks has just got to be easier than putting out —"

Shay smoothly interrupted. "And you're so personable, Morganna, you'll make a ton in tips."

"Right," Barb said with a sneer. "The best tip she'll get will be to *shut up*."

Patti scooted her chair closer to Bryan's. "I've got an interview at a place that makes frames for artwork. It'll be cleaning and putting out supplies, but Shay says if I learn the trade, I might be able to become a saleslady." She scooted closer again, until their chairs bumped. "I think

I'd be good at sales, don't you?"

"I think you'll do well at anything you put your mind to."

It was simple praise, but Patti beamed. "Really?" She leaned closer to Bryan. "I figure sales should be easy. After all, that's what I've always done. Sell myself. This'll just be selling something different." Her hand landed on Bryan's thigh.

Shay stood, took the back of Patti's chair, and dragged her back into place. "We all have seats at the table and we have to stay in them. That's how it's done. Otherwise you'll ruin the arrangement."

"The arrangement?" Bryan said.

"Sure. At all the fancy banquets and stuff, there's always seating arrangements. Hosts try to make sure that the guests are situated in the most advantageous ways to avoid conflicts and keep conversations going."

Barb snorted. "Then Patti needs to be set far away from anything wearing pants."

Ignoring that quip, Bryan eyed Shay. "When was your last fancy banquet?"

She stalled, but quickly recovered. "You can learn anything in a book."

"Damn right," Morganna said, "which is why Shay got us all library cards."

Bryan's eyes nearly crossed. "Library cards?"

Rubbing her hands together, Morganna said, “That’s right. Shay’s taking us to check out some books tonight, after we finish our interviews.”

“I’m not going,” Amy insisted.

“Yes you are,” Barb told her. “We’re all going.”

Bryan met Shay’s gaze across the table. She knew he had a ton of questions, just as she knew she couldn’t answer them yet. She tried for a smile. It wasn’t easy, not with him looking at her like that, like he was both impressed and pleased. Her heart started to beat faster and her breathing deepened.

“Get a room, for crying out loud,” Barb grouched. “How are we supposed to choke down this stupid fancy breakfast with you two panting all over each other?”

Shay turned three shades of red, but Bryan merely said, “Real men do not pant.”

“No?” Patti asked. “What do they do?”

He shrugged. “Growl? Groan? I don’t know. Something manly.”

Morganna burst out laughing. “Then I’ve known a lot of unmanly men.”

“ ’Course you have,” Patti said with a frown. “I imagine we’ve known about every kind of guy there is.”

"The panters aren't so bad," Morganna added. "If they're panting, they get it over with quicker."

Patti raised her glass in a salute.

Bryan, surprising Shay with his lack of discomfort over the bawdy conversation, lifted a bit of fluffy egg on his fork and said, "Delicious. Now you know the way to a man's heart."

"Ha!" Morganna shook her fork at him. "Shay says real men should know how to cook, too."

"She's right." Bryan flashed his grin around the table. "And I do."

"Then what do you need me for?"

Barb's question was sour and hurt and anxious. Bryan reached across the table and took her hand. "You're a better cook, and far more organized. We wouldn't get by without you."

Barb nodded and withdrew her hand.

Shay wanted to melt on the spot. Bryan was so at ease, so natural with the women. And they were responding to him in a most unexpected way. They liked him. They respected him.

They *trusted* him.

What a totally remarkable man.

Amy, her plate still full, slid away from the table.

Startled, Shay laid her napkin aside, but Amy was already ducking through the doorway. "Amy?"

"Breakfast was good," she muttered without stopping. "Thanks." And then she was gone.

Chapter Seven

Twenty minutes later, a horn blared outside, and both Patti and Morganna jumped up from the table. Bryan watched as Patti paused, gave an absurd curtsey, and said, "Excuse us. That's our taxi. Gotta run." She went out the door with a loud bellow for Amy, almost splitting his eardrums.

Morganna bent and gave Shay a hug, squishing her with her impressive bosom. "Sorry to leave ya in a rush, hon, but I don't want to be late. Barb, you outdid yourself, girl. Thanks."

"Tomorrow is your turn," Barb reminded her, and Morganna gave a wave of agreement before she, too, disappeared out the door.

Wearing an apologetic smile, Shay stood and went to the kitchen window. Bryan watched her watching the women. It wasn't curiosity, but rather concern that motivated her. She wanted to see her chicks safely on their way.

Amazing. The women Shay wanted to

protect were more hardened by life than Shay would likely ever be. But she had mother hen tendencies so strong, she'd try to nurture a boar hog if she thought it could use her help. He shook his head in awe, even while admiring her.

In his mind, he went over all the things he knew about Shay, that she was generous, thoughtful, beautiful, kind, strong-willed, independent . . . but he didn't know *her.*

He didn't know where she came from or why she needed to stay in a safe house or why she was so willing to get so involved with women whom other women usually avoided like the plague.

He *needed* to know.

Eating the last bite of egg on his plate, he joined Shay at the window. Morganna sat up front with the cabbie, gabbing all the while. Patti slid into the back, reluctantly followed by Amy. Shay smiled in a pleased, proud way.

From behind them, Barb grouched, "So I guess I get the cleanup from the fancy ta-do? We've got ten times more dishes than we needed. These damn tea parties are a pain in the ass, if you ask me."

Shay's smile never slipped. "After cooking everything, you deserve a break.

Why don't you take the afternoon off and I'll put the kitchen back together?"

Barb's eyes narrowed and slid toward Bryan. "I get paid to clean. That's my job."

"But I don't mind giving you a break, and I'm sure the preacher doesn't mind, either."

Bryan took his cue. "Not at all. I'll even help with the dishes."

"A true manly man," Shay teased.

Barb still hesitated, then with a calculated, exaggerated shrug, she tossed down the dish towel and walked out. The second she was gone, Bryan felt the tension tighten around him.

He'd never survive this.

He still faced the doorway, trying to think of what to say, when he felt Shay's arms slip around him from behind. "I missed you," she whispered while hugging herself against his back. It was such a tender gesture that at the same time set him on fire.

His eyes closed. "Shay, don't." He pried her hands loose and turned to face her. Big mistake. She didn't look discouraged. No, she smiled at him, a knowing smile that made mush of his convictions.

But she also looked adorable in her determination, and he had to smile in return.

It was a novel thing, turning away a woman he wanted so badly — a woman he wanted more than any other.

He touched her nose. "Behave, woman. We have a kitchen to clean, remember?"

She grinned and headed to the table to stack the dishes together. "What do you think? Wasn't it great to see them trying so hard? Barb is the best at remembering her manners, she just doesn't bother to use them very often. And Morganna is trying the hardest. Patti's always so busy flirting that she sometimes forgets."

"And Amy?"

"I'm working on her." Shay turned thoughtful. "She's so shy and withdrawn, it isn't easy. The others accept me. They sort of treat me like one of them."

Bryan carried plates to the sink, then filled it with hot water. "But you aren't?"

"You know I'm not."

"You said you're not a hooker, but that's all I know."

She bumped her hip into his. "So what else is there? You know I like it here, that I'm trying to help." And then with new excitement, "Did you see how great they looked in their new clothes? They weren't crazy about toning it down at first. I mean, they've made a living off of flaunting their bodies. But there's just something about the feel of good clothes that I think won them over."

Bryan was no fashion expert, but even to his less than discerning eye, the outfits had looked like real quality. Shay just confirmed it. So, where the hell did she get the clothes?

Raising crossed fingers, Shay said, "I hope the jobs work out. Morganna especially will be devastated if she doesn't get the position. I told her *no* dirty jokes!" She laughed. "But boy, she has some zingers."

"How'd you get interviews lined up so easily?" Plenty of times, Bruce had tried to get the various area merchants to give the women a chance, but few ever would. Most businesses were afraid of them, afraid of what their clients or customers might think.

"They know me."

"How?"

She lifted one shoulder and began scrubbing plates. Bryan accepted each clean piece to rinse and put in the dish drainer. They worked in silence for a full minute before she finally said, "They've helped me in the past."

So ambiguous. "You've worked for them?"

Her brow furrowed. He could practically

hear her thinking of ways to fashion her reply. He didn't want her to lie to him, so he said, "Never mind."

She bit her lip. "I'm sorry, but —"

He didn't want her to be sorry, either. "You've made a lot of changes in a short time. It's amazing."

Frustration darkened her eyes. "Just superficial stuff. Clothes and makeup can't change the woman. Not that they need to change who they really are. Just maybe how they feel about themselves."

"How do you feel about yourself?"

Again, she bumped her hip playfully into his. "I like me, if that's what you mean."

Her look was so young and carefree, he tensed with emotions he'd never experienced before. In some ways, her natural exuberance for life reminded him of Megan, his wife who'd died far too young. Only Shay seemed infinitely stronger than Megan ever had. And despite her involvement with hookers, she seemed far more ethical. "I like you, too."

A slow, jerky breath expanded her chest, making her breasts rise. "Really?"

Such a simple compliment, but she acted as though he'd just given her diamonds. He looked away from her and put the last glass in the drainer. He tried to sound casual and unaffected, when he felt far from it. "What's not to like?"

"Will you kiss me again?" And before he could deny her, "You know you want to."

His brain scrambled for excuses, reasons to give, when all he really wanted to do was say, "Hell yes." Before he could do more than consider it, she stepped up to him, squeezing in close so that her soft, female scent wrapped around him and her hair brushed his jaw. She was so tall that their bodies aligned perfectly.

Bryan hesitated, but Shay didn't. She wrapped her soapy wet hands around his neck and plastered her mouth to his.

Definitely not a hooker, he thought, amazed at how untutored her kiss seemed. He caught her waist, but not to push her away. He couldn't. He was a man, simple in his needs. And right now, he needed her. Damn near a week away hadn't made any difference.

Bruce had given him permission.

His conscience no longer cared.

Drawing her closer so that she had to tip her head back made it easy for him to take over. He could feel her fast breaths on his cheekbone, feel the press of her belly to his abdomen. She was warm and soft and she smelled so good he wanted to devour her.

His tongue slipped into the heat of her mouth, searching, exploring . . .

The phone rang.

Shay moaned, easing away from him the tiniest bit. Her eyes were heavy with desire, her lips rosy and damp from his kiss. "Ignore it," she whispered against his mouth.

"You know I can't." But God, he wanted to.

"It's no one." Her nose touched his throat; she inhaled, nuzzled. "For two days now it's been ringing and there's never anyone there."

Alarm jerked Bryan out of the sensual haze. Scowling, he set Shay away from him, strode the two steps to the kitchen wall phone and snatched it up. "Hello?"

A split second later, the kitchen window exploded and something hit the wall beside his head.

"Down." The phone dropped from his hand and he tackled Shay to the hard floor. She gave a startled "oof" and started to fight him, but Bryan was already over her, pinning her with his bigger body in an effort to shield her.

Only Shay didn't want to be shielded. Like a crazy woman, she pushed against him, making it hard to control her. "Damn it, Shay, hold still."

He tightened his hold and dropped all his weight on her. Her gasping breaths pelted his ear, her fingers bit into the muscles in his shoulders.

"Bryan."

The agonized panic in her tone sank into him and he allowed her to push his face back, her hands moving over him in a frantic search. Voice shaking, eyes wild, she wailed, *"You're bleeding."*

"I'm fine," he said, but then he saw the streaks of crimson red on her cheek and in her fair hair. What the hell?

"Hold still." He touched one smeared drip near her temple and tested it between his fingers. "Paint."

Confused, Bryan swiped his hand over the side of his own face. He was soaked, though he hadn't realized it until that moment. When the window had shattered, his instincts had kicked in, and his focus had been on protecting Shay.

His palm came away smeared with splotches of bright red. In his rush to protect Shay, he hadn't even felt the splatter.

Shay was nearly sobbing, and he gently shook her. "It's not blood, Shay. It's paint. Just paint."

She went still, her eyes unfocused on his face. "Paint?"

"That's right. Probably from a paintball gun. Someone's idea of a sick joke." He levered away from her. "Don't move."

"Wait!" She sounded breathless and still far too anxious.

Bryan looked at the wall where the receiver hung from the wall unit phone, swinging like a victim of the hangman's noose. From a single deep dent in the plaster, an obscene red spiderweb of paint spread out.

Right next to where his head had been.

If the paintball had hit him, it sure as hell wouldn't have tickled.

He looked down at Shay. She was pale, her breathing shallow. Frowning, he scooted to the side of her. "Hey, you okay?"

Unmindful of the messy paint, she threw her arms around him and squeezed him tight. She didn't cry, but her hold was choking. "I thought —"

"Shhh," Bryan whispered. "I know. I'm sorry." He tucked her hair behind her ear, anxious to investigate outside, but just as anxious to calm Shay. "Did I hurt you when I knocked you down?"

She drew a deep, calming breath, visibly pulling herself together. "Just a little." Her hands touched his face again, as if she had to make sure, one more time, that he wasn't wounded.

Bryan was leveled by her concern. And he didn't have time to be leveled, damn it.

Tucking Shay close, he moved nearer to the wall, away from the broken glass and the view through the window. If anything else was shot in, he didn't want to chance her being hurt. "Stay put while I check it out."

He'd barely moved more than an inch before she snatched him back. "Are you nuts?"

"It's okay," he said, now impatient. "I know what I'm doing."

With a hand fisted in his shirt, she shoved her face close to his. "You're a preacher, Bryan, not a one-man SWAT team! Let's just wait for the cops."

"There won't be any cops. There was no gunshot, no screams."

"Then let's just wait here, where it's safe, until someone comes by."

"Knock it off, Shay." He pried her fingers loose. "I'll be okay. And I mean it, don't you move a single inch."

Indignation replaced her fear. "You're not my boss."

"Shay . . ." Time ticked by, and with it, the chance to find clues.

Her eyes narrowed. "I have many faults, but stupidity isn't one of them. I'm not budging till I know it's clear — and you shouldn't, either."

"We won't know if it's clear until I take a look." Bryan used the sink counter for leverage and slowly pulled himself upward. Glass crunched beneath his boots. The sink was filled with more glass, and the countertop glistened with it. He had to be careful not to cut his fingers.

At an angle, he glanced through the shattered window. It looked clear. Whoever had fired through it was likely gone by now.

But he had to be certain. He went back to Shay, cupped her face and tilted up her chin so she looked at him. "Be right back. Don't move."

"Idiot."

Exasperated, he started to move, but Shay clutched him again. "I'm going to be so mad at you if you get hurt."

That almost had him smiling. "I'll be fine. You have my word."

"And a preacher wouldn't lie."

Bryan shook his head. He wasn't a preacher, but he was a damn fine hunter. In a crouch, he left the kitchen and went into the living room.

Barb stood at the top of the stairs, her hands clasped on the railing. She jumped when she saw him. "What the hell happened? I heard a crash."

"Someone shot out the kitchen window."

"What!"

"Paintball gun, not real bullets. Stay up there while I check things out."

"That ain't no problem! I'm plunking my money-maker right here on the top step and I'm not budging."

At least she didn't argue like Shay. Using the curtain for concealment, Bryan peeked out at the main yard. From this window, he had a better view of the street, but there was no one there. For as far as he could see, the area was clear.

Slowly, as silent as possible, he opened all the locks and ducked outside, then into the bushes. He kept moving, making himself a difficult target in case he missed the obvious and someone lurked within range. In this particular area, people stayed up late and slept late. Most of the houses were still quiet and dark.

He strained to hear the sound of a car, footsteps, anything. All he detected was birds and the street traffic a few blocks away.

After scanning the area, he stepped out

onto the roadway. He was good at what he did, but he couldn't fight ghosts. There were no clues left behind. Just as Bruce had said, the day was sunny, so the ground was dry. There were no footprints to track. Nothing.

Disgust gripped him. He pulled the cell phone from his pocket and put in a call to the police. As usual, they were plenty busy, but someone would drop by soon.

Next, he called Bruce. Rather than answer, his brother stepped out of an alley adjacent to the safe house. "You okay?"

Bryan actually jumped, then cursed. "Goddamnit, what are you doing skulking around out here?"

"Skulking, what else?"

"I didn't see you."

"So maybe I have just enough of you in me to be good at not being seen."

"A scary thought." Bryan folded the phone and tucked it away. "I don't want you to be anything like me."

"Too late."

"What the hell are you doing here?"

Bruce stepped forward, his gaze on the paint smeared over Bryan's face and in his hair. "I wanted to make sure you kept your word about visiting with the women." With his own hair disheveled and his tattered collar turned up, he looked like every other hobo in the area.

"It's not blood."

Bruce nodded. "I know. I heard what you told the police. Funny, I was right there, hanging out in the abandoned building, but after I watched you go in, I stopped paying attention." He sounded disgusted with himself.

"You'd have heard a car, right?"

"I suppose so. I heard you talking on the phone." He propped his hands on his hips. "Is everyone okay?"

"It was a fucking paintball. Can you believe that? Not a bullet. Not something the police will take seriously." Bryan pressed his fist to his forehead, undecided on what to do next. "If the damn thing had hit me, there'd be a dent in my head instead of the wall. But they're not supposed to be lethal. Hell, kids play with the things."

"A warning, maybe?"

"Maybe." His eyes narrowed. "Against you. I guess since beating the hell out of you didn't work, they're stepping it up a notch."

"If it was the same guy. But Bryan, you know as well as I do that random acts of violence aren't uncommon around here."

"No, it was the same guy. I feel it."

"Then I should —"

Shay's anxious voice cut through the hush of their conversation. "Bryan?"

Bruce faded back, but he was smiling and he mimicked, *"Bryan?"* without actually making a sound.

Bryan turned to glare at Shay. "I told you to stay put."

"And I told you that you weren't my boss. Besides, I figured if you could stand in the middle of the street talking, it must be safe." She shielded her eyes from the bright morning sun. "You got a call."

As she spoke, she stared toward the alley Bruce had just slipped into. Bryan could see her frown of curiosity.

He jogged back to the house. "Is it the cops? I talked with them already."

Her lips rolled in and she shook her head. "I don't think so. He said he'd call right back, that I better get you and you better not make him wait."

After digesting that, Bryan grabbed her arm and pulled her back inside the house with him. "How the hell did he call? I left the phone off the hook."

Barb stood at the bottom of the stairs, her arms crossed tight. "I hung it up." And then, with enough belligerence to hide her worry, "There's paint and glass all over the kitchen.

How am I supposed to clean that up?"

"I'll take care of it." He didn't want anyone cleaning it until he could show it to the cops.

Shay asked, "Who were you talking to outside?"

"Just a bystander. He didn't hear a car, so whoever shot in must have been on foot. If I'd gotten out here sooner, I might have caught him." He said that with a glare at her, since she'd kept him inside with her worry.

The phone rang again, forestalling Shay's reply.

Staying out of the way of the window, Bryan reached into the kitchen and snatched up the receiver. He already knew who it'd be. "What?"

His abrupt tone caused a slight pause before the caller growled, "That could be your brains all over the wall."

"Not likely, asshole." Deliberately taunting, Bryan added, "Your aim sucks."

"I missed on purpose!"

Bryan laughed. "Everyone who misses says that."

With a snarl, the man warned, "Close up shop, Preacher. Get the hell out of my town. And leave my girls alone." The line went dead.

Girls? More than one? Squeezing the receiver so hard that his knuckles ached, Bryan turned — and came face-to-face with Shay and Barb. They wore identical expressions of dumbfounded surprise.

Shay cleared her throat. "Asshole?" she asked.

"You egged him on," Barb added. "Are you nuts?"

"Exactly." Shay nodded. "That's what I asked him earlier."

It wasn't easy, but Bryan swallowed down his irritation. He kept forgetting that he wasn't a bounty hunter right now, he was a preacher, but the game kept getting harder and harder to play. He started to make up excuses. Then a new thought intruded. "Ah, hell. Patti, Morganna and Amy are out there."

Shay stiffened. "Do you think they're in danger?"

"He can't know where they are," Barb reasoned.

"He knew I was here." Bryan started for the living room, and Shay jogged to keep up with him.

"But you answered the phone," Shay reasoned. "Maybe that's all he was doing, waiting for you to answer. For a couple of days now, we've been getting empty calls."

"Why the hell didn't you tell me?"
"I didn't think anything of it."
"It could be coincidence, or planned just for me, but I'm not chancing it." He jerked the front door open. "Give me the addresses for where they were going."
"I'll go with you."
Like hell. He wasn't about to risk her more than he already had just by association. "I need you to stay here and talk with the police."
"Barb can do that." She turned to Barb for verification.
Barb nodded. " 'Course I can. Go on." She shooed them away. "Make sure the others are okay."
Bryan wanted to argue, but Shay looked pretty damn set in her decision, and time was again ticking away. *Shit, shit, shit.* "All right. But do everything I tell you."
Shay saluted smartly. "Yes, sir."
Bryan took her arm again and they jogged to the apartment lot three buildings down, where he'd left the wagon parked. When he reached it, his fury exploded. No way could he hold the anger in.
"Son of a bitch."
Shay was too busy staring at the slashed tires to react to his curses. "Should we take the bus?"

"No." He rubbed his head again, more rigid by the moment. "I'll call in a few favors."

"What type of favors are owed a preacher?"

"The best kind." He dialed from his cell phone, turned his back on Shay so she couldn't listen in, and less than a minute later, he'd arranged for all three women to be picked up by men he trusted. He knew Shay was bursting with questions, but he kept her busy calling the establishments were they'd gone, to tell the women what had happened.

Bryan listened as she spoke with the proprietors, and was reminded yet again that she knew all of them personally. She had that easy familiar way of speaking with them that only came through long-standing relationships.

Hopefully those relationships were based on friendship, and not on something more intimate.

Even as he thought that, he knew it shouldn't matter to him.

But it did.

When she'd finished and they were assured the women would be kept safe, they started back to the house.

"All right, Bryan."

He kept his gaze on the area, watching for any sign of trouble. "All right, what?"

"Don't play dumb," she demanded. "What's going on? Who wants to hurt you? And what kind of life did you lead before becoming a preacher?"

Bryan kept his gaze on the surrounding area, watching for any sign of trouble. "You insinuating something, Shay?"

"I'm trying to understand, not judge."

No, Shay wouldn't judge him.

She pursed her mouth in thought. "I think that before you became a preacher, you led a . . . colorful life, and it comes through in your language whenever you get PO'd."

"PO'd?" He grinned. "You mean when I'm royally pissed, don't you?" And then, to cut her off before she got started dissecting him, "If we're going into our pasts, let's start with yours instead. I have plenty of questions already piled up."

Her eyebrows drew down and she quickly ducked her head. Not a single peep escaped her.

"Shay?" he taunted.

"Oh, look." Her expression was falsely bright. "The police are just pulling up. We should go talk to them."

Bryan caught her hand and pulled her to

a halt. His hold was unyielding, but his thumb brushed her knuckles and he kept his tone gentle. "You have to tell me sooner or later."

"I know." And with a hopeful wince: "Can I opt for later?"

The officers were at the front door, waiting with Barb, who promptly pointed him out. Bryan gave up. "All right. But we will talk later. And . . . Shay? Whatever you tell me . . . it won't matter." At least, he hoped it wouldn't.

Shay didn't answer. She strode ahead, taking charge as usual. She invited the officers in and offered to make fresh coffee. Barb, who usually ran the show, just got out of her way. Bryan knew how Barb felt. Once Shay got started, there was no stopping her.

Soon he'd get her started on explanations.

Chapter Eight

Bruce let himself into his cramped, dirty little apartment and promptly relocked the door. Contrary to his brother's perceptions, he wasn't an idiot. He had to be careful and on the lookout — for himself *and* Bryan.

He hated the apartment, but it suited his disguise as one of the more impoverished denizens. He was able to stay close, keeping tabs on his women and on his brother. God understood his concern where Bryan was concerned.

But Bryan wouldn't.

No way was he going to leave his brother's back unprotected. Sure, someone had gotten to him. It happened to the best of them. But he wasn't helpless — not by a long shot.

Bryan wouldn't accept that. He was a protector by nature, as pure in his motives as Bruce could ever be. Not that he'd ever acknowledge any heroic, protective tendencies. Bryan preferred to see himself as the black sheep in a family of snowy white lambs.

Bruce laughed quietly to himself. His brother was really something else. Something *good.*

And Shay. He shook his head. She had Bryan going in circles, and when it all came out in the end, he had no doubt that Bryan would blow his stack. He just hoped Shay had enough fortitude to carry through on her mission.

Yes, he knew her. Not personally, but he'd followed her work in the papers, admired her from afar. She was a remarkable, very giving person, and she'd gotten a bum rap in a situation that wasn't her fault.

Unfortunately, once the media labeled you, no one retrenched. It didn't matter what information was later presented; the ugliest slant was the one that stuck, because it sold the most papers.

Bruce wished her luck, especially now that her newest mission in life seemed to be loving his brother.

For once, the lumpy, smelly bed didn't bother Bruce as he stretched out, already busy formulating plans. He'd protect Bryan the best he could, but he'd also try to protect Shay. She didn't know Bryan the way he did, and she didn't know about Megan and the effect she'd had on someone as proud as Bryan. It all factored in.

The Crown Princess had her work cut out for her this time. But with God's help, and Bruce's interference, his brother would find a "happily ever after" in the end. Bruce would see to it.

The police considered the incident to be no more than a lark by unruly kids that had gotten out of hand. One officer noted that the paintball must have been frozen to travel as far and as hard as it had. He agreed it could have done serious damage had it hit Bryan.

But they also had several cases lined up of idiots in cars shooting paintballs at pedestrians, so this wasn't an isolated case, except that it had come through a window into a home. They took a report, but didn't hold much hope of catching the perpetrator any time soon.

After they left, Bryan realized how quiet Barb had become. She stood alone, propped against the wall, far too introspective for her usual bossy self.

Bryan frowned. Like most of the women, Barb had lived a life of uncertainty and degradation that fostered a sense of low self-esteem. Acting in Bruce's stead, Bryan was supposed to be protecting her now, not exposing her to violence.

Without thinking, he put his hand on her shoulder. She stiffened but didn't pull away. "You okay?" he asked.

Typical of Barb, she snorted rudely. "Of course I am." *Now* she shrugged his hand off.

Bryan grinned. She could be so surly. "Glad to hear it."

She nodded toward the kitchen doorway. "So why'd this happen, you think?"

As if they shared the same thought, Bryan locked gazes with Shay. Almost as one, they said, "Amy."

Barb curled her lip. "Amy? What's she got to do with this? She's with Morganna and Patti."

"I don't mean that she did it," Bryan explained. "Amy wouldn't deliberately hurt anyone." He paced, sharing his thoughts as he sorted through them. "But it concerns her somehow."

"What makes you think that?"

"The guy working her didn't want to let her go. He could still be mad about her escaping here."

Shay spoke up. "And he hurt her. Maybe he's afraid she'll file assault charges after all."

"I doubt it." Barb crossed her arms over her chest in a defensive way. "Most of us have been slapped around before. It comes with the territory. Believe me, the cops don't have much sympathy for us."

Shay pokered up so fast, she somehow made herself look taller, meaner, like an Amazon ready for battle. "*No one* has the right to hurt you. Ever."

Barb just stared at her. "I didn't say I'd put up with it. I'm here, too, remember?"

"The guy who hurt Amy was supposed to be in jail," Bryan explained, interrupting what looked to be a clash of female wills. "But I think I'll check on that. Could be he's loose again. Or he could have some nasty friends or relatives. His kind usually hang out in packs."

Barb rolled her eyes. "You make him sound like a wolf."

"That'd be insulting to a wolf," Shay said, still up in arms over the idea of anyone brutalizing a woman. "I think he should be flogged. He should be locked up for life. He's a waste of humanity."

Seeing Shay so emotional made Bryan want to hold her, to soothe her, but he didn't dare. He couldn't seem to stop with a simple act of comfort, not where Shay was concerned. Because she was so volatile, he kept an eye on her while speaking to Barb. "I'm going to check on things,

Barb, so can you keep an extra close eye on Amy? I'm worried about her."

"Me too," Shay said. "She's younger than the rest of us, and somehow more frail."

"Sure." Barb straightened away from the wall. "I'll watch out for her. But I've had enough for one day. I'm going to a friend's."

Alarmed, Shay took two steps toward her. "A friend?"

In sneering tones, Barb said, "Female friend, Miss Nosy. In these clothes you've got me wearing, I sure as hell couldn't sell anything."

"Oh, Barb, I didn't mean . . ."

"Forget it. Considering what's happened today, I'll call myself a cab." She went upstairs to use a phone in one of the bedrooms.

Shay wilted with guilt. "I insulted her."

"No, Barb just likes to gripe. That's why the others call her Bad Barb."

A sad, reluctant smile curled her mouth. "Just not to her face?"

"Right."

She sighed, wilting right before his eyes. "It has been a long day, and it's not even noon yet."

Bryan hesitated, but in case his instincts

were wrong, he had to cover every possibility. And because he knew so little about her, Shay was a possibility. "I meant what I said, Shay. I want to get to know you better."

Wariness entered her gaze. "In what way?"

In *every* way. "Will you have dinner with me tonight?"

Hope replaced the wariness. "Where?"

He bit the bullet, swallowed down his anticipation, and said calmly enough, "My apartment. It's only a few doors up the street."

A blinding smile chased away all her sadness, all her worry. It even lifted his spirits, when damn it, his spirits didn't need lifting.

"So you really can cook?" she teased.

"Simple stuff. How about chops and baked potatoes?"

"Sounds wonderful. What time?"

In for a penny . . . "It'd be better if the others didn't know."

"I understand. I won't tell a soul."

Anxious to reassure him, she took his hand. And even that, the simple action of holding hands, a damn grade school show of affection, felt like advanced foreplay to his already twitchy libido. Her palm was slim and soft and warm, belying the strength he'd seen in her so far.

It was an appealing combination, that strength and softness. *She* was appealing, in far too many ways.

He carefully disengaged their hands. "Six is good. That'll give you time for your library outing." He backstepped toward the door. "You'll be careful, right?"

"Absolutely. We'll take a cab, stay together. And the library is in a good part of town." With a smile, she added, "What can happen at a library?"

When she intended to take several ex-hookers along? Just about anything. "I'll stop back after you're finished for the day."

Shay turned coy. "I could just come to you, since you don't want anyone to know."

He discarded that idea immediately. With everything that had happened, he didn't want her wandering the streets alone — not even the short distance to his brother's apartment. "That's okay. I want to come by. I've got to admit, I'm curious what books will interest the ladies." And in the meantime, he'd talk with Chili, see if the little weasel knew anything. He'd tried to get in touch with him a couple of times already, but now that he wanted to see

Chili, he seemed to be unavailable.

Shay beamed at him as if he had a halo around his head. "It's wonderful that you're so involved with them."

He wasn't involved, not really. But Bruce would be and he had to be Bruce. Besides, it wouldn't be a hardship to visit. They were starting to grow on him, even Patti and her wandering hands.

The events of the day had left Shay looking adorably disheveled. She'd washed her face, but she still had smears of paint on her shirt, and her hair was mussed. Bryan tucked one long, silky lock behind her ear, and admonished, "Be good."

In her best Morganna impersonation, Shay drawled, "Sugar pie, you'll like me better when I'm bad."

Of that, Bryan had no doubt. But he was afraid that in the long run, it wouldn't matter either way. Good, bad — he just plain liked her. And he wanted her.

Tonight he'd do something about it.

They were all so stupid, not guessing what had happened, acting as if everything was still the same. Or better. What bull.

They deserved what they got. They did.

Just as she had been deserving. But everything was different now, especially the preacher. He hadn't been the same since she *showed up.*

She wasn't like the others. She didn't scare easily, and she never showed hesitation. She wanted something, and just like that, it happened. She made it happen.

Jealousy bit into her, but so what? She'd been jealous most of her life. But no more. From now on, she'd take her share, and to hell with the others. They didn't really care about her anyway. They couldn't.

Could they?

Bryan didn't know which he enjoyed more — the babbling excitement of the women or the beaming satisfaction and pleasure on Shay's face.

Morganna couldn't stop talking — not that her unceasing monologues were anything new. But no one minded this time. She had a "genuine, bona fide, real job," as she put it. The manager had hired her right on the spot, claiming her enthusiasm, ease with new people, and phenomenal memory would be an asset when she took orders.

Bryan hadn't realized she had a phenomenal memory, until he thought of all the jokes she recounted every day.

The uniform, according to Morganna,

wasn't as bad as she'd feared. She held up the white service dress with a dark blue apron, imprinted with the restaurant's logo, for Bryan to see. She wanted his opinion.

He grinned and said, "Men like a woman in uniform."

Laughing, Morganna swatted at him. "Liar!"

"If I get my job," Patti interjected, "I won't have a uniform. Shay says I'll be wearing 'dress casual,' whatever that is."

"I have no idea what it means, either," Bryan admitted, "but I'm betting Shay does."

Patti nodded. "She already offered to help. I think the manager liked me. I should know in a few days."

Bryan watched as she smiled in tremulous hope. No one had entrusted Patti with anything important in too many years to count, but now, thanks to Shay, she'd been given a second chance.

He'd thought about Patti on and off during the day. It had occurred to him that her constant pawing was a type of test. Most men would welcome her advances, even take advantage of her because of her past. But because he dodged her hands without dodging her, he'd earned a measure of friendship.

Seeing the women so happy made him happy, too.

Even Amy, who'd been so reluctant to go, kept smiling shyly. Her job would involve taking inventory for a mechanic. Shay described the owner of the business as a very kind old man. With a dose of cynicism, Amy had quipped that she'd known plenty of old men. But Shay assured her that this old man was different, otherwise she wouldn't have suggested the job.

Amy trusted her.

They all trusted her, and for women conditioned to caution, that said a lot about Shay.

Bryan watched as she refilled Morganna's glass of iced tea. Playing the hostess came as naturally to her as playing mother to a bunch of lusty ex-prostitutes.

He'd stayed busy throughout the afternoon. First he'd had the car tires changed, disgusted with the expense and wishing like hell he could find the one responsible for the damage. But at least he had found Chili.

He was only half drunk, but working on it when Bryan waylaid him in an alley. Twenty bucks hadn't enticed him to talk, so instead Bryan had offered to break his jaw. That got him gabbing real quick, and

Bryan had learned some interesting details.

While he'd been busy siphoning information from Chili, Shay had cleaned up the paint and broken glass, because, as she put it, she didn't want to worry the others unnecessarily. Still, the dent in the wall and the cardboard over the kitchen window couldn't be missed. But they were all more interested in talking about their job possibilities and the books they'd chosen than the menace that had invaded their current home.

And like a ton of bricks, it hit Bryan.

They were so used to having verbal, physical and not-so-tangible threats in their lives, they were able to blow off anything that didn't require immediate attention.

Bryan felt a pain, like a fist tightening in his chest, that almost took his breath away. Something too much like empathy and tenderness and caring began expanding inside him — and Bryan looked at each woman with new eyes.

As a bounty hunter, he never wanted to see anyone hurt unless it was some punk-ass criminal and he was the one doing the hurting. That hadn't changed. He had his own definitions of right and wrong, good and bad, lawful and unlawful. They were ideas he embraced through his work and the constant chase involved in hunting wanted felons. But his attitudes had always been general, not personal. They were peripheral ethics. They didn't touch the core of him, and they didn't hurt him.

But these women were special in different ways. Wounded, but still able to smile. Used, but still fresh with spirit and hope. They now mattered to him, not just as a wrong he wanted to set right, not merely as pawns caught up in his brother's plight.

They were women he now considered under his protection. Almost like family. Definitely like friends.

Shit. Caring too much always complicated things. It muddled the thought processes and weakened reflexes. Instincts got confused with emotions. He was screwed.

And that was before he factored in Shay's effect on him. What the hell was he going to do with her? Every time she looked at him, the need to touch her, to claim her as his own, grew until it was almost unbearable.

No matter how he fought it, she was never far from his mind. And at night, he dreamed about her naked, warm and open to him, accepting him. He wanted to touch her everywhere — her luscious body, but also her mind and heart. He wanted to get between her thighs real bad, feel her clasping him, hear her crying out in pleasure. And he wanted to sit and drink more disgusting tea with her, just to hear her talk.

Hell, he'd be happy just to look at her, to watch her smiles and witness her unself-conscious loving of all those around her.

He'd told himself he'd bed her to build on their intimacy, so that she'd tell him who she really was. To ensure his brother's safety and her own, he needed to know everything about her. It made his motives sound more logical, less carnal. Less emotional. But he wasn't a man who lied to himself; to others, when necessary, but not to himself.

Ever since his conversation with Chili, he'd been anxious to speak with Shay, to share what he'd learned, discuss things with her and get her take on them; to hear her opinion. He'd already told Bruce, but it wasn't the same.

He wanted — *needed* — to be alone with Shay.

Abruptly, he stood. Everyone quieted as their attention focused on him. "I should get going."

Morganna also stood. "But I wanted to show you the books I got!" She bent down and lifted up two paperback novels. "The librarian said they're thrillers with some romance thrown in. What do you think?"

Strange that a woman like Morganna, who was outspoken and ballsy and risqué, would want his approval. But Bryan saw it in her green eyes, in the way she toyed nervously with a long lock of her hair.

He didn't do much reading himself, but he nodded. "The covers are kind of tattered and worn, so I'd say plenty of people must have been checking them out. That has to say something, right?"

Her posture loosened, relaxed. "That's what I thought, too."

Patti waved a cookbook under his nose. "I grabbed this. It has some recipes I want to try. That is, if Shay thinks they're good ones."

Bryan took the book and flipped through it. Cocking a brow, he read, "Pot roast? Chili? Chicken and sage stuffing? Some of my favorites." He handed the book back, saying, "When you try the recipes, make sure I'm invited."

"Really?" Patti actually gulped. "Well, okay." She glanced at Shay. "If Shay helps, then I wouldn't mind letting you try my experiments."

"I'd be happy to help." Shay beamed at Bryan. "And I agree, those are some of my favorites, too."

Bryan glanced at Amy. "Amy? What'd you get?"

She clutched a book to her chest. "Nothing."

Barb laughed. "It's a romance. Mushy stuff."

"Romance is supposed to be mushy," Shay defended. "And that one is my favorite. I've read it at least three times."

That surprised Bryan. "So what's it about?" he asked Shay.

"An English duke who falls in love with the stable master's daughter. It's wonderful — almost like Cinderella but historically accurate."

"I like history," Amy whispered.

"Were dukes allowed to do that? Marry beneath their stations, I mean?" Bryan wondered if that was a personal fantasy of Shay's, to be rescued by a rich man. She'd certainly fit the role of Cinderella, with her sweetness and giving attitude.

Shay said, "I think dukes could do pretty much whatever they wanted, especially in romance novels."

"I got a book on gardening."

Bryan turned to Barb. "Really?"

With a curt nod, she said, "This place looks like a dump. I thought I could maybe plant some flowers out front or something."

His smile spread until he felt ridiculous. "When you decide what type of flowers to get, let me know and we can head to the nursery to get them."

"I'm going up to read," Amy said, and started to leave the room.

Morganna stopped her. "Wait." Amy looked agonized, but Morganna just grinned. "Tomorrow is Amy's birthday. I thought maybe we could do something special."

"I can bake a cake," Barb offered.

"That's not necessary —"

Bryan held up both hands. "How about we all go out for dinner? We can try the new place where Morganna will be working. My treat."

Shay looked thrilled with the suggestion, but the other women shrank back. Morganna actually stammered. "I can't *eat* there."

Shay propped her hands on her hips. "Why not? They have delicious food."

Patti was busy shaking her head. "I don't

know squat about all those fancy forks. No." She shook her head again. "No."

Barb smirked. "Cowards." And then: "*I'll* go."

Amy looked ready to faint. "Oh please, I don't want to make no fuss."

"It's your birthday," Shay insisted. "Of course we have to celebrate."

"But . . ." Amy bit her lip. "No one ever has before."

Bryan took that verbal blow on the chin. Christ. She'd never had a birthday party? Never gotten gifts? His eyes burned with the need to change all that. "Then it's about time, don't you think?"

"It'll be fun," Shay promised. "And ladies, you should never refuse such a nice gesture. It's rude."

Slumping her shoulders, her eyes downcast, Amy shrugged. "I guess it'll be okay."

Morganna and Patti scooted closer to one another, sharing a look of determination. "All right," Morganna said. "We'll go."

Patti nodded.

You'd think he was taking them to the gallows, the way they acted. Bryan shook his head. He promised himself that they'd have a good time. He'd see to it.

He turned to Shay. "You ready?"

Her expression went blank. "Uh . . ."

He looked at the others. "Shay has to get some things and I don't want her out alone. I don't want any of you out alone. Understood?"

"When'd you get so bossy?" Patti asked.

"He was beat up, dummy, remember?" Barb sounded very exasperated. "And now someone shot out the kitchen window. He's always felt responsible for the lot of us."

"That he has," Morganna agreed, and then she winked at Shay. "You be careful, both of you. We'll lock up behind you."

Patti suddenly caught on. "Oh, yeah. I'll get the door." She actually giggled as she trailed behind them, and as they went down the walk, she called out, "Have fun, kids!"

Shay winced, but Bryan didn't react at all. Maybe he hadn't been subtle enough, but then he felt like he'd been waiting forever. He counted himself lucky that he managed to get out of the safe house without confessing outright.

He wanted her.

Tonight, in just a few minutes, he'd have her.

Chapter Nine

Evening began settling over the area, bringing with it a cool, whispering breeze. The sun slowly sank, leaving the sky a spectacular shade of violet streaked with red and pink. One by one, streetlamps flickered on.

Shay tipped her head back and took several deep, invigorating breaths. She felt so good. The library outing had been a blast, and when she'd called Dawn, she found out that her offer for the property down the street had been accepted.

Things were moving right along. "It's pretty here at night, isn't it?"

Bryan gave her an incredulous glance. "We're in the slums, Shay."

"That's not how I see it."

"No?"

She shook her head. "We just left friends." She peeked at him. "You do consider them friends, don't you?"

"Yeah." He smiled, as if the admission amused him. "I do."

"We're both healthy. The sky is spectacular, the crickets are singing, and the present company" — she prodded him with an elbow — "is wonderful. How much nicer could it get?"

"You're ignoring the noise from the bars and the stench from the alleys."

Shay moved along silently beside him, while Bryan spent his time scanning the area, watching for any signs of movement. He was so good at that, at being alert and protective and macho.

"Actually," she whispered, "I've just learned to concentrate on the pleasant parts. There are ugly things everywhere, not just here. People, places, attitudes. Misconceptions. If you dwell on them, it could make you sad. So why not concentrate on the good things instead?"

Bryan's surveillance of the area never wavered, but she felt his heightened attention to her. "Has there been much ugliness in your life?"

In recent times, there'd been plenty — the stain on her name, the discrediting of her efforts. She shook her head. "Nothing I couldn't handle."

He took her upper arm and steered her toward a walkway. "But then, you can handle just about anything, can't you?"

She couldn't tell for sure, but Shay

thought he might have said that facetiously. She lifted her chin and gave him an honest answer. "I like to think so." She sincerely hoped she could handle *him*. More than anything else in her recent experience, he mattered to her.

Bryan reminded her of Sebastian, her sister's husband. He was just as good, just as kindhearted and honest, just as big and macho. But she felt only friendship for Sebastian, whereas Bryan stirred deep, dark emotions within her.

Heading toward a building, he asked, "Do you mind that I told a small lie to the ladies?"

"I thought it was clever," Shay admitted. She glanced up at him. "There are some things I need — from you."

He looked more drawn and urgent by the moment.

Shay smiled. "Do you think any of them bought it?"

"No. They're not idiots." He laced his fingers with hers and for the first time, Shay had hope that he was done fighting her, and done fighting himself. "But I think they approved, given the way they sent us off."

"What about you? Do you approve?"

Bryan tugged her toward a heavy

wooden door. Instead of answering, he said, "I had to insist, but I finally got the landlord to install some flood lamps. This whole yard used to be dark as pitch."

Shay decided not to push him. It was enough that he'd invited her over, that he was holding her hand and chatting with her. "Is this where you got jumped? Were you coming home one night when the guy ambushed you?"

He grunted. "How about we save that conversation until we're inside?"

"All right."

The lobby door didn't close tight and he shoved it open, then led Shay up the stairs to the second floor. With each step they took, her heart beat harder, faster.

"I spoke with Chili today," he said, breaking the silence. "The worm tried to dodge me, but I ran him down."

"He's that little man I met my first night here, right? The smelly, shifty one with the bad hair."

"That's him."

"What do you mean, you ran him down?"

"Tackled him in an alley. He had on dress shoes. Slick as hell, those dress shoes." Bryan opened the locks and pushed the door open. "Wait here."

Slipping inside, he moved silently around the apartment, checking each room and turning on lights in his wake before returning to Shay. "It's clear. Come on in."

She stood there, annoyed and dumbfounded. "Did you expect an intruder?"

"I have reason to be cautious now, that's all." Again, he took her hand in his. "I don't want to see you hurt."

Shay didn't move. "Why?"

Frowning, he tugged her in. "I don't want to talk in the damn hall. The walls are paper thin and anyone could be listening."

"All right." Shay allowed herself to be drawn in, then leaned against the closed door while Bryan clicked all the locks back into place. When he finished, he faced her, and Shay's stomach fluttered with excitement.

Eyes hot and direct, Bryan slowly looked her over, from her feet in flat sandals to her slim jeans and white blouse with the shirttails loose over a white T-shirt.

His gaze locked on hers. In a voice gone rough and deep, he asked, "You hungry, Shay?"

She breathed faster. "Not . . . not especially. You?"

Bryan braced his left hand on the door

beside her head. It was large and rough — such a contrast to her own slim, pale hand. His biceps bulged and flexed as he stared at her mouth. "Not for food."

Her lips parted, her knees locked.

"Maybe," he said, his breath hot on her mouth, "we can eat later?"

"Oh."

His right hand landed on the door, too, and his firm, hair-rough forearms brushed her temples. He was so good, and so strong. So moral, and so sexy. So giving — and now so ready to take.

Like a predator, he had caged her in, watching her with carnal intent. That suited Shay just fine. She wanted to devour him, but . . . was there some sort of decorum involved in loving a preacher? Would he have restrictions that other men didn't have? She didn't want to shock or repulse him.

Shay licked her lips, slid her hands up and over his shoulders to his neck. She decided to move cautiously, until she could determine his mood. "Much later, I hope."

The heat flared. His jaw locked. His eyes blazed.

Then, as if the dam burst, he growled, "Ah . . . Fuck it." And his mouth took hers.

Shocked at his language as well as his sudden hunger, Shay gasped. But that only made it easier for him to deepen the kiss. His velvet tongue licked over hers, teasing, tasting, melting her bones. Oh wow, he smelled so delicious, and tasted even better than that.

Beneath her palms, his shoulders were warm steel and she could feel the shifting of solid muscles over thick bone. His wide chest pressed into her softer curves, thrilling her with the evidence of his tempered power.

Rather than abate, the kiss continued, gaining in intensity until tiny pinpricks of light danced behind her eyelids, leaving her almost dizzy. She tried to draw in more oxygen, but instead she drank in his masculine scent. Her nails dug into his shoulders and she whimpered.

Bryan slanted his head, parting her lips more, holding her closer until their heartbeats mingled. One big hand settled on the back of her head, his fingers sinking into her hair, tangling there so she couldn't move, couldn't retreat at all.

Never in her life had she been consumed like this. She'd had kisses, but in no way could they compare to this.

Obviously, he had no restrictions for her to worry about.

Freed of her reserve, Shay slid her hands over him, seeking an anchor, appeasing her curiosity, loving the feel and texture of his big body.

Bryan took that as an invitation to do the same. One moment he'd be tender, touching her face, tracing her ears with trembling fingertips, then he'd tighten his hold and try dragging her closer when she was already so close that anything more seemed almost impossible.

He wedged a thigh between hers, opening her legs, grinding against her sex. Shay jerked her mouth free and gulped air, amazed at how quickly she spiraled out of control. She dropped her head back on the wooden door with a moan.

"More," he murmured, and with ruthless ease, he took her swollen lips again. It was different now, though. As if her loss of control had appeased him, he softened the kiss, gently soothing her mouth, lazily licking and nibbling.

Bracing his left forearm beside her head freed up his right hand, and he sought out her breast. The very first touch of his hand there electrified her. She opened her eyes and saw that he was watching her, his eyes dark as sin, his long lashes lowered sensually.

"Bryan?" she whispered, shaken by the depth of his look.

"You are so soft and sweet." His hand opened so that his palm brushed over her already stiffened nipple, back and forth, back and forth. "I can't wait to taste you. All of you." His hips pressed in more, both appeasing and increasing the ache. Shay let her head drop back again.

Soft kisses touched her throat and collarbone, drifting here and there, leaving small, heated, damp spots behind.

Her bra offered no barrier at all to his hard fingers. It was thin, a wisp of lace that rasped over her when he caught her nipple, tugging lightly, rolling, applying a modicum of pressure that nearly pushed her over the edge.

"Oh, God." Her hands moved blindly down his back while she arched into him, seeking more pressure from his thigh, pushing her breast into his palm. There was so much of him to enjoy, all solid muscles and incredible strength.

Shay slid her hands down to his waist, around to the small of his back . . .

Her fingers encountered cold, hard steel. Alarmed, she jerked her mouth free. "Bryan?"

"What?" He held tight, licked her ear, nipped her earlobe.

Drugging sensuality mingled with clear-conscious alarm. She closed her hand over the gun and tugged, but it held in the waist holster. Shay met his gaze. "What," she demanded, "are you doing with a weapon?"

The look on his face was comical — for about two seconds. Then he moved back so fast, Shay almost fell to the floor. Their gazes clashed, hers confused and still needy, his hot and . . . angry.

At her?

Using the door for support, stiffening her shaky knees, Shay straightened. She refused to look away. "You're carrying a gun. Why?"

Seconds ticked by while she saw one excuse after another flick across his features. For crying out loud, he was a preacher, not a lawman, not a criminal. "Another lie on the way, Bryan?"

He broke eye contact first, running a hand through his hair and all but growling out his frustration. "No, I'll tell you the truth, at least as much of it as you need to know."

Still he said nothing, and Shay made a sound of exasperation. "Yes?"

"Give me a minute," he snapped. And then, with chagrin, "I'm still a little poleaxed that I forgot the damn thing was there."

"You forgot you were carrying a gun?"

He fried her with his gaze. "Look, I was jumped from behind. Someone shot into the kitchen. You've been getting strange calls and the tires were slashed —"

"So you think to shoot someone?"

His jaw jutted out and his shoulders bunched. "I'll shoot anyone who tries to hurt the safe house or any of the women in it. And that includes you."

Shay sucked in a breath. "You'd shoot me?"

"No!" He looked more frazzled by the moment. "I meant that I'd shoot anyone who tried to hurt you. Jesus, get it straight."

He looked so rattled, she almost laughed. But not quite. "You're a preacher," she reminded him. "What kind of preacher vows to shoot people?"

His eyes narrowed meanly. "I told you from jump, I'm a different kind of preacher."

"A gun-toting preacher, full of righteous fury and defense?"

"If that's what you want to call it." He swallowed, ran a hand through his hair again. "Look, Shay, I'll put the gun away, okay?" He reached back and grabbed a fistful of his shirt, then stripped it off over his head.

Oh, my, my, my. Shay stared at his body

and felt her knees go weak all over again. Gorgeous — incredibly, excitedly gorgeous. His blond hair was in direct contrast to the darker body hair on his wide, muscled chest. It spread from nipple to nipple, then trailed down to his navel and disappeared into his jeans.

Her mouth went dry.

The skin over his shoulders and throat looked smooth and hot, sleek over hard bone and muscle. His abdomen was an enviable six-pack that could have been used in advertisements for a gym. No man, and definitely not a preacher, should be built so utterly perfect.

Keeping his gaze on hers, he began unbuckling a thick black leather belt. Shay opened her mouth twice before she could say, "You're stripping now?" And in a rasp: "Here?"

He flashed her a glare. "No." With one hand behind his back, he held the holster while yanking his belt out. Apparently, that was what held the gun in place. "We'll both strip in a minute. I'm just putting the gun away." He rolled the belt and holster together and strode down the hall with heavy, impatient footfalls.

Unwilling to be left behind, Shay hurried to follow him. His apartment was tidy but dusty, and sparse in the extreme — most definitely a male habitat.

She reached the bedroom doorway in just enough time to see Bryan open a nightstand drawer. He started to drop the gun inside, but the drawer was crowded. Inside were a fat Bible and a large box of condoms.

He stared at the drawer a moment, then his head turned toward her, his dark, fathomless eyes daring her to comment. She didn't have a single thing to say, so he removed the condoms, set them on top of the nightstand and dropped the gun inside.

He snapped the draw shut. "Better?"

Oh, Lord. Shay's stomach tumbled in mingled excitement and uncertainty. The man was such a mystery. She knew a smart woman would be backing away.

Maybe she wasn't so smart, because no way was she walking away now.

Regardless of what she didn't know about him, what she did know was all good. Bryan might not be the stereotypical preacher, but he was definitely a wonderful man. He treated ex-hookers with respect and friendship. He had a protective streak a mile wide. He gave freely of his time and had earned the respect of many in return.

He was, without a doubt, incredible.

Slowly, holding his gaze, Shay stepped in and closed the door behind her. "Much better." And with stark anticipation, she approached him. "Thank you."

Bryan didn't stand as she neared the bed. He was where he wanted them both to be, and he'd be damned if he'd leave it. She could join him. Right now. Before he exploded.

She stopped right in front of him.

Catching her trim hips between his hands, he pulled her to stand between his thighs. "We have a lot to talk about. But it's going to have to wait until after."

"After?" She smiled in a knowing, very female way.

"Damn right." Bryan removed her shirt and let it fall to the floor behind her. Her breathing was fast and deep as he tugged her T-shirt from her jeans and inched it up. He got it only as high as her breasts when he had to lean forward and kiss her midriff. She started to pull back, so he crossed his hands over the small of her back and kept her still. She was all silky skin and womanly fragrance. He nuzzled his mouth, his chin against her.

He wanted to eat her up.

And he would.

Knowing that sent a wave of incredible heat through his muscles.

He stood only long enough to strip the T-shirt over her head. Shay was so tall that it would have been awkward otherwise. In just a bra and jeans, she looked delectable. Moments ago, Bryan had been in such a hurry. Now he wanted to savor the moment.

Eyeing her barely veiled breasts, he asked, "Do your panties match the bra?"

"Yes."

He'd figured as much. Shay was a matching lingerie type of woman. Thinking of the soft lace hugging her ass and crotch got his fingers working again, this time on the snap and zipper of her jeans. He slid off the bed, dropping to one knee in front of her. He worked the denim down her long, sleek thighs, held her with one arm around her hips, and told her, "Lift your foot."

With her cooperation, he stripped off her sandals, then her jeans. When she was left in nothing but her underwear, Bryan slowly straightened and reseated himself.

Looking at her affected him so much, he didn't dare touch her yet. "You are so beautiful."

Her belly hollowed out with a deep

breath. "I . . . I'd rather you like me than find me attractive."

Sometimes the things she said made no sense to him. She'd told him that she got along well with her adoptive family, so why did being liked matter so much to her? During his impersonation of his brother, he'd learned about all kinds of insecurities with the women. Was this Shay's insecurity?

Truthfully, he told her, "I like you a lot."

She took another step closer and slipped her hand over his head, stroking his hair. "Do you mean that?" There was so much yearning in her voice that Bryan paused. "Or are you just saying it because you want to sleep with me?"

It wasn't easy, but he managed to get his eyes off her body and onto her face. "Have other men lied to you to get you into bed?"

His question took her off guard, then she laughed and shoved him backward onto the bed while coming down over him. "You should have been a detective instead of a preacher, do you know that?"

His hands automatically went to her cute rear. Lush, soft flesh filled his palms and made his heart beat a little quicker. "Why?"

"Because you answer every question with another question. You're always digging for information. And you're incredibly suspicious."

Part and parcel with his job, but Bryan wasn't about to tell her that. She had stretched out on top of him, her breasts right there, her belly over his erection, her long legs tangled with his.

In one deft move, he flipped her beneath him. "I didn't lie. I do like you." He cupped her head, smoothed his thumb over her cheekbone. "But you're still beautiful."

"I don't care about that."

He shook his head in wonder. "Funny, but I believe you. If you were any other woman, I might not. But hearing you say it . . . I dunno. It rings true."

"Take your jeans off."

He wasn't a man given to humor, but damn, Shay had him grinning a lot. Apparently she didn't want to talk about her looks anymore. "Yes, ma'am." He rolled to the side of her and did as she asked, even going one further and removing his boxers at the same time.

His cock was thick and hard, more than ready for her. "Better?"

Her incredible blue eyes were bright with inner heat as she stared at him with fascination and lust. She licked her lips and he groaned, anxious to feel that luscious mouth on his dick.

"Much." And before Bryan could move, she was over him again, kissing his throat, his chest, while her hand snaked down his body.

He wasn't sure he'd survive it. "Shay . . ."

"Shh." She moved up and over him, cupping his face and kissing his mouth softly. "I haven't wanted anyone like this in far too long."

His eyes narrowed. "How long?"

Exasperation curled her mouth, but it wasn't quite a smile. "Enough talking, okay?"

Fine by him. "Then let's get you caught up." He reached behind her with one hand and with the flick of two fingers, opened the back clasp of her bra. The cups fell forward, baring her breasts.

"Why, preacher," she teased, "where'd you learn a trick like that?" And she shrugged the bra off.

The sight of her pale, silky breasts and tightly puckered pink nipples had his guts twisting with need. He needed her so badly, it hurt.

Since Shay seemed to enjoy it, Bryan wished he could continue to play. But at the moment, it was well beyond him.

Holding her waist, he pulled her down so he could reach her, and closed his mouth over one taut nipple. Gently, he suckled her, and never wanted to stop.

Shay inhaled sharply and he felt the stiffening of her thighs against his. What he'd imagined so many times became a reality, and he slid his hand down her slim waist, over the rise of her hip — and straight into her lace panties. Everything male within him quickened at the feel of firm, plump flesh, now his to claim. Perfect.

Heart galloping and tension coiling, he explored her from behind, palming one round cheek, letting his fingers sink between. She gasped, stilled in shock, and then he touched her swollen, wet lips.

They both groaned.

Bryan switched to her other breast, drawing that nipple in, sucking hard in reaction to his rising pleasure. Shay rocked against his hand while he insistently worked one thick finger inside her. So hot. So damn slippery wet.

"I've thought about doing this to you at least a hundred times," he growled against her nipple. He worked his finger in deep, slowly drew it out again. Her muscles clenched, trying to hold onto him.

Pressing his finger inside her, he turned

her onto her back so he could watch her face. Her pale hair spread out over his pillows. Her vivid blue eyes closed, her teeth sank into her bottom lip. Bryan watched every nuance of pleasure, excitement and need as it crossed her features.

She was close, he could tell. He worked another finger in, filling her, pumping into her, finger-fucking her while reveling in her reactions. Her neck arched and her fists clenched the sheets.

His hand was bathed in moisture, and he couldn't wait a second more. He kissed her ribs, licked his way down to her cute little belly button, to the ultrasoft skin beneath it.

Shay drew a shuddering, uncertain breath. "Bryan?"

Gently, he pried her thighs farther apart. "I've thought about this, too. About eating you till you scream."

She went mute, from embarrassment or excitement, he didn't know. He didn't care. Holding her legs open, he stared at her sex, flushed dark pink, swollen, her clitoris engorged. A groan rumbled up from deep in his chest and he licked her, from between her slick lips, up and over that ultrasensitive flesh.

"Oh, God," she cried, arching hard, her

legs trying to close automatically.

"No," Bryan said, holding her still and keeping her sprawled wide for his pleasure. "I like looking at you. I like tasting you." He cupped her hips in his hands and lifted her. Her scent was strong, spicy hot and intoxicating. He pressed his face into her, breathing deeply, plunging with his tongue, repeatedly flicking up and over her clitoris, again and again.

Her gasping breaths increased and she started to quiver, signaling the rise of her climax. Her muscles tightened, tightened . . . He closed his mouth around her sweet clit and sucked.

Her low, guttural scream nearly pushed him over the edge. He pressed his cock hard against the mattress and concentrated on not coming until he got inside her, until he could feel her contractions squeezing him tight.

Snatching up a pillow, Shay covered her face to muffle her cries, but Bryan still heard every raw, real sound. Her hips lifted hard against his mouth, her heels dug into the mattress. A rose flush bathed her body.

The moment she sank back to the bed, her trembles now tiny aftershocks and her breathing shallow and fast, he rose up and reached for a condom.

Shay still lay there, her legs open, the pillow hiding her face. She was by far the most beautiful woman he'd ever known, and she hid from him. He wanted to grin but couldn't manage it. With the condom in place, he snatched the pillow away and flung it across the room.

"I want to see you."

Sleepily, her eyes opened — and she held her arms up to him.

His finesse shot to hell, Bryan covered her, clutching her tight to his chest so that her heartbeat matched his, sealing her mouth with his, sinking his tongue past her lips. He thrust into her. Hard and deep.

Shay was so wet that it happened easily, naturally, as if they'd made love a dozen different times. Her nails stung his shoulders. Her legs came up around his waist, hugging him, letting him sink deeper still.

He knew he wouldn't last but he desperately wanted her pleasure again. He slid one hand beneath her ass and tipped her up to give him the best penetration. She groaned into his mouth and struggled to match the rhythm he set. They moved together, more frantic by the moment, hard and fast and deep, and then Shay came again, longer, harder this time. He felt her sweat, tasted it as he opened his mouth on her shoulder and ground out his release with mind-numbing power.

Time seemed to stand still. The air in the room smelled heavy with their combined scents and the scent of sex. From shoulders to hips, their bodies were glued together. Shay's legs slipped from around him to land limp on the mattress. He couldn't pull away. Not yet.

He didn't want to pull away — ever.

Needing time to gather his wits, Bryan kept his face tucked in next to hers. Sated, drained, emotionally rocked, he did no more than stroke her disheveled hair and contemplate what the hell to say.

He heard Shay swallow, felt her bend one leg to get more comfortable. "That was . . ." She sighed, shrugged, kissed his shoulder. "Incredible."

Bryan grinned. Leave it to take-charge Shay to break the uncertainty of the moment. Rejuvenated by her praise, he turned his face to see her. "You're incredible."

Her eyes were closed, but her lips curled in satisfaction. "Help me do that again, and I might believe you."

Laughing, Bryan rolled to his back and pulled her on top of him. She snuggled down and pressed her face into his throat.

After a moment, she whispered, “I hope this wasn’t a one-shot deal, Bryan.”

“No.” He trailed his fingertips down her graceful spine to her bottom. He loved touching her. He loved holding her. He loved . . .

Ah, shit.

“One time?” he asked with mock disbelief. “Hell, no. In fact, give me a few minutes and I’ll be ready again.”

She tweaked his chest hair, soothed the spot with gentle fingers. “Then do you mind if I doze off for a little while? It’s been such a busy day.”

He wanted to tell her to go ahead, that he’d enjoy holding her while she slept. But there were things they had to discuss first. “Sorry honey, but I do mind.”

She raised her face to frown at him. “Don’t tell me I’m too heavy for you.” She poked his chest. “I know I’m not exactly dainty, but you’re hard as bricks. More than sturdy enough to —”

His finger pressed over her lips, shushing her. “We need to talk.”

“Oh.” She retreated — not physically, but emotionally he saw her pulling back and it irritated him. They’d just shared mind-blowing sex — which she’d admitted to, for crying out loud — but she still wanted to keep secrets from him.

He supposed that, whatever problems she had in her life, it would take time for him to overcome them. He bit back his impatience and let her off the hook. "Remember I told you that I'd had a chat with Chili?"

"Oh, yeah." Visibly relaxing, she scooted to his side and sat up.

Now that's a distraction, Bryan thought, looking at her naked body again. She was so unself-conscious with her nudity that it turned him on.

Again.

Already.

He shook his head at himself. "Let me take care of business first." He left the bed and strolled into the bathroom to dispose of the condom. Calling back to Shay, he asked, "You want a drink or something?"

Several seconds passed and then she was there, standing outside the open bathroom door, still bare as a baby. "I could use something cold." Her gaze was on his hands, watching him peel off the condom. "Want me to get us some drinks?"

Did nothing make her uncomfortable? "Why don't we grab some clothes and stay in the kitchen?"

"Why?"

Why, indeed. "If we get back into bed, I'll want you again." He looked over her perfect body. The woman didn't have a single flaw, as far as he could tell. "In fact, if you don't cover up, we won't even make it back to the bed." He forced his attention to her face. "And we really do need to clear up some things."

She seemed to think it over, then shrugged. "Can I borrow a shirt?"

"Help yourself."

They went back into the bedroom and Shay pulled on the T-shirt he'd discarded. She was tall but slender, and it mostly covered her. Yet when she walked, he took tiny peeks at her ass.

Bryan pulled on his boxers. "Still want dinner?"

"Yes. I'm starved." She wrinkled her nose. "But I don't want you to spend your time cooking when we could be spending it other ways."

Hell of an idea. "Okay. So instead of chops, I can pull together some cheese sandwiches."

"Sounds good." She sashayed out of the room, but said over her shoulder, "I do believe I've worked up an appetite. And besides, I don't want you to think I'm a cheap date."

"Never." Bryan frowned at himself, but he knew the truth. How could she be cheap — when she'd just taken his heart?

Chapter Ten

Bryan set a second cheese sandwich in front of Shay. She'd polished off the first in record time.

"Thank you. If Morganna and Patti saw me wolfing down my food, they'd never listen to me about manners."

"Those two, more than most, would understand why you're hungry." He winked at her.

Bryan had been irresistible to her even before he'd begun showing his more playful side. Now that he seemed inclined to tease her, she was a complete and total goner. Who could resist such a strong, capable man, confident enough to care openly for others, and playful to boot? Not her.

And she didn't care. If this was love, then she embraced it. No man had ever affected her as he did. Something — feminine intuition, gut instinct, or good old chemistry — told her that Bryan was her equal in every way that mattered most.

They shared the same objectives. He never bored her with his talk. She adored his tall, strong physique. And making love with him was so powerful, it almost scared her, when nothing ever scared her.

He was her mate — the one man who could make her happy.

One way or another, she'd win his heart. "So what did Chili have to say?"

Bryan took his seat opposite her. "He claims Leigh and Amy had the same pimp."

Startled, she said, "But . . . they each had personal relationships with the guy! Amy thinks she was special to him, and Leigh said he was her boyfriend —"

"Exactly. He manipulated them the same way."

Whenever Shay thought of her childhood, it was the abandonment, the emotional abuse, that cut the most. Bruises to the skin healed, and were much easier to ignore than bruises to the heart. "That bastard."

"Yeah."

Her thoughts spun around, trying to find solid ground. "But the recent stuff can't be because of him. You said he got locked up on a drug arrest."

"That's what I was told. But the legal

system doesn't always work. Could be the son of a bitch is out already."

Food lost all appeal. "You think he's the one who was outside Dawn's when I took Leigh there?"

Bryan nodded. "And I'm betting he's the one who shot the paintball through the window. He wants me to stop helping the women so he can keep working them."

Her blood seemed to congeal in her veins, leaving her cold and uncertain. "This is incredible. And really scary."

Bryan slid his big feet over to encase hers under the table. "Leigh said the guy's name was Freddie. Chili said he's Freddie Baker." His gaze moved over her face. "I need to talk to Amy about it, to ask her a few questions. But I'd like it if you were with me. Amy trusts you more than me."

Shay barely heard him. "We have to stop him."

Bryan's expression hardened and he leaned across the table, palms flattened on the surface. "Wrong. *I* have to stop him. And I will."

He waited for her agreement, so Shay shrugged. "I won't get in your way." But she could hire more people to find him, and more people to watch the women until Freddie was locked away again.

Bryan watched her a moment more, and Shay kept her expression as innocent as possible. Finally, he resided to his seat. "Unfortunately, I don't know where he is. He was supposed to be checking in with his parole officer, but hasn't."

"How do you know that?" And before he could answer, she said, "Right. More contacts?"

"Something like that."

"For a preacher, you sure have a lot of influential friends."

He settled back in his seat, shifting his broad shoulders and said almost reluctantly, "With what I do, those friends come in handy."

"Friends in the police force?"

He shrugged. "And there's always Joe Winston."

"Who?"

Bryan grinned with some fond memory. "The baddest badass of them all. He used to be a bounty hunter — a P.I. and a cop, too. But these days he runs a lake in Visitation, North Carolina, and does his damndest to keep up with Luna."

"Luna?" Such an odd name, Shay thought, but Bryan smiled as he said it.

"His wife. And if that isn't enough, Willow and Austin, his two adopted kids, keep him hopping, too. But I swear, he loves it." Then he added with a chuckle: "The big fraud."

Shay liked his laugh. It was deep and real and natural. "If he lives in North Carolina, how do you know him? Did you used to live there, too?"

His dark eyes filled with mockery. "And you accused me of asking too many questions."

"But mine are just idle curiosity."

"Right."

He didn't buy that for a second, and Shay didn't bother to argue the point. She wanted to know everything about him. And eventually, she'd let him know everything about her.

But not until she knew he cared, and that he'd understand.

"Until he followed Luna to North Carolina, Joe lived in Ohio. I . . . visited him there." He shifted uncomfortably, crossing his arms over the table and visibly chewing his thoughts before deciding to share with her.

Shay braced herself for some grand confession, perhaps that he wasn't a preacher at all.

But instead, he said, "I bought some land in Visitation."

"Really?" Surprise immediately led to worry. Did that mean he planned to relocate? What about his work? What about the women?

She'd just bought property near his safe house. She'd envisioned them working together, united both in convictions and in love.

"Yeah. Not far from where Winston lives now." He shrugged. "It's just an acre, but it's secluded, edged by a farmer's fields. And there's a creek that runs across the back end and a lot of mature trees."

He sounded totally enamored of the land. Alarmed, Shay blurted, "You're not moving, are you?"

"Maybe. Someday." He studied her a moment, then said, "Do you enjoy the country?"

She'd enjoy living anywhere he lived. "Sure. Of course. Why not?"

The way she rushed that answer brought a smile to his mouth. "No malls. Not much entertainment. Just lots of trees and plenty of bugs. But the air is fresh and the creek looks incredible in the sun or under the moonlight. You see deer and coyote and wild turkeys . . ."

"It sounds like you want to be there now."

He hesitated again, frowned, then said, "I'd always planned to live in the country. Away from the smog and the traffic." His gaze sharpened. "But my wife liked the city."

Shay almost fell off her chair. "Your *wife?*"

"She's gone now." He watched her closely while admitting that.

Oh God, she could not possibly be glad about that, but . . . "What happened to her?"

"She was murdered." He slashed a hand through the air. "A bullet meant for someone else hit her instead. She died almost instantly."

Her heart dropped to her knees. She shook her head. "I'm . . . I'm sorry."

Her whispered words seemed to jerk through him. He pushed to his feet. "You done eating?"

With the giant lump in her throat, she'd choke if she tried to swallow another bite. "Yes."

He reached out a hand. "Let's go back to bed."

It wasn't an offer so much as a command. Resolve turned his dark eyes flinty and set his jaw in uncompromising lines. Shay didn't hesitate. She accepted his hand and allowed him to lead her down the hall.

With each step nearer to the bedroom, his urgency grew until she could actually feel it. He vibrated with a mixture of testosterone, savage possessiveness and iron determination. They were barely through the bedroom doorway when he turned and pinned her to the wall. He took her mouth and at the same time, caught her thigh and lifted it up to his hip so she could feel his erection, long and hard, against her.

Just like that, Shay was ready. He could smile at her and set her on fire, but knowing that he needed her, that thoughts of his wife were now driving him toward a distraction, made her feel urgent, too. She wanted to be the woman he turned to. For everything.

Gentling him, she kissed him back, softly, teasing. She stroked down his chest, insinuated her hand between their bodies, and cupped her hand over the fly of his boxers. Her fingers curled around his throbbing length.

Hissing out a breath, Bryan tilted his head back and let her do as she pleased. Against the back of her fingers, his abdomen was rock hard and warm. His cotton boxers were soft, molding to his sex.

She used both hands to stroke and tease.

The tanned skin of his upper chest drew her, and she kissed him there, tasting his flesh, brushing her lips over hard bone and flexing muscles. When she started to slip her hand inside the snug boxers, he stopped her. Their eyes met. His nostrils flared with his deep breaths, and then he had her upper arms, turning her and toppling her into the bed.

"I meant to go slower this time," he rasped while stripping off her shirt and cupping her breasts, stroking her nipples. "Christ, I feel like I'm coming off a year of celibacy."

Shay panted, trying to pull him over her. "I am," she said. "Two years, in fact."

He froze. Jerking up, he looked at her, his brows down, his eyes filled with stunned disbelief.

She didn't care. Touching his lower lip, she whispered, "I was married once, too. It . . . hasn't been easy since then." His expression didn't change. "It doesn't matter if you believe me. You're special, Bryan Kelly. To me. Probably to a lot of people."

More seconds ticked by, then he smoothed her hair from her face, kissed her forehead, and turned to the nightstand for a condom. "Slow," he said, rolling on a condom with ease. "I'll go slow if it kills me."

Shay grinned. "I kind of liked it hard and fast."

He squeezed his eyes shut. "Yeah, me too."

"Then why mess with perfection?"

He struggled with himself, but in the end, he lost. He turned to her with a growl, and then his hands were everywhere, holding her breasts, lightly tormenting her nipples. He stroked down to her belly, slid his fingers through her curls, parted her, pressed in.

His mouth swallowed her groan, and then he was between her legs, pressing her knees apart, and she felt the thick length of his erection sink into her. It was wonderful. It was exciting.

It was fast, as before, but infinitely more tender.

Shay lay curled against him, her head on his shoulder, idly playing with his chest hair. She was boneless, drowsy. Very sweet.

"I care about you, Bryan. A lot."

Bryan squeezed his eyes shut. The woman constantly knocked him off guard with the unexpected. "What happened to your husband?"

"He died a few years ago."

"How?" He no sooner asked it, than he realized how abrupt he sounded. "An accident?"

She shook her head. "Phillip was a really nice man. Gentle. Kind. Everyone loved him."

"Including you?"

"I loved him most of all." She snuggled closer. "He was older than me."

"By much?"

She hesitated. "By a lot, actually."

Bryan didn't ask. He didn't want to know. So, Shay had turned to an older man, probably an authority figure, given her tragic childhood. She'd searched for love and acceptance . . . It didn't work. His stomach churned with disturbing images of Shay desperate for affection. He tightened his arms around her. He wouldn't let her ever feel that way again. Somehow he'd make sure she knew her own worth.

"He had a weak heart and his health suffered for years before he passed away." Shay twisted her head up to see his face. "Was your wife a wonderful person?"

Normally, he hated talking about Megan. But with Shay, everything was different.

He shook his head. “No. No, she wasn't. She was . . . selfish. And confused.”

Again and again, he trailed his fingers through her long, pale hair. It was silken and warm, like Shay. Bryan couldn't stop touching her, couldn't stop the tide of emotions that seemed to be growing more powerful by the moment. “In a lot of ways, she was too naive for her own good. That's what attracted me in the first place.” He considered his words, and then shared things he seldom shared with anyone, even his father or brother. “Dad raised us alone. Did I tell you my dad is a preacher, too?”

“No. You've never mentioned your family much at all.”

She had him there. By necessity, he'd pried into her life while keeping his own very private.

But there were some things he could share. “My mother hated the simple life we had. My dad started out in the service, and Mom thought they'd travel a lot, see the world. But then he got the calling and left the military to become a preacher.”

He rubbed Shay's shoulder, lost in his thoughts. “He's good at what he does, but Mom hated it. Our house was modest, our budget tight. She wanted more, so she split.”

"Do you see her still?"

He shook his head. "Somewhere along the way she remarried, but not long after that she died of cancer. She hadn't ever kept in touch, and she didn't have any other kids. I never really knew her, so I don't miss her, but I decided early on that I'd never fall for a woman who couldn't be content with me and what I do."

"And you thought your wife would be?"

He shrugged. "She was shy and unsure of herself and she needed someone to look after her. I thought that someone would be me."

Shay pressed a warm kiss to his chest, right over his heart. "Do you still love her?"

"No." He thought about Megan, and said, "I feel guilt. I think I'll always feel guilt."

"Because you think you could have saved her?"

"Yeah. I could have." But he hadn't. He'd been too pissed to realize the danger she was in. He had to walk a fine line with this tale, but for some reason, he wanted Shay to understand. "She resented the time I spent working, and felt neglected. Because of that, she got involved with another man. A real low-life scum criminal.

People were hunting him." *Including me.* But he couldn't tell her that. He couldn't tell her that Bruno had used Megan to hurt him, because it would give too much away. "She got caught in the cross fire."

Shay pushed up on his chest to see his face. "So how could you have saved her?"

As amazing as it seemed, he didn't want to ruin Shay's impression of him. He didn't want her to realize that out of all the bastards in the world, he might be the biggest.

But Shay being Shay, she wouldn't give it up. Eventually she'd learn the truth about him, so it was better that she hear bits and pieces early on, to help prepare her.

"You can tell me, you know." She cupped his face in gentle hands, leaned down and kissed him with a tenderness he'd never known. "You can tell me."

With his hands loosely holding her narrow waist, he looked up into her innocent blue eyes and admitted the awful truth. "I knew where they were. I'm the one who sent the authorities after them. I could have warned her first, but I . . . I wanted her to see the drama of a man being captured, dragged in by the police. I wanted her to see . . ." He stopped and looked away.

"You wanted her to see what she'd chosen over you?"

Even in his turmoil, Bryan registered the silky texture of her skin, the heat of her body, her arousing scent. Now, though, instead of exciting him, it comforted him. *She* comforted him. He gave one sharp nod. "That's about it. I never once considered that she might be hurt. I didn't consider anything but feeding my ego, my anger."

"Your hurt." Shay lay back down, this time atop him, giving him a full-body hug. "You're a big, macho tough guy, Bryan, but no one is immune to hurt."

He wanted to deny it, but he knew he couldn't. He'd told Shay enough lies already.

"So," she said, her voice lighter, "did the cops get the guy?"

"No. Once Megan got shot, all their efforts went into helping her, and Bruno got away." He tangled a hand in her hair and tipped her face up so she could see his satisfaction. "I wanted to get him. For Megan and for me. But it was Joe Winston who caught him."

"I'm glad it wasn't you."

"Why?"

"You're a preacher, not a bounty hunter.

You could have been hurt."

"Jesus." He covered his eyes with a hand. Did she have to spell out his lies? Throw them in his face?

"Or," Shay continued, kissing each of his fingers until he removed his hand, "you probably would have hurt Bruno, because you were too emotionally involved. That wouldn't have been good, either. I'm glad Joe Winston is the one who took care of it."

Bryan stared at her, and felt some of the crippling guilt wash away. "Yeah, me too." And for once, he meant it. "Now the creep is rotting in jail."

"Where Freddie Baker should be."

He kissed her mouth. "Don't you worry about Freddie. I'll take care of him."

She started to say something to that, when Bryan's cell phone rang. The fact that it wasn't the landline told him it wasn't one of the women from the safe house. Bryan rolled out from under Shay. "Damn, where the hell are my jeans?"

Shay found them on her side of the bed and handed them to him. Gut instinct told Bryan that something was wrong, that he wouldn't be getting a call now otherwise. After finally wrestling the phone from his pocket, he answered on the forth ring. "Kelly here."

"You're going to love this, Bryan."

"Joe?" Astonished, Bryan glanced at Shay. She sat beside him, totally nude, her legs bent beneath her, her expression reflecting the same curiosity he felt. "Hell of a coincidence."

"I don't believe in coincidence."

"Yeah, I know, but I was just talking about you."

"Riveting conversation, I'm sure," Joe drawled, "but Jamie is here and he's blathering on about you and women you can't trust. He's got himself all excited."

"Jamie? Excited? From what I remember, he's pretty mellow."

"Not this time." There was a pause, a sound of disgust, and Joe said, "Jamie tells me we're interrupting something. Are we?"

His laugh came unexpectedly. The range of Jamie's supposed skills amazed him. "As a matter of fact . . ."

"Great. He just had to be right, didn't he?" And then, "Oh, shut up, Jamie."

Knowing Joe's sour mood was more put on than not, Bryan said, "Give me just a second. I'll be right back." He covered the phone and turned to Shay. "None other than Joe Winston himself is on the line."

Shay stared at him with fascinated glee. "Really?"

"He has some things he needs to tell me. And I imagine the ladies are anxious to see you back, so why don't you get dressed while I talk?"

"You want privacy?"

Hell, no. He wanted to pull her back down in the bed and love her all over again. "No, but I should be getting you back, so get dressed while I finish this conversation, all right?"

"I wish I could stay."

Damn. He wished that, too. Bryan caught the back of her neck and pulled her forward for a soft smooch. He forgot about covering the phone. "Me too, babe. Now get some clothes on before I forget my good intentions."

He heard Joe's laugh, then: "You, good intentions? She doesn't believe that bodacious lie, does she?"

Bryan settled back against the headboard and watched Shay saunter out into the bathroom. " 'Course she does."

"Then she probably doesn't know you that well."

Taking into account the fact that she thought he was a preacher, Bryan could safely say she didn't know him at all. "Probably not."

"That's what I thought. Well, all things

considered, I suppose I should just spit this out."

"Yeah?"

"Jamie thinks a woman is out to hurt you."

He reacted to that idiocy more than he should have. His hand tightened on the phone, his vision narrowed. Hell, he didn't believe in Jamie's ability. Forget that he saw it firsthand, that everyone in the town of Visitation, with the exception of a few men, believed it.

But still the fine hairs on the back of his neck stood on end and a chill ran down his spine. "What the hell are you talking about?"

Joe sighed. "I figured you'd be pissed. Here. I'll let Jamie explain."

"No!" Bryan jerked upright, away from the headboard. "I don't want to talk to that damn nutcase —"

"Something isn't right," Jamie said in his soft, deep voice.

Bryan fell back. Hard. "Here we go." From the little he'd seen of Jamie Creed during his trips to Visitation, once he started on his predictions, the best you could do is hear him out.

"I don't have everything clear yet," Jamie murmured with an air of mystery that few could master, "but you're trusting a woman you shouldn't, a woman who will betray you."

As if summoned by Jamie's words, Shay came back in. She'd splashed her face, leaving it slightly damp, and had her head tilted, untangling her long, fair hair with her fingers. She looked like an angel — a sexy, strong, wonderful angel.

Feeling his gaze, Shay smiled at Bryan, then bent and pulled on her panties.

Oh God, he had it bad. No way could Jamie mean Shay. Sure, Shay had secrets, but that was because of her poor background, her dysfunctional childhood . . .

"Who?" Bryan demanded. Not that he believed anything Jamie said, but he wanted him to confirm that it wasn't Shay.

"That's just it. I don't know. I wish I did. I was going to wait to contact you, but it felt . . . more powerful suddenly. As if things had escalated."

Yeah, escalated into a screaming climax. Twice. An invisible fist squeezed Bryan's heart, and still he said, "I don't believe in mumbo jumbo."

Insults never fazed Jamie. "You don't have to believe. Just be careful."

"I always am."

"No. Not careful enough. In fact, lately

you've been all but blind."

Bryan *hated* insults. "Listen, you damn phantom —"

Joe said, "Forget it, he's gone. You know how Jamie is. He says his piece, then goes off to contrive more ways to torment us."

Bryan's temper suddenly hit the ragged edge. "You don't believe in him any more than I do, so why the hell did you call me?"

"Luna made me." Joe sounded amused by that admission. "She does believe in Jamie. And she's fond of you. I can't have her worrying now, can I?"

Shay had her bra on and was busy slipping her arms into the sleeves of her shirt.

Bryan ate her up with his eyes. He would not start distrusting Shay based on bizarre warnings given by a man who seldom interacted with others. "I'm hanging up now."

"Yeah, right. But Bryan?"

"What?"

"Just in case Jamie's right . . ."

Bryan groaned long and loud and exaggerated. "Don't tell me you're buying into that crap now, too?"

"No. But just in case, watch your back. And if you need me, for anything . . . well, I owe ya one, right? So just let me know."

Bryan considered that offer, knew it was

sincere, just as he knew he couldn't ask for better backup than Joe, and he nodded. "Appreciate that, Joe." And just to tweak him, he added, "Give my love to Luna."

"Hell, no." Joe hung up, leaving Bryan with a grin. Once he got things settled for his brother, maybe he'd take Shay to Visitation for a short vacation. If Jamie met Shay, he'd know she wasn't a threat to anyone.

Fully dressed, Shay sat on the edge of the bed to slip on her sandals. "What was that all about?"

Bryan eyed her, wondered if he should tell her and thought, *Why not?* He was curious to see her reaction to Visitation's living legend. Would she be a believer? Probably. "Down in Visitation, there's this near-silent, mysterious guy named Jamie Creed. He's idolized by the town, at least by the town women. He claims to have some sort of extrasensory perception."

Her eyes widened with interest. "A psychic?"

"Sort of. I don't really know much about how it works, except that, according to the women in the area, Jamie is a romantic specter who only comes down off his mountain when he has dire warnings that usually prove to be on the mark."

Fascinated, Shay asked, "Is he handsome?"

"How the hell would I know?" The sound of police sirens swelled outside. It wasn't uncommon in the area. Sirens could usually be heard most of the night.

Bryan pushed off the bed and located his jeans. It was past time he returned Shay to the safe house.

"Well, what's he look like?"

Lifting one shoulder, Bryan said, "Tall. Dark. Shaggy hair and a beard. I guess he looks like a hermit, but his eyes are dark and intelligent. Nothing vague about him, except the idiotic stuff that spews out of his mouth." Bryan zipped up his jeans and reached for his belt.

A furious pounding on the front door made them both jump. Shay twisted around. Bryan frowned.

And then Patti's frantic, high-pitched voice reached them. "Preacher, Preacher! Come quick."

"Oh, shit." Barefoot and shirtless, Bryan raced out of the room.

Shay was right behind him.

Babbling, Patti said, "He showed up and he tried to grab Amy."

"Who?" Bryan demanded, sticking close as Patti tromped back down the stairs.

"Freddie." Between sobs, she said, "Morganna jumped him, but he hit her and then Barb called the cops and . . . and they're already here, but there are other people, too."

Bryan ran after her, not knowing what he might find but sure that it would be bad. He'd never seen Patti in such a state before. How badly was Morganna hurt? Amy had to be horribly upset. At least Barb had thought to call the police.

Patti shot out the front door and dashed across the yards, with Bryan and Shay following. It was dark outside, yet the front of the safe house was lit up with flashing police lights and the headlights from a white truck with some sort of logo on the side.

Ignoring that for the moment, Bryan anxiously counted heads as he approached.

He could see Barb and Morganna huddled together, neither of them seriously hurt. Amy was wrapped in a blanket next to a cop, and it appeared she was crying but unharmed. They were all safe, thank God.

Towing Shay in his wake, Bryan started toward the cluster of police officers. Two cops had Freddie sprawled out on the street so they could handcuff him. Another stood over him, a hand on his nightstick.

Freddie resisted, cursing up a storm and making vile threats that no one heeded.

Another man in plain clothes stood off to the side, snapping photos of the drama, while another held a microphone, as if waiting his turn. It seemed almost surreal — and too easy to be true. He couldn't easily accept that it was over, and he hadn't even been involved.

Bryan turned to Shay to ask her opinion — and he caught her backing away.

"Shay?"

In a weak protest, she whispered, "I . . . I have to go back to your place." She shook her hand loose from his.

Confused, Bryan saw that her face had gone deathly white and her eyes enormous. Worried, he again captured her hand, halting her retreat. Her fingers were icy. "Shay, everyone's okay, honey. They're arresting Freddie. It's almost over."

He tried to draw her into his arms, but she was trembling and backstepping. She stared at him and bit her lip. "I'm sorry."

Bryan felt his spine stiffen. "For what, exactly?"

The guy with the camera started snapping photos, blinding them both with the flash.

Automatically, Bryan shoved Shay behind him. "What the hell are you doing?"

The microphone got shoved under his nose. "Are you the preacher?"

Bryan felt bizarre, standing there in nothing more than jeans, the cool evening air swirling around him, so many eyes suddenly watching him with regret, curiosity, even eagerness. It was like playing in some cornball play, without knowing his lincs. "Yeah, so?"

The reporter looked beyond him to where Shay huddled. Bryan could feel her fast, warm breaths on his nape, feel her fingers clutching his bare shoulders. Thoughts of Jamie's predictions came back, cramping his guts, filling him with an awful foreboding.

The click of the camera sounded like gunshot. The flash blinded him.

"Is it true that you, the protector of retired prostitutes, are having an affair with the Crown Princess?"

The Crown Princess. The absurd title reverberated through his head, making his brain throb while the photographer moved in for a better angle. *Snap, snap, snap.*

Bryan started to deny the accusation, but nothing emerged from his mouth.

The microphone got passed behind him. "What do you say, Ms. Sommers?"

Sommers. Slowly Bryan turned to face her. Shay Sommers — the Crown Princess. A millionaire. A social butterfly. A woman who ran numerous charities — and had no real need to stay in a shelter.

Unless it was to serve her own ends.

The reporter pushed closer. "Are the hookers your newest project, or is the preacher?"

She shook her head.

"Are you two serious about each other?"

She glanced at Bryan — and then away.

"Is this another stunt to improve your recent bad publicity, to make up for the goof that almost killed that girl?"

Bryan couldn't move, but Shay did. She stepped back, then back again, distancing herself from him. His brain knew he'd been duped, but his heart waited for her to deny it, waited to hear her say something that would make this all a bad dream.

She shook her head — and her chin lifted. In a regal voice worthy of the title *Crown Princess*, she said, "I'm here because these women are my friends."

"Right." The reporter didn't believe that.

Neither did Bryan.

Morganna, Barb and Patti sidled up close to watch the interrogation with awe and horror.

The reporter swept his hand behind him. "Did you dress them?"

By the moment, Shay's expression grew colder and more remote. "They're grown women. They dress themselves."

"But you supplied the clothes. You've gotten them jobs and taught them manners. Isn't that true?"

"Who told you that?" Shay stared directly at the reporter, as if Bryan didn't exist. And he felt like he didn't, like he'd just been sucked into a great void. Damn Jamie. Damn himself for his stupidity.

He should have insisted she share her secrets, he should have done his own investigation. He should have . . . never touched her in the first place.

But that was over and done with, and he had the here-and-now to tend to.

Never mind what lies Shay had told or what she deserved, the women weren't a part of it. It was his job to protect them, and he'd do just that. Bryan stepped in front of the reporter, blocking him from Shay's view. "Get lost."

Undaunted, the reporter asked, "Do you like the idea of Shay Sommers starting a safe house right down the street from you?"

Bryan locked his jaw. "She's not."

"You didn't know?" *Snap, snap.* More pictures were taken. Too damn many pictures, probably showing his shock, his disgust. His hurt. "She's already bought the property. Paid cash for it. Are you concerned that her reputation will taint your good work? Will you two be a team?"

"No." Bryan shoved the reporter out of his way. He caught Morganna's arm, noticed her black eye, and cursed. "Freddie?"

Morganna nodded. She looked as shaken by the events as he felt. With a weak smile, she said, "I gave him one back."

"Good for you. Let's go. Barb? C'mon. Patti, it's okay now." The flash of the camera split the dark night with a strobe effect. Still firing away with his questions, the reporter trotted behind him. Shay didn't. She didn't move. Bryan tried to ignore that, to ignore her. He stopped by Amy's side. "You okay, hon?"

She nodded, but big tears were in her green eyes and her nose was red. "He tried to gr-grab me."

Shay should be soothing her. Shay was good at that. But when Bryan glanced her way, he saw that the reporter had returned to her and was busy trying to bully her into answering his questions. She just stood there, her arms limp at her sides, her face almost expressionless. Bryan wanted to pulverize the guy for bothering her.

He couldn't bear it and he turned away.

Turning to the officer, he asked, "You need to see the women at the station?"

"We do, but there's no rush. We already got statements. They can take a little time to calm down."

"I'll bring them in, say, an hour?"

"Sure."

Barb touched Bryan's shoulder, and that was something she never did. "What about Shay?"

Hell, he didn't know. "After we leave for the station, she can come in and get her things. She doesn't need to be back after that."

Morganna looked ready to cry, and Bryan just knew if she started, they'd all be bawling on him. "It's over," he said, trying for an ounce of levity in a night that felt like death. "Freddie is done harassing us. There'll be nothing but peace from here on out."

The women nodded, but Bryan knew they didn't believe that any more than he did. How could he have peace when Shay had just destroyed him? Damn her.

He hustled the women inside, determined to keep them calm, wishing he'd been with them instead of screwing a woman who'd lied to them all. The last thing he saw before shutting the door to the safe house was the police car driving away with Freddie inside — and Shay facing off with the reporter. She looked so very alone.

Just as he felt.

Chapter Eleven

"Freddie denies shooting the paintball gun or making the phone calls. He says he couldn't care less what Leigh is doing, so why would he have been following you? He says he wasn't the one who hurt the preacher." Amy ducked her head. "He says his only crime was trying to snatch me back."

Shay paused in her work, swiping the back of her forearm across her brow and setting her dust rag aside. The new safe house would be ready soon enough. Right now Amy wanted to talk.

Like the other women, Amy often visited her. At least they hadn't given up all hope on her. "Do you believe him?"

"No."

Well, that was something, at least. Shay prayed daily that Amy would remain strong, and remain safe from the Freddies of the world.

Amy took a turn around the room, staring at her feet. Finally she said, "I like my new job."

"That's great. So it's working out?"

Nodding, Amy said, "I like my new clothes, too. I can't believe you got me so many." She smoothed out the skirt of her dress, admiring the feel and look of the fabric. She hesitated, peeked at Shay, then asked, "Are you really so rich?"

Wrinkling her nose, Shay said, "Disgustingly rich." She waited, but Amy didn't react to that disclosure.

"You were born rich?"

"No. My husband had piles of money, and after he passed away, it all came to me. Phillip didn't have any other relatives. I know he'd have taken real pleasure in how I spend it, though. He was a very wonderful man."

"You loved him?"

Shay turned to stare out the window. She hadn't loved him as a wife loved a husband; they were more like friends or companions. It hadn't mattered to him, so it hadn't mattered to her. "Yeah. I still love him. And I still miss him."

Amy seemed to digest that before changing the subject. "People look at me differently now."

"You're a very pretty, smart young lady. I'm sure they see that."

She nodded, but not really in agreement

— more out of distraction. A blush brightened her face before she whispered, "There's a guy at work . . . he, well, he sort of teases me. In a nice way." She bit off a self-conscious smile, and confided, "He asked me out."

Shay felt like the sun had just shone down on her miserable head. Despite all her current troubles, seeing Amy happy made her happy, too. "He's handsome?"

Amy shrugged. "He has this wonderful smile . . ." With a sigh, she added, "But I'm not ready for that yet. He said he'd wait."

"Smart man." Just about every day, Amy became a happier, more carefree young lady.

At least Freddie was still in jail, and likely to stay there since he couldn't be trusted to check in with his parole officer. He wouldn't be able to bother Amy for a long, long time.

Taking Shay by surprise, Amy threw her arms around her. "It's not the same at the safe house without you. Everyone is doing great — but we miss you. Patti gets sullen and Barb isn't so bossy. The preacher . . . well, he doesn't say much at all. Most of the time. Other times he seems so different."

Shay couldn't talk about Bryan without getting melancholy. She wished she hadn't lied. She wished she'd taken her chances and been honest from the beginning.

She wished she'd never fallen in love with Bryan Kelly.

But she had. And now, as always, she'd have to deal with her actions.

"I can't come back." No matter how badly she wanted to. Bryan had walked away from her without even asking for an explanation. All the time she'd spent with him, when she'd thought they were growing closer, hadn't mattered at all once he'd learned the truth.

Most men would have jumped at the chance to be with her because she was so filthy rich. But Bryan detested her for just that reason. Well, she wouldn't burn the money. Either he wanted her or he didn't.

He didn't — and she'd deal with it. Somehow.

"No, 'course you can't." Amy shrugged. "I mean, you're rich and all that."

Shay said, "Money has nothing to do with it," when in truth, she knew money had a lot to do with it. She could buy anything she wanted, including a man.

Just not the man she wanted.

Shay caught Amy's hands and hoped

she'd believe her. "I had more fun staying with all of you than I have in years."

Dawn walked back in. She had just carried another load of garbage out to the curb. "The kitchen is now completely bare. I thought I'd lend a hand in here."

Amy glanced down at her pretty yellow dress with regret. "I wish I could help. . . ."

"You're dressed way too nice for that," Dawn told her. "And if you don't leave now, you'll miss the bus."

"Then I better go. I don't want to be late for work." She backed toward the door. "I have tomorrow off, so I'll stop by then. I'm good at cleaning. Maybe I'll bring Morganna with me. I think she goes into the restaurant late."

"We'll order in a pizza," Shay promised. "It'll be fun." But after Amy left, Shay leaned against the wall and fought off tears. She missed them all.

Dawn smacked her in the butt with a broom. "Stop moping about how things turned out. Or else make up your mind to change them."

Shay managed a smile that almost hurt. It had been two weeks. Fourteen days without Bryan touching her, smiling at her. She saw him occasionally, but it wasn't the same. Either he looked through her, avoided her, or stared at her with pity.

She couldn't understand it. He almost seemed like two men sometimes. And neither of those two men wanted to be with her. "I'm not moping," she lied. "And there's no way I can change it."

"You can change anything," Dawn told her. "You sure as hell changed me. And Leigh is happier than I ever thought she'd be."

With a snort, Shay said, "You're both wonderful people who remained wonderful people. All I did was lend a small helping hand."

"Then look at Amy. That girl defined sadness not more than a month ago, but she just walked out of here with a big, honest smile. Face it, Shay. You changed all of us. And I happen to believe you can change anything or anyone, including a stubborn preacher."

Shay hugged her best friend. "Thank you, but this time I really blew it."

"Baloney. You only feel that way because you're in love. Your heart's keeping your brain from seeing things clearly. If you looked at this situation the way you look at everything else in life, you'd bulldoze your way through it like *that*." Dawn snapped her fingers.

Shay had to laugh. "Right now, I can't even bulldoze my way through this mess." The house she'd bought was three blocks down from Bryan's safe house. It was plenty big enough to house a dozen women, and once they finished cleaning it and added some fresh paint and carpet, it would look nice. Today she and Dawn were hauling out the biggest piles of junk. With the kitchen finished, Dawn was ready to help her finish tackling one of the downstairs bedrooms.

Dawn looked at Shay, then shook her head. "Look at you. You're exhausted. You should have hired someone to do this."

"I needed something to do. Something physical." *Some way to occupy her mind so she could fight off the need to cry.*

She shooed Dawn with a hand. "But you go on. You don't have to babysit me."

"Honey, someone's got to do it." Dawn threw another stack of newspapers into a large cardboard box. "Know what I think? I think you should jump his bones."

"Jump him, huh? Somehow I don't think that'll work."

"It's all in *how* you do it. Lead with your mouth." Dawn pursed her lips with exaggerated intent. "Kiss first, talk later. And by talk, I mean you talk. Tell him you love him, that you miss him, and if he starts to interrupt, kiss him like no woman has ever kissed him before."

Shay crossed her arms around her middle. That sounded so wonderful. Like an addict, she craved Bryan's touch. A kiss from him, even a small one, would make her feel so much better.

"Do it," Dawn said, "the very next chance you get. Don't let him walk away or give you one of his holier-than-thou looks. Plaster your lips on and don't let go." She lifted the box filled with papers and headed out. The bedroom door was closed, so she balanced the box on one hip and tried to open it. It didn't budge. "Damn old wood. Everything in this house is too tight."

"Including the windows," Shay agreed. "We'll need to have them planed a bit so they're easier to open before anyone moves in."

"I'll add it to the to-do list in just a minute." Dawn set the box down and gripped the doorknob. It wouldn't turn. "Did you lock this?"

Frowning, Shay started toward her. "No, of course not. Amy just left, and it was open then." All of the doors, even the interior ones, had locks with skeleton keys.

The house was old enough to be called quaint despite the problems wrought of age. Crystal doorknobs, high ceilings, and an excess of intricate moldings made the house special.

Even after the incident with the reporter, Shay was determined to make a go of the safe house. The house had been empty, so she'd gotten immediate occupancy.

But after the first article, accompanied by a set of photos, had run in the paper, she'd almost regretted her decision. The article portrayed Shay in the worst possible light. Nothing new in that, but this time they involved Bryan. The heading read: *Preacher Bruce Kelly, newest conquest of the Crown Princess?* Shay felt so guilty. Bryan Bruce Kelly was a special kind of a preacher, and a wonderful man. Yet the papers made him sound like a fool, falling for an evil woman. He'd worked far too hard to be dragged down into her bad press.

It wasn't easy to stick to her guns, but Shay wasn't a quitter. She couldn't quit. So instead, she'd begun working to make the house habitable.

Shay tried the door. "The key's gone."

Dawn suddenly clutched at her arm. "Wait. Do you smell something?"

Shay sniffed the air and froze. "Smoke."

She hated to think beyond the most obvious of explanations. "Maybe someone's burning something outside."

"And we smell it in here with all the windows closed? No." Dawn headed for the window and started trying to tug it up. Of course it stuck. "Someone set a fire."

"But we're . . ."

"Inside. I know." She glanced at Shay over her shoulder, her black eyes solemn with fear and understanding. "Maybe Freddie wasn't the guy hassling the safe house. Maybe it was someone else — and that someone else doesn't want another haven in the area."

"That's reaching." But Shay saw the smoke begin to billow in under the door. "Oh, God." She tried adding her strength to Dawn's but the window was too old and warped to open.

"What are we going to do?"

Her eyes stung and her throat burned. The room quickly filled with more smoke, telling them that the fire was close, probably right out in the hall. They could hear the sounds of wood splintering, the crackle of fire. "Move."

Dawn stepped to the side and Shay hefted the box of newspapers through the window. The glass shattered, allowing fresh air in. Being the smaller of the two, Dawn scampered up and over the high sill with Shay's support.

She moved carefully because of the broken shards of glass still imbedded in the wood. The bushes outside were as aged as the house, a thick, twining tangle of evergreen branches that scratched and tore.

Cursing, her arms already covered in small bloody scrapes, Dawn reached in for Shay's hand — and the door leading to the bedroom collapsed inward.

Flames entered with a threatening whoosh.

Dawn screamed.

And Shay landed face-first in the prickly bushes.

"You're being cruel, when I never thought you could be."

Bryan did his best to ignore Bruce. His brother had become a real pain in the ass, singing Shay's praises while insulting him with great verve. Bruce could like Shay all he wanted. She hadn't lied to *him*. Hadn't slept with *him*.

But she thought she had.

Bryan groaned. In the back of his mind, he knew he was no better than Shay. He'd lied, too. Okay, so his reasons were more valid. But hell, he didn't know what reasons she had.

She hadn't offered them.

He hadn't asked.

He didn't want to get near enough to her to ask. If he did, he'd hold her and kiss her again. He'd be lost.

"Go away, Bruce."

"Ha! You're the one who should go away. I'm back at the safe house now, or at least I am when you're not wandering around there like a lost soul. And why are you still hanging around, anyway?"

Bryan rubbed the back of his neck. He and his brother had switched back to their legitimate places, with Bruce as the preacher and Bryan . . . not sure what to do. But Bruce was right. The apartment sucked.

He strode to the tiny kitchen and got out a long-neck beer. "I can't leave yet. Something doesn't feel right."

He knew Freddie was scum. He knew he'd tried to grab Amy and that he'd socked Morganna, but the rest . . . he couldn't be sure. Someone had followed Shay that day, but was it to get Leigh? Someone had fired into the safe house, making a mess with a paintball. But how would that have helped Freddie's cause?

Freddie denied it all, and for some reason Bryan half believed him. Probably because his instincts said it wasn't over. And until he knew it was over, he wasn't budging.

He wouldn't leave Bruce alone to maybe get jumped again. He wouldn't leave the women alone to possibly be hassled. And Shay . . . damn it, she was just down the street.

More alone than any of them.

"No kidding?" Bruce dropped down into a kitchen chair. "Did Jamie tell you something to make you uncertain?"

Bryan scowled. "No. I haven't talked to him," he lied.

"Maybe you should."

Fed up, Bryan took a long draw on the beer. "You're a preacher. No way do you believe in voodoo."

Bruce shrugged. "God works in mysterious ways. That's what I believe." He eyed Bryan. "You want to know what I think feels wrong?"

"No."

"Could be the way you abandoned Shay to the wolves."

Bryan *hated* melodramatic crap. Almost as much as he hated self-doubt and guilt. "What wolves?"

"Those hideous reporters who are forever trying to discredit her."

Bryan leaned against the sink. If he sat down, Bruce would take away his beer. "She's well acquainted with them. And besides, she discredits herself."

"Yeah? How'd she do that? If you're talking about that past scandal, I followed along. Shay wasn't responsible for what almost happened to that young girl."

"Of course she was. She was in charge."

"Ah. Then I'm responsible for Amy almost getting grabbed? Or Morganna's black eye?"

"No." Bryan stared at the far wall, accepting the truth. "I am."

"You're too smart to be a self-righteous martyr, Bryan. No one can be everywhere at once. We all need to rely on others at times. That's Shay's biggest crime — trusting the wrong people. Believe me, she's more than paid for that. Or haven't you noticed how the papers have crucified her?"

"I noticed." Now that he knew her, it made him sick to think of the hurt she must feel. "But that doesn't explain what she did at the safe house."

"Yeah? What'd she do? Was she hateful to the ladies?"

Bryan tried to ignore him.

"Or do you mean getting them jobs they love, helping them grow as people and gain new self-esteem and respect? Giving them friendship?" He snorted rudely. "Yeah, what a bitch."

Bryan's head snapped up, both out of shock at hearing his brother curse, and raw anger at what he'd just called Shay. "Shut up."

"Your mean tone doesn't work on me. Save it for some poor woman like Shay. God knows you must intimidate her."

"You're going too far, Bruce."

"You went too far when you walked away from her, as if she didn't even exist."

"She's rich enough to buy this whole damn street!"

"And that's a crime? No, wait. You mean she can buy understanding? Sympathy?" He raised a brow and stared at Bryan. "A new man?"

"You don't understand."

"So explain it to me." Bruce leaned forward. "I'm *dying* to understand."

Bryan wasn't in the habit of baring his soul. But his brother deserved some type of explanation, ugly as it might be. Strangling on the words, he rasped, "I told her about Megan."

Bruce couldn't hide his surprise, but it was quickly masked with consideration. "Maybe," he said in a less forceful voice, "you should have told her about *yourself* instead."

Bryan deliberately misunderstood. "You know I couldn't. I was supposed to be you."

"So what? I *want* you to have her. *God* wants you to have her."

Bryan took another long swig of his beer. "Yeah? Did God want me to fuck her, too? Because I did — when I knew damn well I shouldn't have."

Disgusted, Bruce rubbed his forehead. "You *made love* to her, you idiot. There are differences between the two."

"How would you know?" Bryan crossed his arms and tried to steer the conversation in a new direction. "You haven't been laid in too many years to count."

"It doesn't matter." Bruce tried for his most solemn, serious expression. "Come on, Bryan. I know you, and you're in love. Just accept it."

Bryan snorted.

As if that one rude sound was the straw that broke the camel's back, Bruce pushed to his feet. "Fine," he all but shouted. "Be an idiot. Stay here and drink beer. Drink a whole case of beer for all I care. Drown your sorrows if you think that'll make you happy." He turned his back on Bryan and muttered, "Me, I've got better things to do."

"I never get drunk and you know it." But Bruce wasn't listening anymore. His passive, tree-hugging, God-loving brother all but heaved with anger as he stormed out.

Bryan trailed him. "Where are you going?"

"None of your business."

Bryan followed him all the way to the door, through the door, and to the top of the stairs. "Men of God shouldn't stomp."

Bruce turned on the second step, poked Bryan hard in the shoulder, and snarled, "I'm going to do what you should have done."

Uh-oh. He was almost afraid to ask. "And that is?"

"I'm going to tell Shay everything." And with a look of contempt, he said, "Since you're too cowardly to do it."

Sheer stunned surprise kept Bryan's feet glued to the spot. He went mute. His brain staggered. His eyes watched his brother depart, but he couldn't get the rest of his body to do a damn thing.

No, Bruce wouldn't do that.

He couldn't do that.

Bruce was completely out of sight when Bryan realized that, yes, his brother could and would do just as he'd said. Preachers didn't lie.

How would Shay react?

He had to see for himself. He ducked back into the apartment just long enough to grab his gun, a hat and reflective sunglasses. On Bryan's insistence, they still hadn't told anyone that they were brothers. Now that Bruce had shaved and gotten his hair cut — which had forced Bryan to get a haircut, too — they had to be extra careful. It fell on Bryan to don the disguise, and he chose an old favorite: baseball cap and glasses. They worked as well as anything, as long as one didn't look too closely.

Bryan missed the women and he worried about them, so he talked Bruce into letting him make rounds every now and then. It had been awkward a few times, especially with Shay. Bruce tried to show her compassion. Bryan just tried to avoid her.

But now, with Bruce on the loose, avoiding Shay was no longer an option.

Bruce was determined to teach his bullheaded brother a lesson. He'd act in his best interests whether Bryan liked it or not. And helping him to reconcile with Shay was in everyone's best interest.

Regardless of the pretty front, Shay was sad enough to break his heart. She smiled with the women, protecting them from her hurt, but Bruce saw through her. Had she spent her life protecting others? Probably. She was that kind of woman. The kind of bighearted, sweet, wonderful woman that his brother deserved.

And Bryan had told her about Megan. Bruce couldn't get over the shock of that. Bryan *never* talked about his wife.

Yet he'd told Shay.

Whether Bryan wanted to admit it or not, that meant something. A lot. It meant he trusted her on a gut level. And to a man who trusted only a handful of people, a man who lived by his instincts, that should have been all the convincing Bryan needed. But love was strange. It distorted your perspective and played havoc with your logic. Bryan needed someone more levelheaded making his decisions for him right now.

Bruce nominated himself.

Determination rode him so hard that he was practically jogging to the building Shay had bought. It was only a few blocks away and he was more than healthy enough to jog there. He was going over all his righteous statements, working and re-working the explanations in his head in order to deliver them with the best effect.

Then he saw the smoke in the sky and the fire engines parked out front, and his blood ran cold.

Dear God, a fire!

Without really thinking about it, Bruce launched into a dead-run. Panic pushed him, and he skidded to a halt in the front lawn, in the middle of the chaos. The stench was awful. Charred wood littered the area. Hoses were being rewound. Conversation buzzed in high excitement. Neighbors loitered everywhere, gossiping, watching, getting in the way.

It took Bruce a moment to realize the fire was out, that most of the people working were now cleaning up the area, making certain it was safe.

Fire had done major damage to the front of the house, leaving the wooden porch black and bubbled. Fear immobilized Bruce for only a moment. Silently reciting his prayers, he grabbed the nearest firemen. "I'm a close friend." His heart thudded hard, almost hurting. He swallowed. "Was anyone hurt?"

The fireman patted his shoulder. "Take

it easy. Two women were inside, but they're okay. Just a little singed and croaky from inhaling the smoke. Lucky for them, they got out through a window." He pointed past an EMS vehicle. "They're waiting in the minivan there at the curb, just staying out of the mob."

His knees felt like rubber. Shay was okay. Bruce sent some gratitude heavenward, thanked the fireman, and hurried to the passenger door of the minivan. Shay sat with a small, dark woman, talking quietly with her. They both seemed subdued. They had the engine on, probably to run the air-conditioning since there wasn't much fresh air to be found after the fire.

Bruce tapped on the window.

Shay lifted her head — and stared. Pale, singed hair hung limp around her scratched face. Ruined makeup mingled with black soot. She was scratched, maybe bruised. Her eyes had watered and were red and now, while she looked at him, her mouth trembled.

Bruce realized the awkwardness of his timing. Blast Bryan, he should be the one here now. "Could I speak with you a moment?"

Galvanized by his request, the woman in the driver's seat all but leaped out of the van. She circled the hood, stopped in front of Bruce, tangled a fist in the front of his shirt and drew his head down to hers. "She's had a *bad* day, Preacher, you got me?"

"Uh, yes."

"Make her cry again and I'll get ya."

Bruce pulled back in surprise. "No, of course I wouldn't . . ." But obviously Bryan already had. He swallowed and said, "Thank you."

Shay rolled down the window. She was breathing hard, her eyes wide. "Dawn?"

"There are some cute firemen who look like they could use some company." She winked. "If you need me, just honk." And with that, Dawn sauntered away.

Shay bit her bottom lip with visible uncertainty before sliding across the seat to make room.

Bracing himself, Bruce opened the door and climbed in. He closed the door behind him and rolled the window up again to give them a sense of privacy. Where to start? What to say? Her face looked ravaged from lack of sleep, unhappiness, and the scratches from the bushes. His heart turned over. "Shay, are you okay —"

From one second to the next, she launched herself at him. Her arms went around his neck and she squeezed him so tight he couldn't breathe.

Disconcerted by the gesture, Bruce patted her back with ineffectual sympathy. "Shay . . ."

Her lips touched his throat, his jaw, and then they were plastered to his. Bruce, stunned stupid, got the first French kiss he'd had in years.

Wow, he'd forgotten how nice a woman's tongue felt. It was wet and hot — *no.* This was Bryan's woman. And he was a man of high moral beliefs. He didn't . . . ho boy, she had a talented tongue.

"*No.*" He pried her loose, attempting to hold her back the length of his arms. Two deep breaths and a few prayers later, he rasped out, "Please, Shay, let me explain, okay? You need to listen to me . . ."

"Explain later." She slipped her hot little hands inside his shirt and stroked the bare skin of his chest.

Shamefully, Bruce felt his body reacting and almost panicked. "Shay!"

"I need you. Please don't push me away. Not anymore. Not after all I've been through."

He would kick Bryan's butt for this. "No, I wouldn't. I mean, *Bryan* wouldn't. But I —"

"Don't tease, Bryan." And again she

wiggled close enough to kiss him. When he tried to pull back, she bit his bottom lip.

It was . . . quite erotic. Who knew? Biting. Hmmm.

Suddenly the driver's door opened and Bryan slid in. His brother looked like a thundercloud. "Get off her, Bruce."

Bruce almost sputtered. "I'm trying."

Shay jerked back but retained her hold on Bruce.

With a knowing look, Bryan growled, "Honey, let my brother go before he faints."

Shay looked ready to scream. Or pass out. Or both.

To her credit, her wide eyes took in both men, back and forth, one to the other. Her mouth worked, but nothing came out.

Bryan pulled off his sunglasses and waited while Shay figured things out.

She covered her mouth. "What . . . ?"

Bruce nearly melted in relief. " 'Bout time you got here. I'll leave you to it."

Shay jerked around and grabbed at him. "No. Don't go."

Now that Bryan had wisely shown up, Bruce felt much better about things. He squeezed her shoulders and inched her away. "You and Bryan need to talk. It'll be okay now."

But she curled in close to Bruce and looked over her shoulder at Bryan. She seemed afraid — and no wonder, given the black scowl Bryan wore.

Bryan's eyes narrowed even more. "He's my twin, Shay. Not me."

"Not you?" she repeated. She looked between the two of them, her face a mirror of confusion.

After a visible struggle, Bryan brought himself under control. He stroked Shay's frazzled hair, gently touched the scratch on her cheek. "Meet Bruce, my twin brother. The real preacher."

Her eyes widened. "The real preacher? But . . . Then you're . . . ?"

"A bounty hunter." He winced when he saw one particularly nasty scratch on her chin. "I pretended to be him so I could get the bastard who jumped him, the one who was hassling the safe house."

"Freddie?"

He shrugged. "I don't know. I'm not convinced of that yet."

Bryan kept touching her, making Bruce want to whoop in joy. Finally they'd work things out.

Again, Shay looked between them. "I don't know . . . which of you . . . I was . . ."

Bryan cupped the back of her neck, drew

her close, and kissed her. It wasn't an exceptionally long kiss, but it was long enough for Bruce to stare out the window, whistle, and grin.

When Bryan lifted his head, their gazes met. Bryan was blazing again. Shay sighed. "It's you."

"Yeah." He drew a stabilizing breath. "And now that we have that settled . . ." He plopped the cap on Bruce's head and handed him the sunglasses, then reached beyond him to shove open the van door. "Blend in, will ya?"

"Gladly." Grinning, very satisfied with how things had worked out so far, Bruce donned his disguise and slipped out of the van.

No one paid him any mind — at least no one that he noticed.

Chapter Twelve

Blanketed in a surreal cocoon of comfort, Shay settled back into the seat. Twins. One a preacher, one a bounty hunter. It sort of made sense. And yet she couldn't quite bend her mind around it.

But that kiss was all too real. He was the man she wanted, the one she'd fallen so head over heels in love with, almost from first sight.

Relief, happiness and fear all swirled and mixed inside her. She'd been lied to, but would she make the same mistake Bryan had made? Would she condemn him without understanding?

Bryan started to say something, but she held up a hand. When he reached to touch her again, she scuttled back so that she leaned into the corner of the van, between the seat and the door. She couldn't think when he touched her, but if ever a situation called for a clear mind, this was it. She had to deal with Bryan's deception, and she had to deal with the fact of the fire.

A hundred questions clamored for priority, but one more so than the others. Watching him closely, half afraid he'd suddenly leave, or worse, reach for her, she asked, "Why are you here?"

His eyes looked dark and velvet and mesmerizing. "I missed you."

She wanted so badly to believe that.

"I needed to apologize. And explain."

Shay thought about that. "You didn't know about the fire?"

"No. Not until I got here." His jaw locked and again he reached for her. "Are you —"

She raised a hand, halting him in his tracks. "You're really a bounty hunter?"

"Yeah. But I wanted everyone to believe I was Bruce so I could catch the motherfucker who'd hurt him. At first I didn't think about lying to you because I was lying to everyone, but then . . ." He shook his head. "Shay, you've kept so many secrets."

"And so you didn't trust me." That made sense. It was all starting to make sense. His language alone should have clued her in. She felt idiotic — like the biggest fool alive. Frowning, she asked, "You're not mad at me anymore?"

"No." He caught her hand even when

she tried to draw it away. “I had no right to be mad.”

“Why were you?”

“You’re hurt, honey. Can’t we talk about this later?”

“No. We can’t.” Before she moved so much as her pinky toe, she needed to know where they stood with each other. Her heart couldn’t take another break.

“All right.” His thumb rubbed over her knuckles, slowly, gently. It took several moments of thought before he replied. “I haven’t really been involved with a woman since Megan. I’ve fucked women, and I’ve arrested them. But I haven’t been involved.”

Her heart started to race. Apprehension and nervousness rose with hope. “Are we involved?”

His gaze hardened; he leaned closer to her. “Damn right we are. We both lied to each other. I know I felt betrayed, so you have to feel the same. But being away from you has been hell.”

Shay looked around. The house she’d bought was almost gone. Someone had wanted to hurt her. Not just the safe house, not just Bryan — or rather, Bruce — but *her.*

“I don’t know what I feel yet.” Their

eyes met, she lifted one shoulder. "Fear."

"No one will hurt you."

Oh, the easy way he promised that. "You think to protect me now?"

He slid across the seat, crowding into her. "I don't know what the hell I'm doing right now, but I know it isn't over. Not the danger, and not what I feel for you. And no, don't ask what I feel, because as God as my witness, I don't know." His hand tightened on hers. "I just . . . do."

It was a start. She could build from that. She was good at building something big from very little. "All right."

His brows pulled tighter. "All right, what?"

She nodded, trying to form the words, but finally she just said, "Someone locked us in the house."

"Us?"

"Dawn was with me. We were cleaning. I needed . . . needed something to keep me busy so I couldn't keep dwelling on that awful article in the paper and the way I let you down."

"Shhh." He pulled her close, and Shay willingly tucked her head into his broad shoulder. His warmth, his delicious scent, wrapped around her like a protective blanket. "You didn't let anyone down. Definitely not me. The reporter is a jackass." He tipped her back to see her face. "Want me to beat the crap out of him?"

A strangled laugh squeaked out of her. "*No.*"

"Good. I'd probably get arrested." His hand was tangled in her hair, rubbing her scalp, caressing her. "But even while I was reeling from hearing him call you the Crown Princess, I wanted to take him apart. So if you change your mind, just say the word."

"Bryan," she said, by way of chastisement.

He kissed her forehead. "You said you got locked in the house?"

"No, I said someone locked us in there." She eagerly drank in his fresh, clean scent, a direct counterpoint to the smoke clinging to her clothes and hair and skin. She trembled inside, hating to say the worst out loud, but needing it said all the same. "The fire was deliberately set."

Bryan shoved her back. With new eyes, he looked at her hair and skin and reddened eyes. "Son of a bitch."

His whispered anger didn't appease her much. "The fire department and the cops say they're still investigating. They said it could have been faulty wiring."

"You don't believe that?"

She had nothing concrete to go on, but she shook her head. “Bryan . . .” The awful suspicions brought tears to her eyes and made her stomach roil. Agonized at the possibilities, she whispered, “Amy was here. Just chatting. She mentioned Freddie, and she asked me about my money. Then she left, and somehow the door was locked, and . . . and the fire was started.”

His gaze turned glacial. “You think she did it?”

Shay curled close, stealing some of his warmth, taking comfort in his nearness, his strength. “I don’t want to think that. It makes me sick to think it. But . . .”

Almost to himself, Bryan said, “Joe Winston doesn’t believe in coincidences. Neither do I. No one worth his salt does, so don’t feel bad for drawing reasonable conclusions.” Bryan held her for a time, and Shay knew he was thinking, working the facts over in his mind. Finally, with a kiss to her temple, he said, “Tell me who you trust.”

Shay leaned back to stare at him. “What?”

“There are people you trust, right? People you know in your heart, down to the marrow of your bones, would never hurt you. Who are they?”

She didn't understand, but knew instinctively that he was formulating a plan. "There's my family, including my brother-in-law Sebastian. And Dawn and Dr. Martin." An intelligent woman would make an effort to protect herself, to shield a part of her heart, but Shay loved him too much for that. So she added, very softly, "And you."

His gaze locked onto hers. So many emotions crossed his features that Shay couldn't tell what he felt. His nostrils flared, his jaw flexed — and then he grabbed her to him, kissing her hard, ruthlessly taking advantage of her admission.

When he finally lifted his mouth a full minute later, he said against her lips, "I think it's time for us to take a trip to Visitation."

Shay gave him an incredulous look. Leave now, in the middle of everything? "Oh, but —"

One finger pressed over her lips, hushing her. "Sorry, babe. You claimed to trust me. Now you're going to have to prove it." He turned away and opened the van door. "We'll leave tonight."

She wanted it to be over. She wanted things back to normal. She wanted . . . oh, God, so many things. Probably things she no longer deserved, no matter what he told her.

It wasn't until her scalp hurt that she realized she'd tangled both hands in her hair. A sob escaped, but she choked it down. She couldn't risk drawing attention to herself.

They'd duped her for sure. They'd duped everyone. But no more. Now she knew, and she had no choice but to tell. If she didn't, if she kept the information to herself, he'd find out. Then she'd be nowhere again.

She was doing the right thing. She had to be — because if not, she'd never be able to live with herself.

The detective still wasn't entirely convinced that the fire had been deliberate, so he didn't object when Bryan hustled Shay back to his shabby apartment. If they had more questions, they could reach her on his cell phone.

Because Bryan didn't want to take any chances, Dawn agreed to stay with friends for a few days, and Bruce promised to keep a close eye on the women in the safe house. If Amy was involved, and it looked pretty damning for her, then he needed to know where she was at all times. No way was she working alone.

Someone else was involved. Not Freddie.

Then who?

Bryan got ill every time he thought of what could have happened. If Shay had panicked instead of breaking the window, if she'd inhaled too much smoke — if, if, if.

He could have lost her — and that was unbearable.

As he dabbed antiseptic on her scratches, he asked for the hundredth time, "You sure you're okay, honey?"

She gave him a very put-out frown. "I could do that myself."

"Yeah, you could. But I want to do it, so sit still." He needed to touch her. Hell, he didn't ever want to stop touching her. She sat on the lid of the toilet, freshly showered and wrapped in his robe. Even with scratches and red eyes, she looked adorable.

And more than anything else, she was worried about Amy. Shay was such an amazing woman.

The ramshackle apartment didn't even faze her. Shay made herself at home and fit in no matter what her surroundings. She was a woman who always saw the silver lining, and if there wasn't one, she'd be out buying silver paint.

When Bryan finished, he caught her under the arms and pulled her up. "Kiss me again?"

Her cheeks warmed and she ducked her face against his sternum. "I can't believe I kissed your brother."

Bryan couldn't believe it, either. Good thing Bruce was trying to fight her off, or Bryan would have a harder time dealing with it. "It was probably good for his heart. Though it sure as hell set me back on my ass."

She poked his side. "You deserved it." She punctuated that with a groan. "I'm so embarrassed."

"Don't be. Bruce adores you. It was all my fault, and Bruce will gladly tell me so once we get everything sorted and settled."

She grew quiet, then whispered, "I don't like it that someone wants to hurt me. I mean, I'm used to the reporters taking potshots. Not just about my mistakes, but about my marriage, too. But this is different."

Bryan rubbed her slender back a moment, then took her hand and led her to the threadbare couch that came with the apartment. Once she was seated, curled into his side with his arm around her, he said, "Will you tell me about your husband?" He knew very little, except that the guy had been as rich as Midas.

She nodded, but the seconds ticked by without her saying anything.

More frustrated at himself for prying than at her for still keeping secrets, he said, "You don't have to."

"I don't mind. I loved him. He was a wonderful man." She twisted to see his face, her eyes soft and mysterious as only a woman's could be. "It's just . . . I want you to understand. I don't want you to judge me or him."

"Then I won't."

A slight smile lifted the corners of her mouth — and his heart. "All right." She cuddled back into his side before beginning. "We met during a charity event and from the first word, we hit it off. He was twenty years older than me, but not *old*. At least, not in his spirit. But . . . his heart was really bad, and it restricted what he could do. Even the simplest things were often a strain for him. So many times, he wanted to attend events, help people, contribute, but he had to leave that to others to do in his stead. He was the most generous, kindest man I've ever known. And he deserved love."

"You loved him." Bryan felt it in the way

she spoke — and strangely, he suffered no jealousy. If it hadn't been for her deceased husband, he might never have met Shay.

"No, not like a wife. I wanted to take care of him and help him with his work and I loved visiting him and just talking with him. We became inseparable companions. But we were never intimate. He couldn't . . . the strain on his heart would have been too much."

Bryan squeezed her closer. She constantly caught him off guard with the unexpected. She was such a sensual woman, he couldn't imagine her in a nonsexual marriage. The idea seemed almost criminal.

"He slept in a chair, always with oxygen. His nurse lived with us because sometimes he struggled so much to breathe. By the week, he grew more frail."

Her slender fingers curled into his shirt, clutching at him. The new tension in her was palpable, and he knew she was crying, but — typical of Shay — she'd do her best to keep it to herself.

Furtively, she wiped her eyes on Bryan's shoulder. "When he knew he was going to die, he said he wanted me to have his money because he knew I'd spend it well. We went over everything. How much money he wanted to go to different organizations, employees who'd been very loyal to him, memorials he wanted established. I did all that, but there's still so much money." She shook her head. "The house I live in, his house, is enormous and beautiful and so lonely without him that I can't bear being there, but at the same time, I can't bear to sell it because it was his."

Bryan slipped his fingertips inside the sleeve of the robe, seeking out her skin. She glowed with warmth, with love and gentleness, making it impossible not to touch her. "You feel guilty," he guessed.

"He should have had a real wife. A wife who wanted him sexually, not just a pal."

"He couldn't have done anything about it."

"But at least he'd have known he was wanted. That's so important."

Did she know how badly he wanted her? "Sounds to me like he was pretty damn smart. He had you with him for his last days, and now he can rest in peace, knowing you'll continue to give generously in his name."

Her laugh was harsh, unhappy. "Yeah, right. The Crown Princess, the woman who almost let a young pregnant girl die. The woman who brought danger to your brother's safe house."

"The woman who gives so much of herself, there's hardly anything left." Bryan tightened his hold on her, nuzzling with his nose until he found her throat. He felt like a horny goat with no sense of decorum, but her tears, her confessions, even the scratches on her face only made him want her more. The need to comfort her and reclaim her mingled. "I was a complete asshole for how I treated you, Shay. I'm so sorry."

Her laugh this time was of real humor. "Your language is disgraceful."

"Yeah. Bruce tells me that all the time. Sorry." Idiot. He had a hundred things to apologize for. "I'll never curse again." Somehow her robe opened and his nose neared her breast.

"I don't mind. It's part of you." She stroked her fingers through his hair. "You cut it."

"Because Bruce cut his."

"And you had to look alike." Her fingers continued to slide through his hair, rubbing over his scalp, encouraging him. "Will you tell me about being a bounty hunter?"

"Yeah." The single word was hoarse with need. "Later."

He heard her smile when she said, "Then will you make love to me now?"

Her breath shuddered out, and she whispered, "I need you."

He might be an idiot, but he wasn't totally lost to common sense. "Yes." Please don't let her change her mind. "Right now."

Together they left the lumpy couch and headed to the almost as lumpy bed. Bryan kissed her with every step. He kissed her as he lowered her to the mattress. He kissed her as he untied the belt to the robe and spread it wide so he could see every inch of her.

She took his breath away. "So beautiful."

"No, I —"

He pressed a finger to her lips. "Inside and out, Shay. Beautiful inside and out."

Her eyes softened and she tugged at his shirt. More than willing to oblige her, Bryan stood and yanked his shirt off over his head. He had his fingers on his belt buckle when Shay sighed and said, "You're the beautiful one."

He stripped his belt away and eased down his zipper. "If you say so."

"I do. I've never known a man as hard as you, who was also so kind and sensitive and caring."

In a hurry to be inside her, he shoved his jeans down. Lust swirled around him in a red haze, making it difficult to rationalize, but still he felt compelled to remind her of a few basic facts. "My brother is the preacher, babe. He's the one who helps people. I haul their asses — er, butts — back to jail."

He lowered himself over her, settling his hips between her silky thighs, balancing on his elbows so he could cuddle her breasts in his big, hard palms. Her nipples were already drawn tight, begging for his mouth.

"Maybe," she breathed, tipping her head back and offering herself to him. "But you fit the role of preacher *almost* to perfection. Take away the language —" She gasped as his mouth closed around her. He licked, taunted with his teeth, then settled in for a gentle sucking.

Shay groaned. "And you're a natural."

He moved to the other breast. In his mind, there'd been nothing natural about him playing keeper to a bunch of hookers. But they had become friends, and he'd learned a hell of a lot. "If you say so."

Her fingers laced in his hair, holding him tight to her. "I love it when you do that, Bryan."

"This?" He carefully tugged with his teeth, felt her shuddering response, the way she quickened.

"No — but that's good, too." With a hold on his ears, she turned his face up to hers. "I love it when you discount your influence and effect on others. The women all benefited from you being there. They responded to you, and they all love you. No, don't panic." She laughed, kissed his chin. "They're not in love with you. But they really care about you."

"If what we suspect is true, then you have to exclude Amy."

"No." Shay shook her head. "She cares about both of us. She's just confused and feeling lost. Her world hasn't been a nice one. She needs more guidance —"

"You're incredible." Bryan brushed his hand down over her waist, to her hip, then to the inside of her thigh. Her blue eyes darkened and her lips parted. "Now hush and let me make love to you. Concentrate on me and what I'm going to do to you. Not anyone else." His fingers touched her, and she was already slippery wet and hot. Perfect.

"What are you going to do to me?"

"Everything." He pushed one finger barely inside her, teasing, making her squirm. The little catch in her breathing turned him on. Her scent, growing richer by the moment, turned him on. The way she watched him with trusting eyes made him insane with lust.

Bryan didn't mean to say anything else, unless it was the usual murmuring of seductive, sometimes crude sex words. But Shay was under him, trusting and sweet and all his, and he couldn't help but spill his guts. "No one will ever hurt you again, Shay. I promise."

Her breath sighed out. "As long as you don't hurt me, I can handle the rest."

Oh God, was that a promise he could keep? He was still a bounty hunter, and that brought with it a lot of travel, a lot of distraction, and all type of danger. He'd considered retiring to Visitation, but . . . with Shay? Would she even be happy there?

From what he'd seen, she had to be busy helping or she wouldn't be content. He'd never spotted any hookers trolling in Visitation. Maybe she could apply herself to normalizing Jamie Creed. The guy was so weird, it was a task that could take years.

There were far too many unanswered questions for Bryan to box himself in. Rather than reply, he sat up beside Shay, caught her hips, and turned her onto her stomach.

She went motionless for only a moment,

then peered at him over her shoulder. "What are you doing?"

He bent and kissed the small of her back, at the same time wedging his hand between her thighs. "Spread your legs."

Shock rippled through her. "What?"

He didn't wait for her to comply. Instead he caught her legs and drew them wide apart.

Damn, she looked good like that, with her graceful spine exposed, her bottom jutting up and her legs open. "I love your ass."

Enjoying the sight of his dark hand against her pale cheeks, he patted and stroked her bottom, leisurely traced the dark furrow down to her sex, then used his fingertips to part her lips, gently probe and spread her wetness.

Her breathing accelerated, fast and deep, and then he worked two fingers inside her tight little vagina. He heard her raw groan, and smiled in nearly painful pleasure. "Relax and let me touch you, Shay."

Pressing her face into the mattress, knotting her hands in the sheet, she fought the urge to squirm — and lost. She was such a sensual woman, so open and giving.

Bryan traced kisses up and down her spine, from her nape to the small of her back. He nibbled on her full bottom, and he relished the signs of her heightened arousal. When she began shaking all over, her thighs tensed and her breathing harsh, he turned her.

For a time, he simply looked at her, rosy with sexual heat, her sex swollen and wet, her nipples tight.

Promises or not, she was his, damn it. Only his. "Come for me, Shay." He bent and kissed her hard, then thrust his fingers back inside her. Using his thumb, he found and pressed her distended clitoris, working her, urging her. She screamed into his mouth, her hips rising hard against his hand, her fingers tangling tight in his hair. It was wonderful. She was wonderful.

Long moments later, when Shay collapsed, Bryan said, more to himself than the limp woman beside him, "Condom. Can't forget the condom." But it was tempting. He wanted to slide into her, flesh on flesh, to relish the natural friction of her body accepting his. He'd never felt that way before, never once considered tempting fate. But now, with Shay, he hated having any barriers between them.

He dropped the cursed rubber twice before he got the packet open and got it rolled on. His hands were shaking. He was so primed he knew he'd be lucky to last for two full strokes.

He lifted Shay's legs, then draped them over his shoulders. When he leaned forward, her knees pressed into her breasts.

That got her eyes open. In breathless anxiety, she whispered, "Bryan?"

She was wide open, vulnerable to him and what he wanted of her. And he wanted everything.

"It's okay, babe. Relax." Staring down at her lush, pink sex, he positioned his cock and, thanks to the orgasm that had left her creamy and hot, began sinking into heaven. "Jesus. Better than okay." His teeth clenched. "Fucking incredible."

Shay braced her arms against his chest, but she couldn't hold him back. She breathed hard, a little unsure of things, yet he could feel her muscles clamping around his cock, squeezing him, and it just felt too good to stop. "Tell me if I hurt you."

Her nails dug into his pecs. She groaned. He was deep, so damn deep. He pulled back — and thrust in again.

Her slender body arched under his with a gasp.

That was one, he thought, his jaw locked, his forehead damp, his every muscle straining. He rocked in once more, slowly withdrew, back in hard — and her vibrating moan sent him over the edge. Three. A lousy three strokes . . . ah, to hell with it.

He gave himself over to the mind-blowing release, his body draining of energy, tension, need. He growled out his pleasure, pressed as deep inside her as he could get.

And as he went limp over her, she started coming again, too, in small spasms that he felt from inside her. It was enough. It was too much.

Time passed while his mind slowly recovered and his body sank deeper into lethargy.

"Bryan?"

He grunted, which was the best he could manage with her knees still against his ears.

Her fingers glided up and down his back. Her lips pressed into his sweaty shoulder. And in a voice so gentle that he barely recognized it as Shay's, she whispered, "I love you."

Bryan drew out his cell phone and punched in a number he knew by heart.

Joe answered on the first ring. "Winston here."

Skipping common courtesy, Bryan asked, "How bored are you?"

Joe laughed. "I'm married to Luna, remember? Never a dull moment to be had. Why, whatcha got going?"

Though Joe couldn't see him, Bryan shrugged. "A plan to catch a rat bastard who likes to use and hurt women. But I could use a little help."

Joe's voice lowered, probably so Luna wouldn't hear. "Sounds like fun. Count me in."

"You don't even know what you have to do yet."

"Doesn't matter. But then you knew that before you called, right?"

Bryan hadn't had any doubts about Joe lending a hand, but he had expected to do more explaining. Luckily, he didn't have to, since most of Joe's questions would be tough to answer. "Pretty much, yeah."

"That's what I figured." He could almost hear Joe rubbing his hands together in anticipation. "So, you coming here or am I coming there?"

"The first." Bryan glanced down at Shay, curled at his side, almost but not quite asleep. In such a short time, she'd become so precious to him. Just looking at her pleased him. "And I'm bringing Shay with me."

"And Shay is?"

That one was easy enough to answer. "Mine."

"Ah." Amusement filtered into Joe's deep voice. "Gotcha." And then, with a dose of facetious regret, "Alyx will be brokenhearted."

Bryan snorted. Alyx Winston, Joe's kid sister, was a bona fide terror. She'd flirted with him — but then, she flirted with every guy around. He didn't envy the poor sop who ended up with her. She'd be a handful, and then some. "Alyx will survive."

Joe let that go. "So when will you be here?"

"Tonight sometime. I've only got a few more pieces to get in place, then we'll head out."

"Great. Plan on eating dinner with us. Luna will insist."

It was Bryan's turn to be amused. "Sure. Give Luna my love."

"No." Usually Joe would have hung up on him at that point, but this time he said, "Watch your back. At least until you get here and I can watch it for you."

"Thanks." Bryan disconnected the call,

turned to Shay and stroked her hair. "You asleep, babe?"

"Not yet."

His heart clenched at the empty tone of her voice. "Try to rest. We don't have to be anywhere for another hour or so."

She nodded, but she was far too subdued. He was used to Shay's exuberance, her boundless energy. She was a take-charge kind of woman, not the type to sit back while plans were formed around her.

Her declaration of love had left him floundering for a reply, but Shay had eased through the awkward moment without his help. In fact, she'd slugged him in the shoulder and said, rather succinctly, "Get off. You weigh a ton."

She'd even groaned theatrically while straightening out her legs. Then she'd smiled, stretched, and rolled to her side to sleep.

Only she wasn't asleep. She was brooding. Or worrying. And he couldn't bear it. "We'll stop by the safe house last. I want you to tell them all that you're going with me — Bruce — to Visitation until we can find out who tried to hurt you. Bruce will be able to keep an eye on Amy, and if she contacts anyone, or tries to follow, we'll know."

Without opening her eyes, Shay said, "You think she's working with someone?"

"Yeah, I do. Maybe one of Freddie's cronies. Maybe just another goon. I don't know. But either way, I'm not taking any more chances with you. Bruce will keep an eye on things here, and Joe will help keep an eye on us in Visitation. Someone is bound to make a move, and this time, we'll find out exactly who it is."

Shay rolled to her back, sighed, and then sat up beside him. Eyes solemn, expression weary, she said, "I'm not tired, Bryan." She drew a breath. "How about we just get this over with?"

"It's a long drive to North Carolina. Probably five or six hours."

"Then let's go now so we get there before dark." Naked, she climbed out of the bed. "With any luck, we can sleep tonight without any worries."

"You'll sleep with me, either way." He wanted that much to be clear. Problems or not, he wasn't letting her go. Not yet. Maybe not ever.

Shay gave a gentle smile. "I would have insisted, if you hadn't. Now get a move on, lazy. We've got things to do."

She said it with all the take-charge attitude he was used to, but her eyes told the real story. Too much had happened in too short a time, leaving her depleted.

Never mind that he'd rejected her a few weeks ago, he wanted the old Shay back.

Somehow, some way, he'd manage it.

Chapter Thirteen

It hadn't been easy, gathering everyone together. Amy had to leave work early and Morganna would have to go in late. They all clustered around her, full of concern and advice, her *friends,* and Shay refused to believe any of them would do her harm. It just didn't seem possible.

Amy, especially, clung to her side, full of guilt. "I should have stayed with you."

"What good would that have done?" Bryan's tone was casual enough, but Shay saw the speculation in his dark eyes.

"I don't know. The door wasn't locked when I left, but maybe I pulled it closed. Maybe I locked it by accident."

Barb scowled ferociously. "Don't be stupid. It has a key that you have to turn. Did you turn a key? No. So it wasn't your fault."

Normally Barb's lack of patience got on everyone's nerves. But this time, Morganna patted Barb, as if to soothe her. "The preacher's right, Amy. There wasn't anything you could do. We should be thankful that Shay wasn't hurt."

"I *am* thankful," Amy gasped, sounding horrified.

Barb rolled her eyes. "You're all pathetic. I'm going to go put on coffee. Be right back."

"None for us," Bryan said. "We need to get on the road. I'm going to stash Shay with some distant relatives. They live off on some private acreage in Visitation, North Carolina. It's a nice, peaceful little town. Plenty safe." He handed Morganna a slip of paper. "Here's the address, in case the cops need to get in touch with us. My cell phone number is on there, too."

Shay knew he'd given the address for his trailer. Never would Bryan risk leading criminals to his friend's house, especially since Joe and Luna had two kids to protect.

"There are directions on the back." He stared at Amy, alert to any small nuance. "You know, in case the cops need them."

Amy wasn't paying any attention. She was too busy wringing her hands.

Barb snatched the paper away from Morganna. "I'll put this in the kitchen drawer, so we don't lose it. Since I'm the only one here during the day, I'd probably be the one to talk to the cops if they call."

Bryan nodded. "True. Don't lose it, okay?"

Her eyes narrowed. "Why would I lose it?"

Shay smiled. "You wouldn't. Look at how organized you are. You do a great job keeping things in order around here."

Morganna again patted Barb while looking at Shay. "Now that you've taught us how to cook and stuff, we've been pitching in more. It's not fair for all the work to fall on Barb."

"It's my job," Barb protested.

"But we don't mind helping you. It's almost fun." Morganna wrinkled her nose. "Not the cleanup, but we even help with that."

Barb turned on her heel and stalked away.

Sighing, Shay gave up. Barb would always be bristly. She'd hoped to eventually soften her, but while Barb had always been friendly, she continued to snap and growl at everyone within range. Apparently, grouchiness was an innate part of her personality.

Shay embraced Morganna, then Patti, and lastly Amy. "Don't worry, Amy. Everything will be okay. I promise."

Amy shook her head. "I don't know. Every time things look good, something else happens. I wonder if it'll ever end." She held Shay's hand. "North Carolina is so far away. But at least you'll be safe."

"Yeah," Patti added. "Better that you're not here, than to take a chance on getting hurt."

"No one wants that," Morganna agreed. "We all like you too much."

They all sounded so sincere. And yet . . . someone had tried to trap her in the house. Someone had set the fire.

Shay only prayed that someone wasn't Amy.

The minute they hit the highway, Shay fell asleep and stayed asleep for most of the ride. That suited Bryan fine, because she needed the rest and it freed him to keep a close watch on the surrounding traffic. No one followed them.

He didn't know whether he was relieved or disappointed.

Once they hit the older, winding roads, and by necessity had to slow down, Shay stirred and finally awakened. "We're there?"

"Almost. We're in Welcome County. We'll reach Visitation soon." He reached for her hand, rubbed her palm with his thumb.

Sleepily she pushed her hair out of her eyes, then straightened and looked out the window with interest. Sunlight bathed her face, broken only by shadows from the tall trees that bordered either side of the road. The wide highway had turned into a narrow, rough asphalt road with only an occasional house or trailer to be seen along the way. For all intents and purposes, they were away from the real world.

"It's beautiful."

"Yeah," Bryan said, staring at her profile, "very beautiful." She didn't say anything else, and that bugged Bryan. "What are you thinking about?"

"This. Us." She gave up her perusal of the road. "I'm wondering . . ."

"What?"

"Does it still bother you that I'm rich?"

Stunned, Bryan realized he hadn't really thought about the money issue. Mostly he'd concentrated on feeling deceived. But the money *was* something to consider. He was a working-class schmuck, making forty-five grand a year, with an occasional bonus. He lived a frugal life. He had basic tastes. Caviar? Forget it. Mercedes? In his dreams.

The thing was, he couldn't quite picture Shay sucking down fish eggs or trolling around in fancy wheels, either. He knew her simply as Shay, the woman who made herself at home in a safe house and had makeup and tea parties with trollops and chased him to ground with incredible energy.

"Bryan?"

He shrugged. "I dunno," he said, for lack of anything more intelligent. "How rich are you?"

"Filthy rich."

That made him grin. She said it like an admission of murder. "You don't act it — I mean, most wealthy people are snobs."

"Really?" One eyebrow arched up a good inch. "How many wealthy people do you know?"

He had the grace to feel sheepish. "Uh, not many." He could think of only a few. "I nabbed a couple of embezzlers who tried to skip town. They were rich for about two weeks. And there was this one hoity-toity broad who ran off with her Latino gardener. Took me months to track her down and drag her back, kicking and screaming like a banshee."

"So now it's a crime to run off with your lover?"

"Only when you clean out the accounts and steal hubby's car to boot." He smiled at her. "And I know you."

"That's a small percentage of people to use as a measuring stick. I've known plenty, and I can honestly say that sometimes they're snobs, sometimes not."

He squeezed her hand. "You're not."

"No. For the most part, I don't even think about the money except in how it can help make a difference to other people. But I take it for granted, too. Like buying the women clothes . . . It's easy to be generous when all you have to do is make a phone call." She looked down at their twined hands. "It's those people who give their time and their hearts that make a big difference." Her gaze lifted to his. "People like you."

"Bullshit. I was doing a con to catch a criminal, that's all."

"Maybe in the beginning," she agreed. "But you're not fooling me. You care. About all of them. About most people."

"If that's true, then the same can be said of you. Right from jump, you understood the women and what they needed. That takes a special kind of insight and empathy." Damn it, now that he'd accepted how genuine she was, he didn't want her to minimize her contributions.

Whether or not she believed him was anyone's guess, because she changed the subject. Shifting toward him, she said, "I've dated off and on over the years. Some nice men, some total jerks."

"Do I need to hear this?" Bryan hated the idea of her with other men. Her husband was one thing, but just dating for the fun of it? That rankled.

"You're the first guy who was actually turned off by my money. Usually it's the opposite. My money is the big draw."

"Guys chased you for your money?" He hadn't considered that, but it seemed likely. There were a lot of bums in the world.

She nodded. "Men look at me and all they see are dollar signs."

Oh, for the love . . . He snorted. "Babe, I know you don't want to hear this, but you're incredibly sexy."

She slanted him a skeptical look.

"Totally stacked."

She rolled her eyes.

"Hot as hell. Beautiful." He glanced at her, and teased, "Great rack and a killer ass."

That made her laugh.

"Don't you think a few guys probably

chased you for that reason?"

She made a silly face. "I doubt it, but that'd be no better than the other. Looks, money, they don't matter."

"If you say so."

"Do they matter to you?"

His brow arched. "I'm sure as hell not going to complain about your ass." When she started to frown, he said, "All right, all right. Bad joke." He drove in silence for a few seconds, gathering his thoughts, before saying, "I'll admit it was seeing you drunk that totally reeled me in."

"Be serious."

"I am serious. You were so adorable. You'd left yourself totally open to the women. They made you look like a deranged clown, and you didn't mind. You looked at them and saw them as real people with real needs and hopes. You cared. And that made me look at them the same."

A flattered blush colored her cheeks. "I had fun. More fun than I've ever had attending board meetings or trying to squeeze donations out of my acquaintances. In fact, I've been thinking of pawning that part of the job off on Dawn. She's so diplomatic, so easy to be around. She'd be perfect for that end of things."

"I like her." Dawn was a bossy little woman who obviously cared a lot about Shay. And truthfully, he loved the idea of Shay having more time for him.

"Dawn likes you, too — now that I explained everything to her. She saw right off that you were different from any other guy I know."

"Because I'm poor?" She scoffed, but Bryan said, "I'm serious, Shay. The money issue runs both ways. You're in the social spotlight a lot, whereas I'm a social misfit."

Her smile went crooked. "At least I know you don't want me for my money."

"And because of that, you'll overlook the rest?"

She moved her hand to his thigh. "There's also the fact that you're an incredible lover."

His heart jumped. "Glad you noticed."

"So much modesty." She traced little circles on his thigh. "But you know, I do have one complaint."

"Yeah?" His testicles tightened. "What's that?"

Her fingers inched higher, coming dangerously close to the peril point.

"Careful there." He caught her wrist.

"There, you see?"

"I see that I'm trying to drive and you're

trying to make me wreck." It never took much for him to get hard around Shay. A look. A smile. Put her hand millimeters away from his cock, and he was a goner.

He shifted uncomfortably in the restrictive jeans.

"You always take control, Bryan." Shay strained against his hold. "But I want to touch you, too."

A wave of heat swelled and shuddered through him and he nearly groaned. "Fine. You can touch all you want." *Yes.* "But later. When we're in bed. Or at least not in a car."

"You say that *now.* But you always end up doing stuff to me instead." He didn't really put his all in holding her back, and her hand slid up another inch.

Her fingertips touched his scrotum, then gently cupped him.

"Jesus, Shay, honey, give a guy a break, okay?" But he didn't move her hand, and he could have. Hell, he had eighty pounds of muscle on her. He was hard and she was soft and he liked it that she wanted to touch him.

She skirted closer to him, straining her seat belt. Her breasts pressed into his right biceps. In a husky whisper, she said, "You know how you kissed me?"

His jaw clenched. *Don't ask, don't ask . . .* "How?"

She ducked her head, hesitated, then whispered, "Between my legs?"

Oh, shit. His fingers locked around the steering wheel, and his voice went deep and hoarse and raw. "I love how you taste, baby. Especially when you're primed and nearly there and so damn wet —"

Her fingers smashed over his lips. Her fast, hot breath pelted his throat. "Shush, Bryan." She sounded as affected as he felt. "I'm trying to tell you that I want to kiss you like that, too."

Lust hit him like a ton of bricks. If he'd been standing, his knees would have buckled. Shay's mouth on him, sucking, licking? He'd never survive it.

"I want to pleasure you," she whispered, as if she wasn't killing him by small degrees, "the same way you pleasured me."

"Not the same," he groaned.

"I know. It'd definitely be different when you come."

He needed to lie down somewhere.

"But the idea of taking you in my mouth is exciting. I've never done that to anyone before." Her fingers curled around his erection, nearly stopping his heart. "But I'm dying to do it to you."

"Fuck it." He couldn't drive. Hell, he could barely see. "Let's find someplace to pull over. Anyplace. You don't mind a few weeds, do you?"

He sped around the corner, his gaze searching the side of the road for a clearing, and Shay's attention caught on something through the windshield.

She gawked. "Bryan!"

Thank God for sharp reflexes. He saw the man in the road at almost the same time she did. Despite being a little sluggish, thanks to an iron boner, he slammed on his brakes. Gravel and dirt went flying. The car skidded sideways, the tires finally found purchase, and they stopped — about six feet away from the idiot in the road.

Too close, as far as Bryan was concerned.

Without a care in the world, Jamie Creed, the insane recluse, slowly pushed to his feet. He wasn't smiling. He wasn't frowning. He looked as enigmatic as ever.

And he had eyes only for Shay.

In a fury, Bryan shoved the gears into park. He yanked off his seat belt, jerked out of the car and slammed the door behind him.

"God damn it," he roared, "if you want

to get killed, do it on someone else's time!"

Serenity personified, Jamie said, "I had to make sure you'd stop."

Bryan drew himself up. Strangling Jamie would make him feel better, but he had to admit, Jamie was right. If he'd seen him on the side of the road, he would have driven right on by. Not only did he dislike Jamie, but there was that tantalizing suggestion Shay had made. All he needed was a modicum of privacy.

Anger hadn't rid him of his erection. He should get back in his car, drive away . . .

Shay sidled up next to him. "Bryan?"

Oh, hell. He didn't want Shay to meet Jamie. She was in an especially amorous mood at the moment, and women in general tended to see Jamie as a mysterious, romantic figure. If Shay started fluttering her damn eyelashes or swooning, he'd lose it. "Wait in the car."

Her wide-eyed gaze swiveled from Jamie to Bryan, and then narrowed with simmering temper. "Wait in the car?" Her tone was lethal. "No, I don't think so."

Now Jamie smiled. He stepped closer, circling Shay, checking her out up and down and sideways.

A red haze collected in front of Bryan's vision. "I'm going to break your nose."

Jamie didn't even spare Bryan a glance. "No, you're not."

Bryan slumped. No, he probably wasn't.

Jamie circled once more, then stopped in front of Shay, his obsidian eyes direct, his mouth flat and unemotional. "She's the one."

Shay swallowed, blinked twice. "I am?" With so much unwavering attention on her, she twittered nervously.

Maybe he would break his nose after all. "Hell, no."

Bryan grabbed Jamie by the front of the shirt and jerked him around. They were of a similar height, but Bryan had him on meanness, no two ways about it. His lips were so tight, he barely squeezed the words out.

"Don't start with that cryptic bullshit, Jamie. Shay had nothing to do with it." Bryan shook him. "Do you hear me?"

Jamie tilted his head — and closed his hand around Bryan's wrist. His grip was stronger than a hermit's should be. "You misunderstand."

"The hell I do." Bryan struggled to keep his tone below a shout. "You said a woman was involved."

"One is."

His head throbbed. "It's *not* Shay."

"No. It's not."

One good punch, that's all it'd take. "Then why did you just —"

"I said she was *the one*. The one you'll stay with. The one for you." When Bryan stared, with a blank expression on his face, Jamie sighed. "The *perfect* one." Jamie didn't smile, but Bryan still caught his amusement. It showed in his blacker than black eyes. "Your soul mate."

Oh, hell. Bryan glanced at Shay, curious as to how she'd take that bit of sage prophecy concerning their future, but she was too busy ogling Jamie to react.

And Jamie didn't seem to mind.

"You're good for him," Jamie told her. He leaned closer and in a stage whisper, said, "Don't give up."

Shay twittered again. "No, I won't."

Bryan wanted to puke. He wanted to toss Shay's sexy twittering ass back into the car. He wanted to pulverize Jamie.

Why did full-grown, mature, reasonable women act like giggly little girls whenever Jamie showed up? It sure as hell couldn't be his thick mountain-man beard or his stilted conversational skills. And he wasn't exactly a slave to fashion. Today his dark hair was pulled back into an unkempt ponytail. He wore a plain gray T-shirt, which was probably one of three T-shirts that he owned: white, gray and black. According to the weather, he sometimes had a frayed flannel over the T-shirt. His jeans had to be ten years old, because no way had he paid extra for the "fashionably worn" look. His brown leather lace-up boots were sturdy, meant for hiking up and down the damned mountain, whenever the mood struck him to annoy the males of Visitation.

Bryan didn't want to, but he had to ask. "So you still think a woman is involved?"

Where Jamie was concerned, there was no "think" about it. He gave an emphatic reply. "One is."

"Amy?"

Shrugging, Jamie pulled Bryan's hand away from the front of his shirt. "Describe her."

Shay hurried to do his bidding. "Shy, slim, blond with green eyes —"

"No. It's not her."

Fascinated, Shay said, "Thank God." Then: "So who is it?"

Bryan's jaw fell open. "You believe him? Just like that?"

"Don't you?"

Damn it, he sort of did.

Ignoring them both, his head down, his hands in his back pockets, Jamie paced a small circle in the road. "I don't know yet. But she'll come to you when you need her."

"When I *need* her?" Bryan shared a quizzical glance with Shay. "What the hell does that mean?"

Jamie shrugged again. "I don't —"

"Yeah, yeah. You don't know." Bryan caught Shay's arm. "C'mon. Let's get out of here." He took two long steps, hauling Shay with him.

"The real threat is a man."

Ignore him, ignore him, ignore . . . Bryan did an about-face. "*What* man?"

"Not one you'd expect." Jamie rubbed his head, deep in thought. It was almost eerie to watch him, as if you could see the visions passing before him.

Idiotic.

"Are you done?"

Jamie nodded. "Yes. It'll all be okay. I'm not worried now."

"Well, gee, *you're* not worried? What a relief." Sarcasm dripped from Bryan's every word. "I'll just tell Joe to forget the whole thing, then."

"No, you won't." Sarcasm never bothered Jamie.

Shay pressed forward. "Could you call us if you think of anything else?"

As if he'd forgotten she was there, Jamie glanced up, and slowly his expression cleared. "Can't. I don't have a phone." He turned and started down the road. He headed into the bright red, setting sun, and it made a black silhouette of his lean body.

Incredulous, Shay blinked. Mindful of Jamie's nonexistent feelings, she leaned in close to whisper, "He doesn't have a phone?"

"Nope." He half grinned. "No car, either. He lives up on that mountain somewhere, all by himself. I told you he was strange."

Of course, she got defensive. "I like him."

"You like everyone."

"Including you?" Her tone dared him to explain that one — and he couldn't. He had no idea what she saw in him. Annoyed, Shay said, "The very least you could do is thank him."

"Not possible." Bryan propped his hands on his hips and contemplated the cloudless sky, which was now a dusky gray. Sweat gathered on his shoulder blades and in the middle of his chest. It was a damn hot evening.

"No? Why not?"

He took great satisfaction in saying, "He's gone."

Shay whipped around, searched the area, and then asked in surprise, "Where'd he go?"

"Who the hell knows? Who cares?" Done with Jamie Creed for the moment, Bryan caught her hand and pulled her back to the car. "He does that disappearing trick all the time. One minute he's there, and the next, poof. He's gone. It's annoying. He's annoying. Let's go. I'm getting hungry, and Joe Winston isn't a man to be kept waiting. Not for dinner, and not for anything else."

And after dinner, when he got Shay alone at his trailer, he'd remind her of what she wanted to do to him. He had a feeling he'd be semihard until then.

Even though he looked nothing like she'd imagined, Shay recognized Joe Winston the second they pulled down the long gravel drive. Whenever Bryan spoke of him, he'd sounded . . . meaner. Not that she knew anything about Joe's temperament, of course. But right now, standing there waiting for them, he looked domestic and friendly, not at all like a convict.

She'd half expected him to be scarred, to maybe heave with menace, to snarl like a rabid dog. This man was smiling — and he was incredibly, knock-you-off-your-feet gorgeous.

He had one long, heavily muscled arm draped around a woman, presumably his wife. Two kids hovered on the porch behind them — a young, pretty girl on the steps and a boy in a porch swing. Both kids had the palest blond hair Shay had ever seen. The girl's was long and shiny, the boy's short and mussed.

Flowers grew up a trellis on one side of the house. Lush green grass grew in and around a profusion of enormous trees. Birds sang and squirrels played. In the background, the surface of a large lake rippled with the gentle breeze. The house was big and stately and looked like Shay's idea of home. It exuded warmth, unlike her mansion — a.k.a. mausoleum — back in Ohio.

A bit envious, she said, "It's a Kodak moment."

"Yeah." Bryan grinned. "That's Joe and Luna, and Austin and Willow on the porch. They make a nice family, huh?"

Shay nodded, more emotional by the moment. She wanted what they had. She wanted to smile with that type of satisfaction. She wanted to be that content. "They all look happy."

"Joe wouldn't have it any other way." Bryan turned off the car and walked around to her door. "Come on. You'll love Luna."

She barely had time to step out before they were descended upon.

"You're finally here!" Luna held out her arms, and Bryan obligingly gave her a quick hug. Shay noticed that Joe watched him with narrow-eyed menace the whole time.

Not the least worried about her husband's imposing audience, Bryan asked, "Is that shades of blue I see in your hair, Luna?"

She swatted at him. "It's called plum." And then to Shay, "I like changing my hair sometimes, and every guy around thinks that's a reason to poke fun."

Shay stared at Luna with awe. She *did* have blue streaks in her hair, but it wasn't unattractive. In fact, it was kind of nice the way her hair matched the polish on her fingernails and toenails. "It looks beautiful."

"Thank you. I thought so, too. This is my husband Joe." Luna hugged herself around his massive biceps and pulled him forward. "Say hello, Joe."

"Hello, Joe." The dark hulk reached out

and caught Shay's hand. "Well." He looked Shay up and down. "I can see why the mighty has fallen." Then to Bryan: "You didn't say she was beautiful."

A little stunned by that outrageous compliment, Shay glanced at Luna, who nodded enthusiastically. "You really are stunning."

Wearing a frown, Bryan tucked Shay into his side. "She doesn't like for you to mention that."

Shay felt her face go hot. "I don't?"

He glared at her. "You didn't want me to mention it."

Joe and Luna listened with avid curiosity.

"Bryan," Shay complained under her breath, more than a little embarrassed. "That's because I wanted you to like me, not just be attracted to me."

Bryan scowled. "Of course I like you."

Laughing, Joe slapped Bryan on the shoulder, and since Shay was plastered to his side, it nearly knocked her off balance. "Was all this in doubt?" Joe asked. "Amazing. You must not be nearly as accomplished as I figured, Bryan. We'll talk later and I'll give you some pointers."

Another car pulled into the drive. Slowly. Quietly. Joe suddenly sharpened.

Now he looked like a convict.

Both Willow and Austin joined the adults.

Luna put her arm around the girl and said, "This is our daughter, Willow."

The little boy puffed out his chest. "I'm Austin."

"Nice to meet you both," Shay said.

Austin turned to Bryan. "You shoot anybody lately?"

"Sorry, no."

Shay started to laugh at the crestfallen look on Austin's face, but she managed to hold it back.

A car door closed.

"Here comes Clay," Austin explained. "He's Willow's boyfriend."

"Willow's only fifteen," Joe corrected. "Too young to have a boyfriend."

Willow just rolled her eyes, but Luna rounded on Joe. "Do. Not. Start. I mean it, Joe. If you embarrass her —"

Willow hooked her arm through Joe's. "He won't."

Clay stepped up in front of them. "Hello Joe, Luna." He cleared his throat. "Thanks for letting Luna go to the school dance with me."

Luna beamed. "She'll have a wonderful time."

"She better," Joe warned.

Luna's eyes narrowed. "*Joe.*"

Clay just grinned. Apparently he was used to Joe's gruff protectiveness. "I'll see to it, and I'll have her home by nine."

Willow turned and gave Joe a loud kiss on the cheek. She hugged Luna next, then said to Shay, "It was nice to meet you. Bye, Bryan." And off she went, hand in hand with Clay.

Shay didn't think she'd ever been that young and carefree. For as long as she could remember, she'd been driven to do, to make a difference.

To justify her own good fortune.

Maybe it was past time to hand the reins over to Dawn. Maybe it was time for her to get her own life in order. After all, how could she help make others happy if she wasn't happy herself? And she had to admit, without Bryan, she wouldn't be happy. She hadn't realized that until she met him, hadn't even known that anything was missing in her life until he helped fill it up. But now she did know, and not being a dummy, she had to do something about it.

She'd still keep an eye on things, but she trusted Dawn to disperse the money charitably, to make wise decisions.

Then she'd be free to concentrate on

getting Bryan out of "in the moment" and into the "forever and always."

"When we gonna eat?" Austin demanded. "I'm starving."

Luna ruffled his fair hair. "You're a bottomless pit. Go on in and wash up and I'll get dinner on the table."

Austin ran off with more energy than a young jackrabbit. The adults followed at a more leisurely pace.

Shay could see why Bryan wanted to stay in Visitation — because now she wanted to stay, too.

Back in his old hobo disguise, Bruce lingered in the shadows outside the safe house. He'd been at it for hours now, waiting, watching. Amy was the only one home now, since Patti and Morganna had headed off to work and Barb had left to go shopping.

He felt like a failure — a washout as a preacher and a miserable excuse for a protector. He'd made horrendous mistakes. By harboring a dangerous woman, he'd put the other women at risk. *Dear God, Shay could have been killed.*

He'd known that Amy was more troubled than the others, but like an arrogant, conceited jerk, he thought he could make everything right just by befriending her. He thought . . . His face warmed and disgust washed through him, but . . . he'd thought that he could be in her life, and it'd somehow be better. Somehow be good enough that she'd be able to turn things around.

What a jackass.

In a very short time, Shay had done more good than he managed in a year.

Maybe he should just talk to Amy — no. He'd promised Bryan to go along with the game, but now it just didn't sit right. He couldn't bear the thought of Amy being so deceitful. What if she had done things because she'd felt threatened? Maybe she *had* been threatened. Bryan didn't think she was working alone, but with Freddie locked up, who else was there?

The house was awfully quiet. It had been quiet for hours. What if Amy had somehow managed to slip out without him noticing?

Once he thought it, he couldn't stop worrying about it. If only Barb would get back — she'd been gone for hours already — then he could confide in her, ask her for help. With Barb on the inside and him on the outside, they could make sure that Amy went nowhere unnoticed.

He was so lost in thought that when the

cell phone rang, he jumped a foot. Every awful scenario imaginable ran through his mind. Somehow, Bryan had been hurt. Or one of the women. He pulled it from his pocket and answered it on the second ring. "Hello?"

"Preacher? This is Eve Martin."

"Dr. Martin?" A new fear exploded and he said, "Leigh! Is she all right?"

"Leigh's fine. She's right here, with me." Eve stopped to draw a deep breath. "I don't want to alarm you, but remember you asked Leigh if she was one of Freddie's girls? That is, if she worked for him?"

Never had he heard Eve speak so fast. She sounded frazzled, when usually she was too controlling to be frazzled.

"I remember." It had actually been Bryan who asked, but they'd kept each other appraised of things as they went along. What difference did it make now, though?

"This is surprising, to say the least, but I thought you should know. Freddie had a damn harem going, apparently. There's another woman he had working for him."

Another woman working for Freddie? The man spread himself pretty thin. Bryan started to ask, "Who?" but before he could get the word out, the front door of the safe house opened and Amy came running out.

She looked startled.

She looked afraid.

Another woman . . . Everything clicked into place. Bruce said, "Oh, hell," and didn't even care that he'd cursed.

Chapter Fourteen

Whenever Bryan stayed at the trailer, he felt at peace, like the weight of the world and all its responsibilities had just melted away. He could relax. He could enjoy life. It was a feeling he hadn't gotten anywhere else.

Except when he was with Shay.

Now, having her at the trailer, peace was the farthest thing from his mind. While they'd visited with Joe and Luna, the sky had darkened to black velvet, glistening with a million bright stars. The stream out back gurgled as melodically as ever. Owls whispered from the trees. Crickets chirped.

And Bryan couldn't appreciate any of it. Shay stood there, her fair hair lit by the moon, her skin opalescent, her scent carried to him on a gentle breeze. He wanted to rush her inside, strip her naked, and continue their conversation from the car. Or better yet, not talk, just *do*.

But at the same time, he saw the trailer as she might see it — older, small and shabby. Shay had probably never stayed in a trailer in her entire life. Hell, his house back in Ohio would probably fit in her foyer, but at least it wasn't metal.

Shay held up her arms as if embracing the night. "Bryan, this is . . . incredible. I feel so small standing here." She dropped her arms to hug herself. "And the air smells so good. Like water and trees and rich dirt."

"Yeah." His cock throbbed and his muscles twitched. He needed her. Bad. They'd lingered too long after dinner. Joe had wanted to go over every detail of the plans, and Shay seemed to be enjoying herself with Luna, so he'd hated to drag her away.

But now he felt like he'd suffered four hours of foreplay.

Bruce hadn't called yet, so he knew everything was okay back in Ohio. He had Shay to himself for once.

She turned to face him. "Let's go down to the creek."

He nearly groaned aloud. He didn't want to sightsee tonight. "Don't you want to check out the trailer?"

"I do." He could see her eyes shining, knew she was smiling at him. "Later. Maybe you could run in and grab a blanket."

He caught her waist and pulled her closer. "Why?"

"I've never made love outside. Have you?"

He had, but he shook his head, more than willing to indulge her. "The bugs will eat you alive."

"Wimp. What's a few bug bites?"

Bryan grinned. Damn, he lo . . . No. He shook his head again, afraid even to think about his emotions when he was so primed. He cared about her. He wanted her. It was enough for the moment.

Liar. Nothing with Shay would ever be enough.

But that realization disturbed him, too, so he yanked her close and kissed her. When she softened against him, he lifted his head. "If I'm a wimp, then you're a hussy. What if someone sees us?"

"Who? A fish? An owl?" And then, with her eyes wider, "Your friend Jamie won't show up, will he?"

Bryan tasted the soft, fragrant skin where her throat met her shoulder. "He's not my friend, Shay, and no, he won't show up. Not if he knows what's good for him."

"Well, then . . ." She walked her fingers down his chest to his crotch. "I have some experimenting to do, remember?"

As if he could ever forget. "Anywhere, anytime, honey."

"The stream, and right now, please."

He had to be the luckiest bastard alive. "If that's what you really want, I'm game."

"I really do." She gave him two encouraging strokes to get him hustling.

Bryan grabbed her hand, turned and headed for the trailer. It was one of those old bullet-shaped, silver jobs — ugly, but functional enough to meet his needs. Large trees towered over it, keeping it cool in the summer heat.

He'd made a wooden, two-step platform that sat in front of the door, and he bounded up to it with a lot of haste. He held Shay with one hand and was reaching for the knob with the other, when every instinct he owned went on alert.

Something was wrong. Bad wrong. He could feel it.

Shay patted his butt. "Hurry up."

"Shhh." Slowly, silently, Bryan started to step back, urging Shay to the ground. He'd put her in the car and then investigate. . . . The door swung open.

The trailer was dark, with only the glow of the moon and the stars providing illumination. But it was enough for Bryan to make out the features of the man in the doorframe.

Chili's eyes gleamed in fanatical delight.

He shifted, and Bryan's attention was drawn to his right hand and the Beretta nine-millimeter. Aimed at Shay.

"Not so fast, Preacher."

Without conscious thought, Bryan put himself in front of Shay. A hundred and one possibilities ran through his mind even as he said, "You son of a bitch."

"My mother was a saint," Chili yelled, and he lifted the gun toward Bryan's face.

Smirking, Bryan said, "It wasn't a personal comment on your lineage, you idiot, just a reference to your character."

That stymied Chili. His eyes narrowed. "Step away from the bitch."

"I don't think so." Bryan felt Shay's hands clutch at his back, and he knew, knew, damn it, that she'd try to protect him. His gun was at the small of his back. With the way she pressed against him, there was no way for her to be unaware of it. But Shay had never been in his world. She didn't handle guns, had probably never fired one in her life.

If she attempted to draw it out of his holster, Chili would shoot her.

Bryan reached back and grabbed her arm. His knuckles brushed the butt of the Smith and Wesson. "Not a single damn step, Shay, you got me?"

Her forehead pressed against his back. She nodded.

But he still didn't trust her. "What do you want, Chili? What the hell are you doing here?"

Chili slouched onto one hip in a negligent pose. "You don't talk like a preacher. All those whores, claiming you're good as God, so righteous and all. Hell, you're no better than most other man."

"No," Bryan agreed, "but I'm a helluva sight better than you."

Chili straightened again. "Shut up."

"You use women, Chili, don't you? What'd Freddie do, give you a finder's fee? Is that why you were checking out Shay that first night? Hoped to tell Freddie about her and get yourself a little on the side for free?"

"Shut up."

"No woman would touch you otherwise, huh? Not even the two-bit hookers. Why take money from a slimeball like you when another man — a *real* man — is right around the corner?"

He released Shay so that he could move when the time came. Chili got more rattled by the second, which meant emotion was clouding his judgment, and his aim would be sloppy. Bryan knew how to manipulate spineless cretins like Chili. He'd lose control, act hastily, and then Bryan would have him.

If he caught a bullet in the process, well, he'd get Chili first. Shay would be safe.

Bryan doubted he'd have time to get his gun out of his holster and fire a clean shot, but he was all set to throw himself at Chili when suddenly a light came on in the trailer. Momentarily blinded, Bryan shielded his eyes, and there she stood.

Barb.

He blinked twice to make sure he wasn't just seeing things, but no, there was no mistaking that sour expression.

Barb had her arms crossed under her large boobs, her hip jutting out to one side, a mean sneer on her lips. She stared at Bryan over Chili's shoulder — and then she winked.

Bryan's jaw loosened. What the hell?

"Chili, calm down." Barb acted bored with all the drama. "You were going to bring them inside, remember?"

Shay stepped to the side of Bryan. "Barb?"

Bryan used the distraction to open the holster. If he could just get his gun . . .

"Yeah, it's me. Not that simpleton Amy." Barb made a rude sound. "Amy can barely talk without stammering. Why the hell would you think she could plan anything?"

Shay breathed hard. Bryan knew she was hurt at the betrayal, and that made him furious. But . . . Shay hadn't seen that wink. What did it mean?

He hadn't been all that sharp since meeting Shay. Damn, but she kept him off balance, otherwise he would have considered Barb. Not because Barb seemed a likely suspect, but hell, he'd gone through a similar situation with Joe Winston not that long ago. Joe had been just as arrogant in his presumptions, never guessing that a woman, especially a woman he thought liked him, could pull such a stunt.

Men could be such dumbasses sometimes.

Then he thought of Jamie's prediction, that the woman involved would help them when they needed it. He hoped like hell that Jamie was right. Maybe Barb would pull through in the end. But just in case, he needed his gun.

His hand closed around it . . .

Suddenly Chili said, "Ah, ah, ah. No guns, Preacher, at least not for you. Get your hands where I can see them. Barb, get that from him, will ya?"

Barb made a face, part apology, part

annoyance. "Turn around, Preacher."

With Chili's gun aimed at Shay, Bryan had no choice. He turned.

Barb slipped the gun free, hesitated, but Chili grabbed it away from her and shoved it into his pants pocket. "Now get out of my way."

Barb faded back into the trailer. "Bring them in."

"Why?" Shay swallowed, her gaze never leaving Barb, her tone haunted. "What did I ever do to you?"

Surprisingly, Barb shoved Chili to the side and jutted her chin toward Shay. "You took over! It was *my* job" — she jabbed a thumb into her chest — "to run things, to make the safe house nice. Everyone relied on me, and they were happy with how I worked till you came in and started criticizing."

"I didn't," Shay whispered.

"The hell you didn't. The food wasn't good enough. Our manners weren't good enough. We had to dress different, talk different. You changed everything."

"I thought you had fun."

"The others did, so I played along. But it was all a waste of time."

"Barb," Shay implored, "I only wanted to help."

"Yeah, right. And that got Morganna thinking I needed her help, too. Even Patti pitched in. Pretty soon, there wasn't anything for me to do." Barb gulped down air, her bottom lip quivering. "It was the only real job I'd ever had, but why would the preacher need to keep me around anymore?"

Shay started to go to Barb, but Bryan stopped her. "He's your friend, Barb."

Chili laughed. "Save your breath, bitch. She's not that dumb."

Barb lifted her chin. "No, I'm not."

"Barb knew all along she'd never cut it as a housekeeper. What bullshit. She works best on her back, and she knows it. That's why she stayed in touch with me, letting me know where Leigh got off to. That little whore still owed me."

The more Chili talked, the more devastated Barb looked. Bryan wanted to kill him. "You're a sick bastard."

Chili put his arm low on Barb's waist, then fondled her butt. "I'm smart, not sick. I sent customers to Freddie, helped him spot the right girls to recruit, and in turn he let me sample the merchandise whenever I wanted."

Barb didn't smile. "And he wanted to, a lot."

"Damn right." Chili slapped her hip. "When Freddie got locked up on that stupid drug bust, he put me — *me* — in charge of the girls. Only between the two of you, there weren't hardly any girls left. Just the real pathetic ones, and I didn't want them."

"What about your wife?" Shay asked. "What about her?"

Chili pulled back, full of affront. "She's not a slut."

"I get it," Bryan said. "Your wife doesn't want to fuck you, either." He laughed. "Have you offered to pay her?"

Chili actually trembled with that insult. In a rasping whisper, he said, "By God, I'll kill you right now and be done with it."

Bryan braced himself, more than ready to lunge, but Barb nudged Chili. "I thought you wanted to have some fun first."

Slowly, the anger faded away until he was once again grinning with malicious delight. "That's right. I do."

Bryan stared at Barb. "You overheard Shay tell me about Leigh, didn't you?"

Guilt flashed over Barb's face for only an instant. She shrugged. "That's how Chili knew to follow Shay. Only you followed her, too. And then you hid Leigh. . . ."

"Enough standing around out here," Chili said.

"Right." Relieved, Barb gestured them both inside. "Come on."

"No." Chili backed Bryan and Shay away from the steps by waving the gun. "The bitch wants to go to the stream for a nature fuck. So that's what we'll do."

That threw Barb. "But you had it all planned. . . ."

"I changed the plans," Chili snapped, then nodded to Bryan. "I was listening. It's a hell of an idea. I wanna watch." He leered at Shay, licked his lips. "Then I'll take my turn with her."

"Not in this lifetime," Bryan told him, and meant it. His weapon might be gone, but unless Chili managed a fatal wound, and Bryan doubted he could, he was such a putz, he'd still have the advantage. He'd beat Chili to death with his bare hands before he let him touch Shay.

Barb, her mouth opening like a fish, looked from one person to the next. "But you said —"

"Shut up!" Chili immediately collected himself after that outburst. He was still breathing hard as he smoothed his hair and straightened his glasses. "Go get a flashlight."

Defeated, Barb disappeared into the trailer.

Bryan had backed up several feet. He stood two steps ahead of Shay, a little to her left. He could feel her tension, her fear. Should he take his chances on tackling Chili?

Barb reappeared with a heavy industrial flashlight. She watched Chili, hefted the light in her palm, and narrowed her eyes.

"Move it," Chili said.

Bryan situated himself a little more to the left, making sure Shay would be blocked by his body. His muscles tensed — and his cell phone rang.

Threatened, Chili took a step back and aimed. "Who the hell would be calling you? Who knows you're here beside the whores?"

Bryan shrugged. "The police. But it's probably Joe Winston." Bryan doubted Chili knew Joe, but he had to give a name other than that of his brother. If Chili found out he wasn't the preacher, he'd probably shoot him on the spot. "He lives close by. If I don't answer it, he'll know something is wrong."

Ready to have a full-fledged temper tantrum, Chili snarled, narrowed his eyes, then snapped, "Answer it, damn it. But make it quick. And don't try to warn anyone, or I'll blow her brains out." He moved to Shay's side and pointed the end of the gun at her head. "I could always put you with Barb instead. Hell, Barb would love it, I bet. But I'd prefer to see you on Shay, so don't give me a reason to kill her now."

Barb had always looked cross and a little mean.

Now she looked downright evil.

The second Bryan said hello, Bruce blurted, "It's Barb. Not Amy. And she left hours ago and —"

"No shit."

That lethally calm reply filled Bruce with sick dread. Worry became a lead weight in his stomach. "She's there?"

"Yeah."

Oh God, oh God, oh God. "With someone?"

"You betcha."

Bruce was driving like a madman, holding the phone with one hand, choking the steering wheel with the other. At her insistence, Amy rode with him. He hadn't at first wanted to tell Amy that they had suspected her, but after she'd found Barb's room empty, her things gone, he'd had to explain.

Think, Bruce. Don't waste time. "Hang on,

Bryan. I already called Joe. He's on his way. He said he'd take care of the backup, but I still had to call. I hoped to catch you in time . . ."

"You didn't, but don't worry about it. I'll figure something out."

His brother was always so confident, so capable. Bruce envied him — and respected him more than any other man he knew.

Bruce heard someone hiss, "That's enough. Hang up," and he started praying. "I'll be there as quick as I can, Bryan. We're already on the way —"

The phone went dead.

Numb, sick at heart, Bruce handed it to Amy. "She's already there."

Amy sat as still as a frightened rabbit, then she seemed to calm. "It'll be okay." She looked at him and took a deep breath. "Barb is . . . different. Harder. But she's vulnerable, too. I don't know what it is, maybe the way she always watched Shay. But Shay has helped me to see everything differently, including people. I know Barb won't hurt her. She won't."

Bruce reached for her hand. "I pray you're right."

Barb held the flashlight, leading the way to the creek. With every step she took, she grumbled and groused, so typical of Barb. Shay stared at her back and wanted to weep. She'd thought Barb was a friend. She'd thought Barb liked her.

Bryan followed behind Shay, with Chili trailing them all. Shay was very aware of the gun, of how easy it would be for Chili to lose his fragile grasp on control and hurt, or even kill one of them. Her life had been an odd one, filled with the pleasure of giving and the heartache of insults and misunderstandings. But not since she'd been adopted had she dealt with any violence.

That was Bryan's forte, and she sincerely hoped he knew what to do, because she didn't.

Like a line of soldiers, they made their way across the dew-wet grass. Insects buzzed around them. An occasional bat scooped low and then soared away. The creek, sparkling with the reflection of a million stars and a fat bright moon, was about eight feet wide, winding and twisting across the land.

Chili said, "That's far enough." His voice was high with excitement, making Shay's stomach churn. "Turn around." He breathed hard with glee. Licked his lips. "Now get naked."

The air crackled with menace.

Bryan stood very close to Shay, half shielding her with his wide shoulders. "I don't think so."

"I wasn't talking to you!" Flustered and too anxious, Chili waved the gun around. "I want to see her. From the first night she showed up, soaked to the skin, I've been planning this. If you hadn't interfered, she'd have been mine that night."

Though her muscles felt brittle with fear and her throat was dry, Shay managed a credible laugh. "Not a chance."

"I wouldn't have given you a choice, bitch." He stared at her breasts. "Lose the clothes."

Shay lifted her chin. "No."

Barb moved to Chili's side, holding the light at her side. She didn't shine it on them, but then, the night was so bright, and they were in such a wide clearing, that it didn't matter.

Shay didn't know what to do, so she took her cues from Bryan. He had a plan, she just knew he did. What, she couldn't imagine, but she refused to believe there'd be any outcome other than good over evil.

The way Barb watched her, like she wanted her to understand, tore at Shay. She knew she couldn't get through to

Chili, but perhaps Barb would relent. "I'm your friend, Barb."

Barb shook her head. "You put up a good show, I'll give you that. But sooner or later, you'd have moved on. Real friends don't do that."

"No, they don't," Shay agreed. "Just as real friends don't betray you. Or threaten to shoot you, or —"

"Christ," Chili yelled. "Quit yakking and get the clothes off."

Shay took comfort in Bryan's nearness, in the knowledge that he dealt with criminals all the time. "Frankly, I'd rather be shot than do that."

As if his patience had reached an end, Chili huffed. "Stupid whore."

"Pathetic excuse for a man."

He actually staggered back. He wasn't used to women standing up to him. His mouth opened twice, and nothing came out.

Barb stared at Shay, too, but with exasperated disapproval. When Shay met her gaze, Barb gave a small, urgent shake of her head. But Shay had no time to ponder Barb's silent message.

"You don't want to play nice?" Chili whispered. "I'll just shoot *him*, then." He turned the gun on Bryan, and Shay saw the intent in his gaze.

"No, wait!" He wouldn't shoot her, Shay decided, not until he got what he wanted. At least, Shay hoped that was the case, because she didn't want to die like this. Not when she'd just found Bryan.

She threw herself in front of Bryan, watching Chili in case he squeezed the trigger. Did it really matter if he saw her nude? Undressing would give Bryan more time to figure out how to get them out of this mess.

Bryan all but tossed her behind him. "Damn it, Shay, don't do that."

To put off the inevitable — her nakedness — Shay squared off with Bryan. "Stop trying to boss me around. You're always doing that and I'm sick of it."

Bryan looked first incredulous, then thunderous. Through set teeth, he growled, "Do what I tell you."

"I'll do what I think is right. Chili wants to see me naked, don't you, Chili?" She glanced at him, saw that Chili was excited by their argument, and said, "There. See?" She reached for the top button of her blouse. Maybe she could do this *really* slow. Like . . . take forever. "He won't shoot me, so it makes sense for me — oof!"

Bryan jerked her around behind him. Shay had never seen him so livid. His eyes fairly glowed with menace, his face was dark with rage. "Don't . . ." His jaw worked. "Don't do that." He gave her a hard shake, practically rattling her teeth. "Trust me, God damn it."

"Hey," Chili complained. "I can't see her. Move."

Bryan lowered his nose to hers. "Everything will be okay." He drew a breath, and their lips almost touched. "When I turn back around, run. It's dark, they won't see you."

"I can't hear you," Chili complained. "Stop that damn whispering."

Appalled, Shay realized that Bryan planned to sacrifice himself. The big dope. "No, I will not run. I'm not leaving you behind." And then, softer still, "I love you, remember?"

Chili bounded forward two steps. "Enough of that shit. I'm done waiting."

Bryan closed his eyes, pained. "Shay, when I get us out of this . . ."

"Unless you want your blood all over her, Preacher, you better move away. Right *now*."

Slowly, Bryan opened his eyes, and Shay saw in his gaze that he did indeed have a plan. But what could it be? To sacrifice himself so she could scurry off like a coward?

Bryan was already turning, his gaze sharp with purpose, his muscles tensed. Poised to lunge.

Chili laughed, held the gun in both hands to steady it, and began to squeeze the trigger.

Everything seemed to happen at once.

Barb screamed, so high and shrill that the treetops came alive with birds or bats fleeing into the night sky.

Like a great hulking shadow of death, Joe Winston exploded from the bushes. In a blur of motion, a knife left his hand to sail through the air and sink deep into Chili's upper arm.

The gun went off, the blast echoing around the area again and again, before Chili howled and dropped the weapon.

All of this happened in an instant, and then Bryan's body hit Shay hard, taking them both to the ground with bone-jarring impact.

He didn't just land with her, but rolled until she was pinned under him with his arms clamped around her head, his body completely blanketing hers. Her nose was smashed into his granite chest while sticks and pebbles dug into her spine.

But not for long.

"Stay down," Bryan ordered, and then

he was gone, moving with lightning speed. An approaching siren split the night, and new voices began shouting.

Chili, silent as death and just as resolute, was up on his knees. His glasses were askew, and Shay couldn't see his eyes behind the lenses, but his mouth was twisted, his expression a frozen mask of hatred. His left arm gushed blood from the knife wound, but he'd retrieved Bryan's 9mm from his pocket, and had it aimed point-blank at Bryan's head.

Bryan's thunderous footfalls rattled the earth as he took a running tackle toward Chili. Shay knew he'd never reach him in time. She struggled to her feet.

Then a wild banshee cry split the night, and Barb swung the heavy flashlight at Chili's head. The light danced wildly around the clearing, Chili ducked, and the light connected with his shoulder. He howled again — and the light died out.

Everything looked even more macabre in the moonlight.

Bryan plowed into Chili, taking him to his back. The gun flew out of his hand. Shay didn't get a chance to scream. Bryan's fist pulled back, and landed with bone-crushing impact. Once, twice.

Joe yelled, "That's enough, Bryan. Leave

something to send to jail."

Barb slumped back. She was crying, great tearing sobs. "I'm sorry. I'm sorry. I had it all planned out. When he took you into the trailer, I was going to hit him with the cast-iron skillet, but then he didn't come back inside and I didn't know what to do. I didn't know what to do! I thought he was just going to drive you away." She gulped more tears, babbling, sobbing. "When I found out he planned to shoot you, I came with him. I came along to *help*. I swear it. I'm sorry. I'm sorry."

Joe leaped over Chili and Bryan, caught Barb's shoulders and pushed her to the ground. Shay heard him say, "Ah, shit."

Barb continued to chatter and explain even as Joe restrained her. With Chili knocked out cold, Bryan retrieved his weapon, then checked Chili's pulse. "He'll live. The bastard."

Shay didn't spare Chili a single thought. Bryan could have been killed. If Barb hadn't hit him with the light . . .

Then Bryan was there, wrapping his arms around her, holding her back. "It's okay, Shay. We're okay."

She gripped him tight. She felt like she should cry, yet no tears came. "Bryan . . ." she ran her hands over him, his chest, his throat, his beautiful face. "Oh God, Bryan . . ."

"Shh. I'm here. I'm all right. I swear."

Barb let out a long moan.

"Oh no," Shay said, her concern shifting. Barb had helped them, just as Jamie Creed said she would. But Joe didn't understand. He would hurt her. She started to pull away from Bryan, only he wouldn't let her.

He was still squeezing her tight. "Joe knows what he's doing."

"He's hurting her."

"No, baby." He caught her face in both hands, his dark eyes boring into hers, forcing her to comprehend. "He's trying to stop the bleeding."

"The bleeding? But . . ." Shay's heart stuttered to a standstill, then lurched back into a frantic pace. *Chili had fired the gun.* "Barb!"

Bryan didn't let her go. "You'll only get in the way, Shay. Hear the sirens? That'd be Scott, the deputy. They'll get her to the hospital."

A terrible chill went through Shay. "We have to go with her."

"Of course we will." Bryan rubbed his hands up and down her arms, kissed her temple, then her cheek.

Shay knew she was shaking all over, but

she couldn't seem to stop. They'd almost been shot. Barb could still die.

Joe pulled Barb's blouse loose, then stripped it away from her chest. "I think it went through her shoulder," he shouted. He whipped his own shirt off in record time and began wadding it up. The deputy's car pulled right up into the lot and stopped with the headlights shining on them. Thankfully, he silenced the siren.

Activity erupted all around. The deputy was speaking to the ambulance, Joe issued orders — and Chili came around. He saw the chaos and tried to creep away. He hadn't gotten farther than a foot or two when Bryan kissed Shay's cheek and said, "Hold on, honey. I'll be right back."

Chili was on his knees now, holding his injured arm, almost into the thick tangle of bushes that lined the creek. His glasses were gone and blood from his nose smeared the left half of his face.

Grinning, Bryan stepped over him, then crouched down. "Give me a reason, you bastard. Any reason."

Chili cowered.

Grabbing him by the shirt, Bryan hauled him to his feet. Chili kicked and struggled, but he was no match for Bryan. Finally, he tried to lurch free and run.

Bryan said, "Thanks." And hit him hard in the gut. Wheezing, Chili slumped over, but Bryan held him upright by his shirt.

Joe glanced up. "You probably shouldn't have done that."

"Probably not."

"I'd have been happy to do it for you."

"Yeah, I know."

Neither of the men acted like anything out of the ordinary had happened, while Shay felt nauseous and cold and shaken to her core. Never in her life had she felt so ineffectual. Her knees were so weak, she either had to kneel down or collapse.

Bryan frowned at her, then just let Chili drop. He reached Shay in two steps. "Hey," He knelt down by her. "You okay, baby?"

Barb had stopped crying and now just stared at Joe with wide-eyed awe. Joe crooned to her, reassuring her as he kept pressure on her wound, and Shay could have almost sworn she heard Barb sighing.

Shay didn't realize that tears were tracking her cheeks until Bryan pulled her into his lap and brushed them away. Loudly, he said, "Tell her you're all right, Barb."

"I'm . . . I'm okay." Barb winced. "Really."

"There, you see?" And to Barb, "Hang in there, kiddo. The ambulance is on its way."

Barb nodded, never once taking her gaze off Joe. Or rather, Joe's chest.

Shay shook her head in wonder. Even a wounded woman was gaping at Joe Winston. "She tried to help us, just as Jamie said she would."

"Yeah." Bryan pressed his face into her neck and rocked her gently. "God, I've never been so scared in my life."

Shay started. "What?" He hadn't been frightened. Mad, yes, but not scared.

Suddenly he had her shoulders in his hands and he looked fierce again. "Damn you, don't you ever pull another stunt like that, do you hear me?"

Shay blinked at him. He was shouting so loud, no doubt everyone for a mile heard him.

"You could have been the one shot." He shook her. "The next time I tell you to run, you damn well better *run*."

Strangely enough, his loss of control helped her. The shock faded. It became easier to breathe. "There won't be a next time," she reasoned. Surely this was the end of it. They deserved peace and quiet and happily ever after now. "Besides, I couldn't leave you alone with him. . . ."

"I wouldn't have been alone. I knew Joe was there."

"You did?" How had he known? Shay hadn't heard or seen a thing. Joe was damn sneaky, as far as she could tell.

"You didn't?" He sounded incredulous.

Shay shook her head.

"Well, I heard him. I saw him. That's what I do, Shay. And I'm good at it." He pulled her close and kissed her hard. "For the rest of your life, for the rest of *our* lives, you will trust me."

The evening felt very cold to her now and she curled in against Bryan's chest, seeking his warmth and the comfort he always gave. Giving him some comfort as well. "I promise."

Like steel bands, his arms tightened on her. "Ah, damn, Shay. What am I going to do with you?"

She had a few suggestions. Like love her. Maybe marry her. Be a father to her children . . .

The ambulance screeched into the yard. One man ran to Barb, and with Joe's help, put her on a stretcher. Her voice was weak with pain, but still, in typical Barb fashion, she began to complain.

Chili was louder and whinier. The deputy knelt down beside him. Joe had already filled him in on the phone, and he began reading Chili his rights.

Shirtless, his powerful chest lined in moonlight, Joe sauntered over to them. "What now?"

Bryan stood and, amazingly enough, kept Shay in his arms. She wasn't exactly a dainty little thing, and his strength never ceased to amaze her. "We're going to the hospital with Barb."

Joe glanced up at the moon. "I'll hang around till everyone is loaded up, just to help you keep an eye on your little friend."

Remembering the look on Chili's face made Shay's stomach lurch. "He's insane. He's sick."

"He'll be locked up soon as his arm heals," Bryan promised.

"Probably gotta let his nose heal now, too," Joe added. And he grinned.

With Barb loaded into the ambulance and Chili in restraints in the back of the car, the deputy joined them. He started to hold out a hand to Bryan, saw he had his arms full, and frowned instead. "Bryan," he said by way of greeting.

Bryan nodded. "Scott, this is Shay Sommers. Shay, Scott's the local law around here."

"Ma'am," he said, and actually tipped his hat. Charmed, Shay noted that he was a handsome man with sandy brown hair and gentle blue eyes, and he looked very nice in his uniform. "Sorry I didn't get here sooner. Joe likes to act first, and call me second."

"But I did call ya," Joe reminded him in good humor.

Scott looked aggrieved. "You know, Bryan, it's bad enough when this jackass" — he tipped his head toward Joe — "brings all kinds of trouble with him. Don't you start, too."

Joe laughed. "Hey, I'm a happily married domestic man now. My trouble is all at an end."

"Right." The deputy gave him a long look. "Does that mean your sister won't be back?"

"Ah, you mean *that* trouble." Joe chuckled. "You know, I think Alyx said she'd be visiting again next week."

Scott propped his hands on his hips, dropped his head forward and groaned. "God help me."

Shay looked at Bryan. "His sister?"

"A female Joe, actually."

"Hey!" Joe said, "That's my baby sister you're maligning." But he grinned, too.

The paramedics were ready to go. Joe slapped Bryan on the back. "I'm heading home. The wife will be waiting." He walked off, a man without a care.

Incredible.

Scott eyed the protective way that Bryan held Shay. "Does she need medical attention?"

Shay shook her head. "No, *she* is fine. And Bryan can certainly put me down now."

But he didn't. Not until he set her inside his car, buckled her in and kissed her forehead. He was treating her like fine china, and for the moment, Shay didn't mind.

It meant he cared. How much, she didn't yet know. But he had mentioned the rest of their lives. That sounded like a fine place to start.

Chapter Fifteen

Scott gave them an escort to the hospital. Trailing the deputy with lights and sirens blazing, they made good time. During the drive, Shay used Bryan's cell phone to call Bruce to let him know they were all right.

His first reaction was, "Thank God." Then, with wry relief, "I guess I can slow down to a more reasonable speed. I never did understand the thrill of racing."

"Don't speed," Shay agreed, "but I have some bad news, too." She hated to say it out loud, but they needed to know about Barb. She told what she knew, explaining that Barb had been shot, but it appeared she'd be okay. Bruce felt the same as Shay did. He wanted to see Barb for himself, and he wanted to be with her, to let her know she still had friends. The extent of his giving had no boundaries.

Amy, especially, thought she could empathize with Barb. Their ETA was still a few hours away.

Bryan and Shay arrived at the hospital

right behind the ambulance. Barb couldn't quite meet Shay's gaze, and it wasn't until some hours later, after the doctor had treated her and she'd been admitted for the night for observation, that Shay really got to speak to her.

Shay sat beside her bed and reached for Barb's hand. As usual, Barb was uncomfortable with being touched, but she didn't pull away. "It's going to be okay."

Barb stared at the far wall. "You always say that, even when you don't know what you're talking about."

It was so nice to have Bad Barb back and in fighting form, that Shay chuckled. That startled Barb, but she ended up grinning, too, then quickly sobered. "I really, really am sorry. I was stupid. Chili kept telling me . . ." Her hand tightened on Shay's and she shook her head. "Never mind. It doesn't matter now."

But Shay couldn't let it go. "He made you think you didn't deserve friends."

Covering her blush with a black frown, Barb said, "And I don't. I helped him try to drive you away just because I was afraid you'd take my place. I ratted out Leigh just to keep him happy. I'm a . . . a miserable person."

"No, you're not." Bryan had been

standing quietly near the door, but now he approached Barb's bed and stood glaring down at her. "You made some bad choices, but no more, right?"

"Uh, right."

"And you were unsure of yourself, but now you know that you're needed at the safe house and that people care about you, right?"

She gave one small nod.

"Bruce wouldn't have it any other way."

Confused, Barb said, "Bruce?"

Bryan sighed. "Not a single one of us has been honest lately."

"That's right," Shay agreed. "I lied to all of you."

"For good reasons." Barb attempted to smooth the ugly hospital gown, but the IV got in her way. And she didn't seem inclined to release Shay's hand. "You were sort of undercover."

"Maybe." Shay shrugged. "But you lied out of fear and, trust me, fear is as valid, maybe more so, than anything else."

"I was undercover too," Bryan said. "I lied to help my brother."

"Your brother?"

"Bruce. The real preacher." To Shay's surprise, he told Barb all about the deception he and his brother had set up. As he spoke, Barb's eyes bulged and her face went pale. "He should be here soon. Both he and Amy are very concerned about you."

Barb stared at Bryan in disbelief. "There are *two* of you? No shit?"

"No shit," Bryan promised.

Shay laughed. "Fun, huh?"

"Two." Barb looked utterly boggled by the possibility. "A preacher and a bounty hunter." She slowly shook her head. "That's . . . well, I don't know what to think." Her brow furrowed. "But you did act awful strange, at least part of the time. The preacher sure never discussed underwear with us."

Bryan laughed. "Yeah, that was me. Scintillating conversations you gals have." He winked. "There was a time or two I would have gladly strangled Bruce."

Shay punched his arm, laughing.

Suddenly Barb grew solemn again. "I can't believe you're both here, still talking to me after what I did."

"You saved us," Shay reminded her. "That's what you did."

"And we have to talk to you," Bryan said. "If we don't talk to you, how can we invite you to the wedding?"

Shay almost fell over. She didn't move,

didn't even breathe. But inside she was reeling. Marry! He wanted to marry her?

Getting drowsy from her pain medication, Barb smiled. "So it's like that, huh?"

"Exactly like that." Bryan smoothed Barb's hair with real affection. "You crazy broad. You fucked up, but you won't do it again, right?"

Tears filled Barb's eyes. "No, I swear." She yawned. "Please tell the preacher that he can count on me, if he wants to maybe try giving me another chance."

"You can tell him yourself." Bryan glanced at his watch. "He should be here any minute."

Shay was ready to start weeping again. "We're getting married?"

Instead of answering, Bryan put his heavy arm around her, then nodded to Barb. "See ya in the morning. Be good and don't scare the doctors."

Barb snorted.

"And be nice to Bruce. He's a good guy. An innocent guy. He's not made of the same mettle that I am."

Barb actually laughed. "Yeah, I'll remember that. But you know you better hitch up quick, because once Patti finds out you're not a preacher, she's going to get grabby again."

* * *

They were in Bryan's car before Shay found her voice. Bryan was really starting to sweat it. She'd said she loved him, but that didn't necessarily mean she wanted to stay with him forever.

Now all she did was yawn and say, "I'm so tired. What an unbelievable day."

Primed, edgy, Bryan struggled to rein himself in. He felt like a starving junkyard dog, ready to attack a succulent bone. Shay epitomized everything good that he wanted to have in his life. Even her money didn't bother him, since she wasn't a snob about it.

She had to be damned upset after everything that had occurred. She wasn't like him, wasn't from his world where every other person you came into contact with had a weapon and was anxious to use it. Every time he thought of Chili aiming that gun at her, again and again, he wanted to shout out his rage. But Shay needed him calm, not furious. "We could stay with Joe and Luna tonight if you feel funny about going back to the —"

"No. I still haven't seen the inside of your trailer."

Bryan swallowed twice. He wanted to be alone with her, but he didn't want her to suffer even a single second more of anxiety. "Whatever you want, honey."

"Is that a promise?"

His hands flexed on the steering wheel. "Yeah. Sure."

"Then tell me you love me."

He almost wrecked the car. Thank God they'd reached the trailer. Bryan pulled into the yard, and parked the car beneath a tall walnut tree. He looked at Shay in the darkness, could feel her attentiveness, and growled, "I love you."

He got out and walked around to her door. Shay climbed out and smiled at him. "I like the sound of that."

Any second now, he'd implode. "Come on. Let's get you inside." For the second time that night, he led her up the steps and then inside. He switched on all the lights and secured the door behind her.

Out of necessity, they stood close together. The trailer was cramped, filled to overflowing with a soft couch and easy chair, a television and a stereo. "The trailer is temporary," he felt pushed to explain. "I'm going to build a house —"

"Can it be a ranch?" Shay edged around him and walked the length of the trailer, peeked into his john, peered at the double bed, then returned to the tiny kitchen.

"With a wraparound porch so we can see all the beautiful woods no matter where we sit?"

He stared at her. She was planning a future he hadn't been sure she'd accept. "A ranch?"

"You did just promise to give me anything."

She looked so beautiful — scratched and bruised, with tangled hair and smudged makeup and dark circles under her eyes. But beautiful. "Yeah. Sure. A ranch."

"A gazebo down by the creek would be wonderful, too. I want one of those."

"All right." Hell, he'd build her twenty gazebos all along the creek if it'd make her happy.

A bright smile lit up her face. She made a fist, punched it into the air, and shouted, "We're getting married."

There. She'd said it. Did that mean she agreed? "I want you with me forever, Shay." And again, making damn sure she understood: "I love you."

She threw her arms around his waist. "I'm glad. We'll live here, okay? I'm going to put Dawn in charge of things back in Ohio. She'll love it. Can you do your work from here?"

Just like Shay, to move at Mach speed.

He could barely keep up. "I dunno." But he didn't want to disappoint her, so he added, "Probably."

Shay pulled his shirt out of his jeans, then up and over his head. Obligingly, he raised his arms. "I might just retire. Find something else to do."

Her busy fingers went to his jeans. "Do you think we'll both fit in that minuscule shower?"

Bryan caught her face in his hands. She wanted to shower with him? Now? "Shay, what are you doing?"

The smile faded. "I need you. I need to know that we're both okay and healthy and that you really do love me."

"More than life," he promised.

Her hands opened on his chest, stroked up and over his shoulders, touching him, feeling him. "I need to show you how much I love you, too."

His breath caught. His heart swelled. "Fuckin-A, we'll fit in the shower." Being loved by Shay had to be the biggest mind-blow ever. He'd need a lifetime just to get used to how right it seemed and how good it felt.

Epilogue

The wedding, which started out simple enough, given the fact that they'd organized it in less than a month, ended up being a gigantic party. Relatives, friends and neighbors all attended.

Bryan's dad married them, and Bruce was the best man, with Scott and Joe as ushers. The bride's side of the wedding party outnumbered the groom's — not that anyone minded.

Dawn stood as Shay's maid of honor, and Barb, Amy, Leigh, Morganna and Patti all made stunning bridesmaids. Shay's sister, Brandi, also attended. Being nearly nine months pregnant, she was more comfortable sitting on her husband's lap than standing through the ceremony.

Shay's mother cried, her father beamed with pride, and they all claimed to love Bryan right off. After all, he'd done the impossible. He'd actually managed to snare Shay, when they all knew her as an unstoppable force.

Amy's new boyfriend came with her, but the rest of the women were flying solo. Unfortunately Dr. Martin couldn't make it. She sent her sincere apologies and a very large gift. Shay knew Dr. Martin seldom ever left the clinic unattended. She was too dedicated to her work.

Shay had picked out beautiful dresses for the ladies, classy and simple and altered to fit just right. Only the women didn't care for the less-than-plunging necklines and knee-covering hems. So they did a few alterations of their own. As a result, Shay had the sexiest bridal party in the history of Visitation.

To their credit, the women were on pretty good behavior. Someone had spiked the punch, but Bryan said he thought that was Joe. And Austin, Joe's son who was almost ten, kept his ears cocked for anything anyone might say, so foul language and sexual innuendoes were kept at a minimum.

Barb still had some shoulder discomfort, and she had to take it easy. But despite that, she took her community service, assigned to her for her part in the crimes committed against the safe house, very seriously. She was working hard to make amends, and she finally seemed happy.

They still called her Bad Barb, but only because she took so much pleasure in bossing everyone around.

Scott stood next to Joe. They were both in suits, both pulling at their ties, and both watching the party with varying degrees of interest. "Visitation is never going to be the same."

Joe cocked a brow. "It has been livened up some."

Scott nursed his beer, belched discreetly, and narrowed his eyes. "Your sister seems to fit right in with Bruce's women."

That had Joe choking, but he only said, "I can't get over the way the preacher refers to them as 'his.' Like he has a damn harem or something."

"More like he's a proud papa." Scott shook his head. "Not that I've got anything against the women. They're all nice enough — although that Patti has grabbed my ass about ten times now. I think your sister might be putting her up to it."

Joe slanted him a look. "*Just* your ass? Lucky you."

That made Scott laugh. "I'm quicker than you, obviously."

"Or maybe she just knows I have more to offer."

Luna stepped between the two men with

a *tsking* sound. "I can't believe it. You're standing here debating who is more irresistible?"

"No!"

"Of course not."

She said, "Uh-huh," and they both grumbled guiltily. "Well, if you look, you'll see that Jamie is really the man of the hour." Luna hooked her arms through theirs. "They're all after him."

Joe squinted in Jamie's direction, then grinned hugely. Jamie, without his typical poker face, kept backing away from a small group of females. He hadn't worn a suit, just black jeans and a white shirt, but that was enough to give a start, considering how he usually dressed. Now, with several women advancing on him, he appeared more grim than ever.

"He looks panicked." Scott scowled. "But I don't see him disappearing, now, do you?"

"Nope. Maybe he's enjoying the attention."

They all laughed at that.

"You're both evil." Luna, proving she could be evil, too, said, "Did you know that Alyx is real curious about the life of prostitution? Morganna has been telling her all kinds of stories, and Alyx is just hanging on every word. You'd think she was writing a book or maybe researching an upcoming event."

"Son of a . . ." Scott shoved his drink into Joe's free hand and stomped off in search of Alyx. Under his breath, he muttered something about needing overtime pay whenever Alyx Winston came to visit.

Joe hugged his wife. "That was mean."

"Just helping Alyx with her cause."

"To drive Scott crazy?" His hand slid down to casually fondle her bottom. "As I said, mean."

Bryan strode up with Shay tucked in close to his side. He shook hands with Joe. "Thank you again for letting us use the lake for the reception."

"It is absolutely beautiful," Shay told them. "I can't imagine a nicer setting anywhere."

"You're welcome anytime," Joe told them. "And just as an FYI, the boathouse makes a nice private place to rendezvous whenever kids are underfoot."

Bryan cleared his throat. "Well, I did see Willow headed in there with Clay just a few minutes ago."

Joe dropped his drink. It hit the mossy ground with a dull thud. Eyes narrowed and mean, Joe started off — but Luna caught him before he could take more than a single stomping step. With her hands latched onto the back of his belt, she said, "Joe. He's a very nice young man."

Incredulous, Joe looked at her over his shoulder. "Exactly. He's young and male. A bad combination."

Bryan rubbed the back of his neck. "I kind of have to agree with that."

Shay elbowed Bryan. "Even if he's a typical guy, you have to trust Willow to make smart decisions."

Just then, Willow and Clay came into view. They were in a rowboat, heading out to the middle of the lake, taking advantage of the beautiful fall day. Luna raised a brow at Joe. "There, you see?"

"I see that for now, he's allowed to stay." Joe straightened his tie. "But I think I'll mosey down that way, just so he knows I'm keeping an eye on things."

To Shay, Luna said, "As if he had any doubt?" She caught Joe's hand. "I'd better go, too. Poor Clay is still a little awed by Joe."

As Shay watched them head off, she leaned into Bryan. "I can understand that."

Bryan leaned forward to nuzzle Shay's

ear. "What's this? Should I be jealous?"

"No. Never." Then she sighed. "They are such a happy couple, though."

"And what are we?"

Shay turned in his arms, looped her arms around his neck, and said, "Delirious? Euphoric?"

"Right." His hand went to the small of her back. "Can we escape now?"

From behind him, Jamie Creed said, "Not yet."

Pained, Bryan slowly turned to face Jamie. "You still here?"

"It wasn't time for me to go yet. I needed to tell Shay that she's made all the right decisions. Don't ever doubt that. Bruce's decisions have nothing to do with yours."

Bryan didn't like the way Jamie said that. "What the hell does that mean?"

He turned to Bryan. "Everyone who comes to Visitation wants to stay." His eyes darkened until you couldn't see his pupils, until they were just black and mysterious and so damn deep, you felt lost looking at him. "Me, you and now even your brother, Bruce."

"Did Bruce tell you that?"

"No." His expression gentled when he looked at Shay. "But she has things well under control, so now your brother feels free to . . . explore."

"Explore what?"

Black eyes coasted over Bryan's face. Jamie looked away and shrugged. "Women."

"The hell you say!" Bryan didn't know if he should laugh or be insulted on Bruce's behalf.

Shay smiled. "But he always deals with women."

"No." Jamie glanced up at the sky, as if judging the time. "Now he's free to be a man, not just a preacher."

Bryan and Shay looked at each other. Shay covered her mouth with a hand. "Maybe since you're married, it's got him . . . thinking about it."

Frowning, Bryan said, "More like it's that damn kiss you gave him after the fire." Then under his breath, "Hell, no man could be immune to you."

Ignoring that, Shay turned to demand that Jamie explain — but he was already gone. "Oh, my. He *did* just disappear."

"Forget it," Bryan said. "It's a parlor trick. Now what did he mean? What decisions have you made?"

She bit her lip. "I know you have a few cases to finish up, but then surely we could start building here. And since Dawn is thrilled to take over for me in Ohio, I thought I'd dive into some of the local projects. For instance, Scott says they need new equipment at the sheriff's station. He said that with you and Joe in town, they could really use some bulletproof vests."

"Bastard." But Bryan was grinning.

"And the nearest firehouse is too far away to be of much help to anyone living this far out. So if I could put up the building and get the equipment, we could probably get volunteer firefighters, or better yet, certified firefighters. That'd bring more jobs into the area."

Watching Shay's excitement grow always amused Bryan. She never did anything halfway. Which was good, since she loved as hard as she did anything, and she loved *him*.

She caught her breath before continuing. "And I met this very nice teacher, Julie Rose, who hopes to get some new educational programs started in town. She normally teaches in a much ritzier area, but she's been helping out with the summer school here, and you know, I think she might want to move here, too. It's just like Jamie said, everyone who comes here —"

Bryan put a finger to her lips. "We'll definitely stay, as long as you don't mind living in the trailer while we build a more suitable house." He waited to see if she'd insist on using her money for something fancier, but Shay seldom thought of her own comfort where her money was concerned.

"Close quarters," she purred with a smile. "You'll get no complaints from me."

What a woman. And she was all his. "I've decided to open my own business, too. It's something I've been considering for a while. Being a bounty hunter keeps me more on the road than not and I'm damn tired of always moving around, not to mention I want to spend more time with my wife."

"And don't discount the awful danger." She shuddered, but new excitement sparkled in her eyes. "So what kind of business?"

"Security equipment. Because of my job, I've always owned my share, and lately I've thought about selling it. I use it in the field, so I know what works and what doesn't. Your brother-in-law, Sebastian, gave me some tips on setting up shop. I didn't realize he had his own personal security business."

"It never came up, but yes, he's very successful."

He was also honorable and friendly, and if the situation called for it, Bryan knew he'd be able to hold his own. "I like your folks and your sister, too." He laughed. "When you call her your little sister, you aren't kidding."

"Brandi's small like the rest of the family."

"You're both beautiful, but in different ways." Bryan had been amazed at how Brandi's husband towered over her — not that Brandi seemed to notice. She didn't look like Shay, but it was clear right off that she had as much grit.

Shay was still considering Bryan's news. "I remember Luna saying that they had to drive two hours to get their security equipment for the lake."

"Right. There's a warehouse south of here, but I'll set up about an hour north, so the competition won't be too stiff. And since I'll carry better equipment, I'll draw customers from all over. I figured I'd add a mail-order catalog and something on the net, too."

Shay gave him a beaming smile. "It's a wonderful idea."

"I thought you'd like it." He walked her to the back porch where he produced a long sheath of papers, rolled together and tied with a ribbon. "I've got something to show you."

"What is it?" Shay asked.

"My wedding gift to you." Bryan opened the papers with a flourish and spread them out on a picnic table. "House plans. Not as fancy as what you already have, but just as you described to me."

Her eyes widened and her bottom lip quivered as she stared down at the blue-prints.

Bryan got uneasy. It wasn't a small house, but compared to what her first husband had left her . . . no, Shay wouldn't care about that. "Nothing is set in stone yet, so you can still change things if you want."

She didn't say a word.

"You don't like it?"

She dashed the tears away. "I never cried until I met you."

Shit. He set the plans aside and cradled her close. "I don't ever want you to cry, babe."

She sniffed and laughed and squeezed him tight. "But don't you see? My life has always been full. I've stayed busy and been happy. But I never, ever felt so much until you. Happy was just happy, not deliriously, mind-blowing happy. Sad was just a moment to get through, not a heartbreaker. And love was what I felt for my family, my work. With you, it's so much more. It's so strong it takes my knees out and makes me want to shout and cry and laugh."

"Let's go with the laughing or shouting. No tears, okay?"

She *did* laugh, but it was a watery sound. "You make me feel more of everything, and that makes me whole. Because I'm with you, I'm not lost anymore."

"You're staying with me, too. Forever."

"Yes." She peeked up at him. "Let's go back to the trailer, get a blanket and go down by the creek."

Being wanted by Shay nearly took *his* knees out. "Damn," he said, while leading her across the yard so they could say their good-byes. "I'm really glad I'm not a preacher."

Shay just laughed. "Preacher, bounty hunter, businessman. Doesn't matter to me — as long as you're mine."

Bruce stayed in the shadows, a place with which he'd become familiar while trading places with his brother. He had a sappy, melancholy smile on his face.

So Shay didn't care what Bryan did, as long as he stayed with her? When he found a woman to love, he hoped she felt the same. He'd always be a preacher, and that might turn some young ladies away, just as it had their mother.

But now he knew the truth, too. He had a streak of wildness, just as his brother did. For once in his life, he was free to indulge it.

What better place than Visitation?

The employees of Thorndike Press hope you have enjoyed this Large Print book. All our Thorndike and Wheeler Large Print titles are designed for easy reading, and all our books are made to last. Other Thorndike Press Large Print books are available at your library, through selected bookstores, or directly from us.

For information about titles, please call:

(800) 223-1244

or visit our Web site at:

www.gale.com/thorndike
www.gale.com/wheeler

To share your comments, please write:

Publisher
Thorndike Press
295 Kennedy Memorial Drive
Waterville, ME 04901